I would like to dedicate this book
to the Tuesday Night Titans—Smurf, Oger, Tater,
Boo Boo and Aaron—even though we mostly play
on Monday nights these days.
Also, this one is dedicated to RP of Millstadt,
my first, truest love.

Withdrawn from Stock

D0755635

chapter 1

Their screams echoed down the hall, creating a cacophony that was overwhelming. The man walking down it, a burly specimen of manhood, winced at the sound. He increased his speed a bit, going from a shuffling saunter to a near-jog. Medium-length brown hair cascaded down to his broad shoulders, framing his blunt-featured face. He was not unattractive, with bright blue eyes and a strong jaw, but his looks were unconventional, possibly intimidating. Stubble on his face indicated that he had skipped shaving that morning, and he jabbed his tongue out of the corner of his mouth, poking at a whisker that was troubling him.

He continued down the faded green tiles, the sounds made by his size-sixteen sneakers muffled by the dissonance spilling from the room at the end of the hall. He passed by a bulletin board decorated with pictures of turkeys. The artwork was clearly done by young children who had dipped their hands into brown paint and then slapped them onto a piece of construction paper. Poorly scrawled names were written in tall letters across the bottom of the pictures.

Upon reaching his destination, he gripped the doorknob with a large hand and pulled it open. The sound seemed to envelop him, increasing in volume as he removed the barrier. Through the door, a multitude of young children were playing, running, and screaming with great enthusiasm. A young boy with blond hair and large blue eyes ran up toward him, throwing his arms about the man's leg and giving him a fierce hug.

"Mr. Steve!" he said. "You're late, Mr. Steve!"

"I know, Darrien," said Steve, patting the boy on his back. He looked up from the young child's face to regard the decidedly angry woman sitting behind the teacher's desk.

"When you called," she said in a dry voice, "you said you would only be ten minutes late."

She was an older woman, her wizened face pockmarked with old acne scars. Her hair was thick, curly and dark brown, with bits of gray showing at her roots. She wore a cozy-looking sweater with a depiction of a Native American child on it. The crude stereotype it portrayed raised his ire a bit, but he was careful to keep his displeasure off of his face.

"I'm sorry. Most of my street is still torn up. I had to go three blocks out of my way just to catch a train."

"Your street has been under construction for two months now. I would think that by now you would have learned to wake up a little earlier."

"Yeah." Steve scratched behind his head. "I know. I'm sorry."

"Try not to be late. I have important things to do in the office. I can't waste my time here watching children because their teacher is incapable of maintaining a schedule."

She rose to her feet, snagging a cordless phone and jamming it into her corduroy pants. She walked stiffly out of the room, her face crossed by clouds blacker than Steve's chalkboard.

He sighed, picking up a clipboard from his cluttered desk. He noted that attendance had already been taken, made a quick head count to ensure it was accurate, and looked out over his classroom. Dodging past the chaotic, zigzagging bodies in his path, he walked over to a battered CD player covered in a great deal of duct tape. He pressed the play button and a jaunty tune emanated from it.

"It's clean up time!" said Steve at the top of his lungs. The children, many of whom did not notice his late entrance to the room, grew even louder in their enthusiasm to greet him.

"Mr. Steve! Hey, Mr. Steve is here!"

"All right! Mr. Steve!"

"I love you, Mr. Steve!"

"I'm glad Miss Stone left, she's mean!"

"Do we have to take a nap today?"

He was swarmed by their tiny bodies, a half dozen of them squeezing his legs in bear hugs. He patted as many of them on the back as he could in rapid succession, a wide smile on his face.

"Okay, okay," he said after a few minutes of being grappled. "We're running late today, so let's get cleaned up for circle time!"

With some more coaxing from the tall man, they were soon duteously picking up toys, hanging up play clothes, and wiping up finger paint. Steve pitched in at several areas that were rife with spilled toys, his blue eyes narrowing.

"How many times do I have to tell you guys *not* to just dump the baskets out? Why can't you just take the toys you want?"

He did not expect an answer, and did not receive one. He rose to his feet, dusting off his knees a bit, and noticed a serious-looking young girl with pale blond hair and wide green eyes approaching him. She gazed up at his face, her tone plaintive.

"Mr. Steve," she said. "Jaws is dead."

"What?" asked Steve, glancing at the small aquarium in the corner. There was, indeed, an orange-scaled fish floating belly-up. "Oh, crap."

"Jaws is dead?"

"Nooooo!"

"Give him mouth to mouth!"

"Mr. Steve knows CCR!"

"It's CPR, not CCR!"

"You're not the boss of me!"

"Calm down!" said Steve at a high volume, catching most of their collective attention. When all of their large, wide-open eyes were focused on him, he continued in a more normal tone of voice.

"Sarah, you're flag helper today," he said, taking down a rolled-up American flag from the top of a tall metal cabinet. He handed it off to a pudgy blond girl in a pink taffeta dress. "Everybody on the circle time rug! Find your spot and park your butt on it!"

Most of the children complied immediately, going to the front of the room and arranging themselves on a wide blue rug decorated with the alphabet and numbers up to twenty. A few children lingered in play areas, and he increased his volume while keeping his tone positive.

"Look at Robert," he said. "Robert's a good listener — he's sitting on the carpet."

Several of the stragglers hurried over to the rug, finding their places on the brightly colored surface.

"Here comes Samantha and Demarco," he said as two swarthy students eagerly found their spots. "They're being good listeners now."

"What about me?" said Darrien, sitting up on his knees to see over the low bookshelf bordering the circle time area.

"You're a good listener, too, Darrien," said Steve as he scooped out Mr. Jaws with a small green net. He opened the door to his classroom and spotted the staff bathroom across the hall. With a flick of his wrist he sent the piscine missile arcing across the vomit green tiles, trailing droplets of water behind it. Mr. Jaws dived into a new pool of water, this one attached to the commode. Regretting that he could not flush the toilet without leaving his children unattended, he closed the door and returned his attention to his charges.

"All right!" he said when he noticed that all twenty of the kindergarten students were lined up in a circle on the rug. "Let's get started with the Pledge of Allegiance."

"Mr. Steve!" said Darrien, bouncing up and down on his bottom. "Mr. Steve, can I go back on green?"

"What?" Steve asked, squinting his eyes as he peered across the room at a row of brightly painted lockers. There was a name tag shaped like a turkey affixed to the front of each with the child's name written across it in their own hand. Just above the name tag (and the reach of small hands) there was a cardboard cutout of a traffic signal light. On most of them, a small clothespin was hanging from the topmost, green light. From Darrien's light, the clip was firmly affixed to the red one.

"What'd you do to get on red already?" Steve asked, directing his gaze back to Darrien.

"I was being loud," said Darrien.

"You didn't hit anyone?" said Steve.

Darrien shook his head vehemently. Steve scanned the faces of the other students, to see if they would dispute Darrien's claim, but none of them did.

"All right. Be a good listener for circle time, and *maybe* I'll put it back on green."

"Okay, Mr. Steve!" The boy sat down instantly, focused upon being good with concentration so intense it crossed the boy's eyes.

Thanks, kid, thought Steve, *you just made life seem a little less like hell!*

"All right," said Steve, "Let's start with the pledge! Put your right hand over your heart…"

"What about Mr. Jaws?" asked a young girl with a trembling lip.

"Well," said Steve, sighing and scratching the back of his head. He suddenly laughed at them with a sly grin on his face. "The thing about goldfish is they're what we call…*disposable* pets."

"What does disposable mean?" Sarah asked, still gripping the unfurled flag in her small hand.

"It means that they swim around for a while, and you enjoy looking at them, but then they die, and you go out and get a new goldfish."

The children were silent for a moment, then there was a dissonant rush of their enthusiastic voices.

"I wanna name it!"

"I wanna pick it out!"

"I don't want a fish, I want a snake!"

"I just want Mr. Jaws back…"

"Let's name it Jaws II!"

"That's a stupid name!"

"You're stupid!"

"Settle down!" said Steve in a firm, loud voice. The voices stopped almost immediately. "Now, we all miss Mr. Jaws, but he wouldn't want us to not have class time! Put your right hands over your hearts, and let's say the pledge—your other right, Cole. Now, I pledge allegiance to the flag…"

Steve led the class through his circle time lesson, which centered on turkeys. He used a poster board chart the children had colored to point out the parts of the bird, and asked them to gobble and move like turkeys. They complied with great enthusiasm, traipsing about the carpet and classroom while flapping their arms like wings. The few children too tired or bashful to pantomime America's largest game bird were encouraged by Steve's willingness to walk with knees bent, arms held at his sides like wings. After several minutes he recalled them to the carpet, and after giving them a few moments to recover their wind and the natural pallor of their cheeks (as well as his own), they sang a song about Thanksgiving.

After circle time, he engaged in the frustrating task of teaching them their letters. They were on the letter T, a symbol Steve had found easy to impart in the past. For some reason, many of his children seemed to struggle with their printing, and he strove to keep his tone light and uplifting as he corrected them.

They broke for lunch, giving him about twenty minutes to prepare notes for their lockers concerning an upcoming field trip. After an aide led them back into the classroom, he directed them to the rug so he could set out their rugs for nap time.

After nap, he had no lessons to teach, so he engaged several children in a game of *Chutes and Ladders*, celebrating his own spins and not allowing them to cheat.

"Yes!" he said. "I'm gonna win, I'm gonna *win!*" He held up his hands clasped over his head and shook them as if he had just scored the winning touchdown on Super-Bowl Sunday.

"You're mean, Mr. Steve," said Darrien.

"Yeah," said another girl, her hair in cornrows. "You should let us win!"

"How is that gonna teach you anything?" Steve was grinning from ear to ear. "In the real world, *nobody* just lets you win. You have to earn it."

"My dad lets me win," said the girl.

"That's his business, and my classroom is mine."

"I wanna win all the time," said Darrien, pouting.

"Oh, really?" said Steve with exaggerated slowness. "You want? Well, you know what happens when you talk about what you *want...*"

Darrien clapped his palms over his ears, shaking his head.

"No!" said the little girl plaintively, though a fierce smile was on her face.

"You can't always get what ya waaant," sang Steve.

Steve shouldered the thin door to his apartment open, his hands burdened by plastic shopping bags. He struggled for a moment to flip on the light switch, cursing as he dropped one of the bags noisily to the floor. The room was suddenly bathed in light from an overhead fixture. The apartment was small, with a living room area right inside the door. An old suede sofa patched with several strips of duct tape sat in front of a thirty-two-inch LCD TV. He grabbed a white remote, pressed one of the brightly colored buttons, and the screen came to life a moment later. A newscaster appeared in front of a map of the New York/New Jersey area. He only glanced at the image for a moment before walking the short distance to his tiny kitchenette. Using the meager counter space not taken up by his coffee maker and microwave, he set the bags down and put away his groceries. He kept out a twenty-four-ounce can of beer, popping it open as he approached the sofa. The view out the single dingy window in the living room was of a train track a short distance away, largely blocking his view of the street below.

He plopped down on the couch, cursing as some suds foamed up off the can and slopped onto his collared shirt. He hastily sipped the beverage to prevent another mishap, flipping through his channel guide as he went.

"Ain't shit on Fridays," he said with a sneer.

He eventually settled on a college football game, more for background noise than anything else. He drained the can of beer and stretched out on the couch, his eyes slowly drooping until he was snoring softly.

He awakened less than thirty minutes later when his unseen cell phone rang. He groaned as he rose, knocking over the beer can with a large socked foot. Stumbling in his thick-headed, groggy state, he zigzagged around the small apartment until he located the phone, which was still in his jacket pocket.

The phone had gone to voice mail at that point, and as he stared darkly at the screen with bloodshot eyes it rang again.

"Yeah?" he said, his tone clearly irritated even though he strove not to sound that way.

"Hey, hey, hey," came a young woman's voice from the other end. "It lives!"

"What's up, Susie?" said Steve, rubbing the back of his hand across his mouth to mop up drool.

"Dad's in town," said Susan, her voice cheerful.

"Yippee," said Steve. "I had a long week and I'm really tired. I'm hanging up now —"

"Oh, come on, don't be an asshole. He misses you. We're meeting at Stuckey's for dinner in an hour. Come out and join us."

"I'd like to, but I'm tired."

"Tired doing what?" said Susan. "You're a glorified babysitter. That's not work!"

"It's harder than it looks," said Steve with irritation, his blue eyes narrowing.

"Whatever. Are you coming out?" she asked.

"I don't think so," he said, face contorting with guilt.

"I knew I was going to have to do this," she said with a sigh.

"Do what?" he asked.

"You remember my Death and Dying professor, Darla Rhodes?"

"Yeah," said Steve, a small smile on his face. "Yeah, she's kind of hard to forget."

"Well, she happens to be a *huge* wrestling fan, so when I said my dad was the Deathslayer, she just couldn't *wait* to come out tonight," she said.

"Really?" he said, straightening up. "At Stuckey's, you say? I'll be there in a bit."

"Dad's buying us dinner, so I hope you like mozzarella sticks and hot wings!"

"Are you kidding?" he said with a chuckle. "You and I ate so much bar food growing up that we sweat fryer oil!"

"We'll see you there. Bye."

"Bye," he said, turning off the phone. Dancing a little jig, he raced into the bathroom adjacent to his sleeping area, peering into the mirror with skepticism. He stripped off his shirt, revealing a muscular if hairy chest, and squirted a curl of shaving cream into the palm of one hand.

He hummed to himself as he completed his grooming, brushing out his hair and using a spritz of hairspray. He slapped on cologne from a dark green bottle, hissing as his skin burned, and picked at a bit of corn stuck between two teeth.

"Hey there," he said lasciviously, as if he were speaking to a woman. "What do I do for a living? Oh, I'm a teacher. Yep, that's right, I'm good with kids."

He flexed a bicep before the mirror in a pantomime of a body builder.

"Yes, those *are* twenty-two-inch guns. Careful, they might go off."

His gaze dropped from his relatively muscular arms and shoulders, across his hairy chest, and down to the bit of paunch he was developing. He blew out a long sigh, seeming to deflate as he did so.

"Who are you kidding?" he said, no longer able to look in the mirror.

With a heavy heart and hands that seemed made of lead, he put on socks and shoes. Slipping on a white tank top first, he donned a dark blue button-up shirt. He considered a tie, but seemed unable to get the top button closed, so he tossed it back into his messy closet.

Finally prepared, he grabbed his coat from the chair back he'd flung it over and headed out the door. Ignoring loud shouting from another apartment, he walked through the hallway and went down a flight of creaky stairs and was soon standing on the street. The night air was cool, but not cold, so he decided to walk the three blocks to Stuckey's.

As he made his journey, he passed throngs of people gathered on the sidewalk. He noticed with chagrin that many of the more provocatively dressed young women seemed to look right through him. He felt old, much older than his thirty-three years, as he passed couples younger than himself holding hands, lost in each other's world.

His brows were low over his blue eyes, square jaw set hard. He swung open the battered and scarred door to Stuckey's. The bar and grill was cozy, not more than twenty feet wide and only half that long. Sports memorabilia decorated the walls, primarily featuring boxing and professional wrestling but with the odd baseball bat or jersey thrown in. It was still early in the evening, so the establishment was sparsely populated. Across a room of empty tables he saw a young woman stand up and enthusiastically wave at him.

She was very young, barely into her twenties. She had a slender, athletic build, evident in the way she lithely gained her feet as she stood up from her chair. She had the same long nose as Steve, but her eyes were wider and a deep green. Her light brown hair framed a face with a few girlish freckles on the cheeks, split wide in a smile.

"You made it," she said, giving him a tight hug.

"Yeah, well," said Steve, a bit embarrassed as he returned the embrace, "I figure I blew off Dad the last couple times, so…"

"You're only here because I lied to you," she said, sticking her tongue out at him.

"You lied?" he asked, confusion crossing his face. Realization dawned, and he grimaced at her. "Not cool."

"It was the only way that I could get you to come out," she said with a pout.

Steve rolled his eyes and picked up a menu off the graffiti laden table.

"Where is Pop?" he asked as his eyes scanned it.

"He'll be here soon. He had to sign autographs at some comic book store on the Upper East Side."

"Great, I drop everything just to see him, and he blows me off. Just like always."

"Quit being a dick," said Susan, pretty face scrunching up. "Besides, what were you doing? Passing out drunk in front of the TV again?"

He glared at her as a waitress approached. He stopped long enough to order a beer, then went back to sulking.

"I thought family was supposed to be supportive," he said ruefully.

"I *am* being supportive," she said, shaking his arm roughly. "I got you to come outside into the real world, didn't I?"

"I go out in the real world all the time," he said, arching an eyebrow.

"You go out on a pub crawl with Phillip like once or twice a year."

"Once every other month and holidays. Hell, I hang out with Phil and his buddy Rich all the time."

"Playing *Dungeons and Dragons* once a week in somebody's basement does not count as a social life, Steve," she said somberly. "How are you going to meet a nice girl?"

"Don't forget the strip clubs. And besides, who says I want to meet a nice girl?" he said. "I'd rather meet a dirty girl."

He laughed harshly at his own joke as the beer arrived, causing Susan to roll her eyes to the ceiling.

"That's part of your problem," she said sadly. "You're stuck in the mentality of a twelve-year-old. That's why you hang out with twenty-somethings, date chicks ten years younger than you are—"

"Hey, your professor is about my age."

"Actually, she's older," said Susan, "and we all know that's the exception. You need to get yourself out there, on the market, or no one's gonna take you home."

"On the market," he said snidely, taking a long pull of his beer. "How asinine. What am I, a hunk of meat? A prize bull being auctioned off for the slaughter? Whatever happened to just meeting someone and *connecting* with them. Why do I have to sell myself at all?"

Susan drained the last of her white soda, setting the heavy glass down carefully on the worn tabletop. She fixed him with a serious gaze that held tinges of sadness as well.

"You shouldn't have to," she said kindly, "and *I* know what a great guy you are. But it's a new era. Facebook, Twitter, and eHarmony have changed the way the dating scene works. People expect you to brag about yourself a little bit."

Steve rolled his eyes, hands coming down on the table on either side of his drink.

"How do people do that? How do people act so goddamn full of shit without being consciously aware that they're being full of shit? I can't help it if I'm for real and I say and think things that make the rest of the world uncomfortable."

"Being for real is one thing. You *enjoy* making people squirm. You go out of your way to do it."

"Maybe I do! Maybe the rest of the world deserves to suffer a little bit, so they know how I feel."

Susan's mouth twitched, and she glared at him from narrowed eyes.

"Oh, it's not like you were abused or something. Mom and Dad always made sure we had what we needed."

"Yeah, they made sure we had clothes, that we made it to school, that we had cars on our sixteenth birthdays," he said angrily. "But what about all the other parts of being a parent? What about teaching your son how to be a man? Because I have no clue if I'm doing it right."

Susan opened her mouth to respond, but the wide smile bursting forth on her face cut off any intelligible rebuttal. She stared over Steve's head, eyes lighting up in delight.

"Daddy!" Susan leaped out of her chair so quickly it dumped backward to land hard on the floor.

Steve turned in his seat to look at the man's approach. He was tall, taller than Steve by almost a foot, built like a linebacker. Long, scraggly hair dyed black hung down on either side of his haggard face in tight curls. A handlebar mustache decorated his lip, perched over a mouth that was long and thin but expressive. It widened into a warm smile at Susan's approach, and he wrapped his thick arms about her in a tight hug.

"Pumpkin!" he said warmly in a husky, deep voice.

Steve rose out of his chair and went to the old man.

"Steve," his father said as they shook hands. "How have you been?"

"Little of this, little of that," said Steve, smiling. "How are you holding up?"

"Going on one more tour to shore up my 401(k)," he said with a wink.

"You always say it's the last tour," said Susan.

"And one of these days I'll be right," he said with a grin. "I've been lucky, you know. No major surgeries, and my knees and back are holding up all right."

The three of them sat down, their father eschewing a menu and ordering from memory. The big man drew a number of stares, both due to his size and perhaps his fame. They made small talk while they waited for the food to arrive. Steve had a difficult time meeting his father's eyes, and the senior man behaved likewise.

"So I figure I'll be taking only six credit hours next semester, to give me time to train," said Susan, wrapping up her dissertation.

"You're gonna get hurt, you know," Steve said.

"Yes," said his father, meeting his gaze with stern eyes, "she will. But she can take it. She's a Borgia, after all."

Susan crossed her arms over her small but firm breasts and stuck out her tongue at Steve.

"It's your life," said Steve, going to his beer but finding it empty.

"How's your life, son?" the big man asked with warmth. "We barely even talk on the phone anymore."

"I just been busy, Pop," he said, ordering another drink. "You know, with teaching."

"He just earned tenure last year," said Susan, elbowing Steve playfully in the ribs.

"That's great!" Deathslayer cocked his head to the side and arched an eyebrow. "What's tenure?"

"It means—" Steve turned his head so his father would not see him roll his eyes "—that I'd have to haul off and punch somebody to lose my job at this point. Honestly, you can go on for twenty minutes about the nuances of a Japanese sleeper hold, but you don't know what tenure is?"

"No such thing as tenure in my profession," said his father with a snicker. "Ain't no retirement plan, either, which is why my old ass still tours."

"I didn't mean it like that," said Steve with a sigh. "You know I'm grateful for all the help you've given me, financial and otherwise."

"You're not paying me back for grad school," said his father.

"C'mon, Pop, it's not like I can't afford it." He chuckled sardonically. "I sure ain't spending my money on some woman, so why shouldn't you have it?"

The big man fixed him with brows hanging low over his eyes. His nostrils flared, and his hands clenched into fists.

"Because a man is supposed to pay for his child's education. And that's that!"

Despite being in his thirties, Steve was amazed at how the big man could still put his foot down. Deathslayer was old-fashioned to the core; his wife did not have to work, and his children were to be taken care of entirely, including their secondary education. Steve still felt a pang of guilt, even as he threw up his hands in surrender. His mother was more forthcoming about finances, and his father's recent comeback tour did not have nearly as much to do with nostalgia as the big man wanted them to believe.

Their food arrived, and conversation turned to lighter subjects. Susan did most of the talking, eliciting a constant stream of laughter from the big man. Steven mostly sulked through the meal, finishing off two more beers.

Several hours later, the bar was beginning to bustle with activity and nearly every table was full. They had no sooner stood up from the table than a waitress hastily cleaned it, giving them dirty glances.

"Are you coming to the Garden tomorrow night?" their father asked as he tossed several bills on the table.

"I gotta work, Daddy," said Susan, "but Steve'll be there, right, Steve?"

She fixed him with an accusatory stare, under which he folded.

"Yeah, I'll be there," he said.

"Great!" said the big man, digging in his coat pocket for something. He eventually extracted a pair of tickets creased down the middle.

"Here," he said, "bring a date. Best seats in the house! Come around back and say hey to the boys, will ya? Some of 'em ain't seen you since you was knee high to a grasshopper!"

"Yeah, maybe," said Steve, shoving the tickets in his pocket. After an awkward, stiff-armed embrace, he and his father parted company, going different directions in the night.

chapter 2

Steve grumbled as he waited in line at the coffee shop, his stomach rumbling loudly. The mass of humanity had spilled out of the serpentine and was backed up all the way to the glass double doors. With growing impatience, he noted that the line was not moving much at all. A few patrons actually left the line, the rest of it scrunching up to fill the gaps.

When he was a few people from the front, he could hear the barista's voice as she attempted to handle a complicated order.

"Vanilla latte, double-shot espresso, extra-large," she said, her voice fraught with stress.

"No," said the angry heavyset man at the front of the line. "Vanilla *steamer*, one shot of espresso, extra-large."

"Sorry, sir," she said. "I'm new here."

Steve strained to see the barista's face, but the fat man was nearly as tall as he was, and she was granted total concealment by his corpulent mass.

"Sorry doesn't fix it," said the man, turning away from her with his drink wedged between pudgy fingers. "I intend to speak with the manager about this!"

The man left, people shrinking to get out of his way. Steve was able to see the barista at last. His breath caught in his throat. She had black hair done up in pigtails that cascaded down her slim shoulders. Her eyes were a soft, rich brown, with a slight almond shape to them. Her tan complexion was even and attractive, from her dark brows past her thin, Roman nose, and down to her wide, feminine lips. She had a metal hoop pierced through her right eyebrow and a golden stud gleaming over one nostril. The black sweater she wore under her red coffee house apron had the sleeves rolled up the elbows, revealing several tattoos. He could only see her from the waist up, but she had moderately large breasts that strained against the layers of fabric atop them.

The girl took two more orders while Steve stood enthralled. When it was his turn, he was still staring at her. She raised an eyebrow, finally heaving an exasperated sigh and asking, "Can I help you, or are you just trying to catch flies with your mouth?"

"Huh?" he said, sputtering. "Oh, sorry!"

He quickly moved to the counter, offering her a nervous smile. She glanced back at him, one eyebrow arched, as he continued to stare.

"This is the part where you tell me your order," she said sarcastically.

"What?"

"Your order? You know, you, the consumer, tell me, the barista, what you want to drink and I make it for you. Are you a foreigner?"

"A foreigner?" he said, his voice breaking.

"No, you speak English too good." She cocked her head to the side a bit. "Are you autistic or something, like Rain Man?"

"Uh, no," he said with a slight chuckle.

"Then what's the hold up?"

"Sorry. I'll have the usual."

"That's great," she said with mock sincerity, "except that I'm new here and have no frame of reference as to what your 'usual' is."

"Oh." Steve swallowed and glanced at the menu above his head though he didn't need to. "A large Colombian dark, with four sugars and six creams."

"Holy crap," she said with a short bark of laughter, "You even like the taste of coffee?"

"I'm in a coffee shop, ain't I?" said Steve, growing perturbed.

"Yeah," she said, preparing his order, "you are at that."

She put the cup on the counter and eyed him expectantly.

"This is where you pay."

"Oh, right." Steve dug into his front pocket. Change spilled out of his hand and onto the counter. He cursed as he strove to collect the pieces of silver as they rolled around at his feet. The barista snickered as he frantically bent over, his butt facing toward her. The frustrated patrons behind him were giving him dark glowers. Had he not been so large a fellow, no doubt some may have been moved to verbally berate him.

"*You fucked up,*" the barista said in a singsong, sports-crowd manner, "*you fucked up, you fucked up!*"

Several of the people behind Steve in line gasped, horrified that a sales clerk would curse so readily in front of customers, particularly in such a mocking manner. Steve, however, was overcome with laughter, actually dropping more of his change in his mirth.

"Old *ECW* chant," he said, finally giving her the correct amount. "Nice! Haven't heard that since back in the day."

"You like wrestling?" she asked, filling an umbra paper cup with dark coffee.

"I actually used to be a wrestler, for a little while."

"Really?" She slapped a plastic lid on the cup with some awkwardness. "You don't seem the type…What made you quit?"

"Well," said Steve, collecting his coffee and a hand full of condiments, "I—"

"Yo, buddy," said a man in a flannel vest a few spaces behind Steve, "flirt on your own time! I gots to get to work!"

Several others, emboldened by the tubby man, added their voices to the chorus.

"Uh," said Steve, staring into the woman's eyes. He again found himself lost in them, not quite sure knowing why, or caring. "Uh, I—"

"Sorry, sugar," said the woman with a wink, staring past him at the next customer. "I gotta earn my bread. My name's Autumn, in case you can't read my name tag, and that's Autumn like the season, not Auggie like the hideously deformed kid from *Wonder*, you dig? I work most Tuesdays and Thursdays, so come in and say hey if you want. Or not."

Autumn kept her eyes focused on the next customer as she spoke, and her verbal barbs kept him somewhat off balance. He numbly walked out of the café, wondering if he should get back in line. He was certain there was a mutual attraction, but decided that such a tactic might seem desperate. Befuddled, but with a bit of a genuine smile on his face for the first time in days, he sipped at his coffee. He spat it out a minute later, realizing he had forgotten to doctor it.

Phillip pushed his horn rim glasses back up his nose with his index finger. Casting his gaze longingly out the open window adjacent to his elbow, he struggled to pay attention to the old man droning on at the front of the table. He looked past the bored faces of his coworkers seated adjacent to him. They all looked as if they felt like busting out the windows of the meeting room and making a break for it. The meeting showed no signs of stopping anytime soon.

Phillip was not a large man, not even reaching six feet tall. He was also slimly built, and the glasses which conspired to hide his handsome brown eyes seemed to cement his geek status. His face was attractive enough, but the portrait he created was not overtly manly (particularly in his own opinion).

He scribbled a bit on the notepad before him, though most of the other attendees were using laptops or tablets. He sketched out a picture of a knight astride a mighty steed, steam blowing from its nostrils. He added a big-busted maid staring up at the knight with adoration, her gown possessing a plunging neckline. Phillip was starting to flesh out her body with some sketchy lines when he felt a hard slap on his shoulder.

"Hey, Picasso!" came a loud voice at his ear. He lifted his head, blinking in confusion, as most of the people at the table were making their way out the door. Phil had become so engrossed in his drawing, he had not even noticed that the meeting had come to an end. He turned his head to regard the speaker, a young man of about his own height but possessed of a more muscular build. His hair had been dyed platinum blond and was lightly frosted, gel holding it up in a disarrayed pattern.

"I'm hardly an abstract artist, Rich," he said, "so calling me that isn't appropriate."

"Whatever, dork. What are you drawing anyway?"

He snatched up the notepad, slapping Phil on the back of the hand when the bespectacled man tried to intercept.

"Nice tits," he said, tossing the pad back onto the table.

"Thanks, I suppose." Phil gave him a narrow-eyed stare.

"So what are you doing tonight?" Rich stared out the window at the street four stories below.

"Got game, then maybe we're gonna sneak in a practice," said Phil quickly, "so I'm pretty busy."

"You're such a nerd."

"Not everyone spends their Saturday night getting blasted and trolling for skanks, Rich." Phil patiently gathered up his papers and stowed them in a briefcase.

"Oh, c'mon," said Rich, dismissing his concerns with a wave of his hand. "We had to work on a weekend, for fuck's sake. That almost *demands* a night out drinking and whoring!"

Phil rose to his feet and fixed the other man with a glower.

"We had a meeting, and it didn't even last very long. You literally have the whole day left to do whatever you want."

"What I want is to get laid tonight. Something that will never happen to you since you sadly like to spend your time pretending to skewer dragons on graph paper."

"Unlike you, Rich, I don't base my entire worth as a human being upon my ability to get pussy."

"How else do you measure it?"

Phil didn't answer, just kept moving down the hallway. They reached a row of three elevators and he pushed the down button as Rich continued to drone on.

"You're a hard guy to get a lead on. I mean, you're in a band, which normally would have you rolling in pussy, but you play *Dungeons and Dragons*, which makes chicks avoid your pecker like it was made of uranium."

"Uranium isn't dangerous in its raw form," said Phil as the metal door slid open. "It only becomes radioactive after it's been refined."

Rich stared at him for a long moment, finally wrapping his muscular arm around the other man in a headlock. He gave the bespectacled man a vigorous noogie, messing up Phil's carefully combed hair.

"Nerd! NERD NERD NERD—"

"Ow, cut it out, asshole!" said Phil, extricating himself and shoving the other man in the chest. The doors slid open just as Rich's back hit the wall of the elevator. Shooting Phil a grin with a wicked gleam in his eye, Rich allowed himself to slide down to his bottom.

"Ow!" he said in a plaintive voice, drawing raised eyebrows from several of the people waiting to ride the car. "Why do you always have to pick on me, you big bully?"

"Yeah, keep your hands to yourself," said a cute young woman in a skirt suit. Her eyes bored into Phil as she moved past him to help Rich to his feet.

"Are you all right?"

"I think I might have some swelling…"

With a grunt of frustration, Phil tore out of the elevator and stormed across the office building's foyer, not stopping until he was on the street. He angrily waved down a cab and went through the frustrating and grueling process of imparting his destination to the non-English-speaking driver.

Thus, he was in a truly dark mood when the cab pulled up outside a two-story house in Queens. He looked outside at the brick and mortar structure, a short driveway leading to a garage that had been converted into an apartment. After paying his fare, he walked up the concrete path, stepping over an oil slick, and banged on the door.

"Enter," came a cheerful voice from within. He opened the flimsy door and blinked as his eyes adjusted to the gloom. A small room lay before him, dominated by two pieces of furniture: a king-sized bed with its box springs set directly on the floor, and a mahogany dinner table that had seen much better days, or at least more attentive owners. Stacks of books and brightly colored polyhedron dice were haphazardly arranged on its surface. Led Zeppelin wafted through the air from old stereo speakers set up high on the wall.

"'Sup," said Steve, engaged in the task of getting himself a beer. Not far from the big man was a heavyset fellow with a prominent bald spot, though his hair hung down to his back otherwise. He was wearing sweat pants and a wife beater, his hairy arms and chest on full pudgy display. He grinned a gap-toothed smile at Phil as the latter set his briefcase on the table.

"Gentlemen," said Phil as he sat down.

"What?" said Steve, intently searching behind himself. "Where?"

"I think he means us, old boy," said the bald man with a faux accent.

"Oh, quite right, master Rex," said Steve in kind. "Bully day, isn't it?"

Phil ignored their banter, snapping open his briefcase and taking out a form scrawled with numerous notations and eraser marks. He slapped it on the table, then eyed them both quizzically.

"Where's Tobias?"

"Got himself a woman," said Steve, a touch of bitterness in his tone, "so I doubt we'll be seeing him for game night much."

"Yeah," said Rex, "until she gets a good look at that needle dick of his!"

All three men engaged in a laugh, though Phil stopped first.

"How does that douchebag always get a woman?" he asked with frustration. "He's vile, chauvinistic, conceited—"

"He actually *talks* to them," said Rex. "You think I landed Becky just because I'm so pretty?"

"I talk to women," said Phil, miffed.

"Chicks you talk to on *World of Warcraft* don't count," said Steve.

"Oh, like you're so much better," said Rex with a sneer. "It's been, what, a year since you broke up with what's her name?"

"Cathy," said Steve, wincing a bit as he recalled the painful memory. "Thanks, buddy, why don't you run a cheese grater on my sack and dip it in kerosene while you're feeling so spry?"

"Oh, go home and change your tampon, Steve," said Rex, rolling his eyes.

"I'd be happy just to get a date," said Phil, sadly.

"Oh, buck up, little trooper," said Rex, slapping him on his slender arm. "Let's play some D and D and forget about it."

"Easy for you to say," said Steve, "you have in-house pussy!"

"Don't I know it," said Rex with a smile. It faded, and he put his arms akimbo and shook his head. "Cocksucker."

"Now you know how it feels," said Steve with a shrug.

"Where did we leave off last time?" Phil asked, as much to distract the men from their argument as anything.

"Uh, think we just came across those Goblins we were looking for," said Steve, arching an eyebrow at Rex.

"No, that was the week before last," said Rex. "You actually found out that the goblins worked for the Black Tusk King…"

Several hours and many dice rolls later, the three men sat laughing loudly around the table. Steve checked his cell phone, picking it up from where it lay on the table. He stood up quickly, cursing to himself.

"Fuck! I have to go; it's damn near six already."

"Yeah," said Rex, glaring hard at Phil, "*somebody* kept us waiting."

"Not my fault there was a meeting," said Phil. "If you guys had real jobs, you'd understand."

"Ouch," said Rex.

"Sand in your vagina, Phil?" said Steve, shaking his head.

Steve took his leave, while the other two men cleared the table off. Working in tandem, they moved it to an area adjacent to the bed, stowing it under a wooden staircase with numerous cobwebs clinging to it. Phil shuddered as one of the gray gossamer strands brushed against his face.

"Quit being a pussy," Rex said.

"As long as there are no spiders in those webs, we're fine," Phil said.

Rex laughed at his discomfort.

"You're what now, twenty-five?" he said. "Don't you think it's high time you stopped being afraid of teeny, tiny bugs? It's not like they can hurt you."

"Some of them are poisonous," Phil said.

"But most of 'em aren't," Rex said.

"It's not the danger they present," Phil said. "It's all those, those *legs*. And the shape of their bodies. I don't know, it just triggers something primal in me."

The two men dragged amplifiers out from behind the staircase, straining with the burden. Rex went back one more time and returned with a bass guitar. It was a long-necked, darkly stained Les Paul, scratches just above the bridge displaying its veteran status. Phil opened a cabinet a few feet from the table, squatting low to peer within. He withdrew a thick, heavy keyboard, nearly as long as the ivories on a full-sized piano. Something brushed against his hand and he panicked, nearly dropping the instrument.

"Did you get shocked?" Rex asked, looking up in alarm as he tuned the bass.

"No," said Phil, carefully checking his hand for damage.

"You thought you had a spider crawling on you," said Rex with a snicker. "Pussy."

Rex's pocket glowed a split second before the cellphone within rang. He extracted the rectangular device, hampered by the size of his hairy hands. He at last put it up to his ear and spoke.

"Hello?" he said.

Phil could just barely make out the voice on the other line and loudly said, "Hey, John."

"Did you hear that?" said Rex. "Yeah, that was Phil."

Rex's eyes narrowed, and his tone grew plaintive.

"What?" he asked. "Why? Whaddaya mean we ain't going nowhere? I'm trying to land us a gig, man, I'm trying, but there's so many cover — what? Yeah, I take it seriously! We all take it —"

Rex grew silent for a time as the other voice droned on for several seconds.

"Yeah," he said harshly, "whatever, man, good luck with those assholes. Have a nice life."

Rex shut the phone off and rudely shoved it back into his pocket, plopping down heavily in a chair after he had done so.

"Oh man, oh man, what are we gonna do?" he asked.

"What?" Phil asked, eyes narrowing. "What's going on? Is he not coming to practice?"

"Yeah," said Rex. "He ain't never coming to practice again. Found another band that's more 'serious' than we are."

"I never liked him anyway," said Phil. "We'll just find someone else."

"Find someone else?" said Rex incredulously. "What the fuck you mean, find someone else? Sure, John was an asshole, but he could *play*. Where are we gonna find a new guitarist who —" he ticked his points off on his fingers "— one, can play decently; two, will actually join our pathetic cover band; and three, can stand all of the shit we throw around the basement?"

"Well," said Phil, "let's call up Sven and see if he knows someone."

"Maybe," said Rex with cautious optimism, "but I ain't holding my breath!"

Steve put on his denim jacket, eschewing the buttons as the evening was yet warm. He stared at his face in the bathroom mirror. Though he had a bit of a five o'clock shadow, he decided to skip shaving. A brief, fleeting hope came and went that he would run into the strange woman he had met at the coffee shop. Her name had been something strange…Autumn. The memory of her deep brown eyes came to him, and on a whim he went back into the bathroom and gave himself a quick shave. He had to change his shirt because of a dollop of shaving cream, and he was running late by the time he slapped on cologne.

As he hopped on the subway and began his rumble from the Bronx to the Garden, he knew he would not be able to see his father before the show. He cursed at himself, thinking the old man would probably believe Steve was punishing him.

Steve slowed his pace as he approached the milling throng of humanity haphazardly lined up outside the ticket booth. He was glad he did not have to wait, and was doubly so when a booming voice echoed over the sidewalk, declaring that the tickets had sold out. A general groan rolled from the crowd. It dispersed raggedly, spilling angry patrons in myriad directions. Steve's eyes were drawn to a sight he had not truly expected to see: Autumn, complaining loudly to the night air about missing out on the show.

She was dressed in a knee-length wool coat, black as midnight in hue. The coat was unbuttoned, revealing a black V-neck shirt unbuttoned far enough to show just a slight bit of her cleavage. He struggled not to stare at her bustline, forcing his gaze downward to the black leather belt decorated with silver studs. It was looped through a red plaid skirt that terminated just above the knee. Underneath she had worn fishnet stockings which disappeared into calf-high leather Doc Martens. Skull earrings dangled prettily from her lobes, and a matching silver necklace hung just below her clavicle.

His feet propelled him toward her, and he tried to will his heart to stop beating so hard in his chest.

You can do this, he thought to himself. *Just like riding a bicycle.*

"Hey," she said, smiling with a hint of nervousness, "it's the guy who fucked up in the coffee shop!"

"Hey," he said, feeling that his voice was banal. "You look great."

"Thanks," she said, smiling a bit wider. Then her lips twisted in a sneer. "Shut up."

"Shut up?"

"It was sweet," she said, "but it's totally something you'd say on a date, and I don't even know your name, so…"

"Steve," he said, offering his hand for a shake. She took it, and he marveled at the tiny thrill that raced down his spine. "Nice to meet you, uh…again. I take it you couldn't get tickets?"

"Yeah, bunch of punk ass kids, just want to go there so they can tweet OMG I'M SO INTO WRESTLING. Poseurs!"

"I know, right? And they don't know about guys like Bruno Sammartino and Harley Race."

"Oh, god! I used to have such a crush on Bruno!"

"Really?"

"Oh, hell yeah. When I was a girl, I wanted so bad to just run my hands through his chest hair."

"Yeah, back then men were men and steroids was just a funny word."

"Deathslayer is a guy I grew up watching too," said Autumn when she finished laughing at Steve's quip. "Damn, this might be my last chance to see him before he retires, and they're sold out."

"Uhm, hey, uh…this sounds like a horrible pick-up line, but I actually do happen to have an extra ticket."

"Shut up," said Autumn, punching him in the arm. "You'll so be my hero if you really do, though!"

"I really do." Steve held up the foil embossed tickets. An image of his father drawn to cartoonish proportions and smashing the Empire State Building was depicted on its surface.

"Duh, dun dun duh duh," he said, imitating the *Superman* theme.

"Cool," said Autumn, visibly trying to play down her enthusiasm. "So are those like, nosebleeds, or…"

"Front row."

"Holy shit, front row?" said Autumn, grabbing the tickets in her hand and staring at them as if they were exalted relics. "Who did you have to kill? You know what, I don't care! I'm going to sit front row for Battlebrawl!"

She glanced up at Steve sheepishly, handing him back the tickets.

"Uh, thanks, Steve. I appreciate this. Just…don't go getting cocky, because this does not count as a date."

"Uh, sure," said Steve, trying to be nonchalant, but his dashed hopes were all over his face.

"Oh, don't look so disappointed." They walked toward the entrance. "I'm a pain in the ass anyway."

"Most people are."

"Yeah, true." Her large brown eyes were shining with excitement. "But you have no idea how much more qualified for the position I am."

They both laughed, his own guffaws spontaneous while she joined in a moment later.

"You been watching wrestling long?" she asked.

"I guess you could say that I've been watching it my whole life."

"Yeah, you must be an über-fan to get front row tickets. What'd you have to do, pay five thousand bucks for them on eBay?"

"No." They paused their conversation while Steve handed the usher their tickets. After giving Autumn her stub, he took a deep breath and said in a rush, "My dad's the Deathslayer. He got me the tickets."

Autumn stared at him wide-eyed for a moment, then burst into laughter.

"Yeah, right! I bet that line's a panty peeler, though!"

Steve sighed, giving her a tired smile. "No one ever believes me, but I have his nose, and his eyes."

He turned his visage to her. She peered at it intently, even putting her palms on either side of his cheeks and patting them.

"You know...I think I *do* see it! You have his Neanderthal brow ridges, too. And you're a freakin' giant..."

"I'm only six-five. Pop's seven feet tall. He said I got my mom's genes; her family were a bunch of midgets by comparison."

Autumn put her hand on his forearm and gave it a quick squeeze.

"I can't believe that *you're* the Deathslayer's kid! That must have been so cool having him as your dad!"

Steve smiled, chuckling as he was on familiar ground.

"It had its perks."

"Yeah, I'll bet. If any kid gave you a hard time on the playground you could have had him come to school and say his catchphrase."

Autumn adopted a gravelly, harsh-sounding voice and a narrow-eyed glare. Her face contorted in an almost grotesque manner, seeming quite similar to the carefree spirit displayed by his students. The sinister grimace made him laugh and warmed his heart at the same time.

"You will BURN...IN...HELL!"

"That's pretty good! A lot of women wouldn't have gone all the way with the face."

"A lot of women are shallow bitches. I am what I am. Lots of guys have found me attractive."

"So does this one."

"Okay...changing conversation off of 'date mode.' So, your mom wasn't a wrestler, I take it? Uh..." She looked at him, lines knitting her brow. "Is your mom, uh...is she still alive?"

"Oh yeah. She and Pop live out in Cali, where it's warm all the time. How they made it work for so long with him constantly on the road is beyond me."

"That's true love for you." Autumn's tone held a note of bitterness, and her gaze seemed far away for a moment.

He raised his eyebrow at her tone, but she fell silent again. After a few quiet moments, he cleared his throat.

"What about your parents?"

She glanced at him sharply, her lips drawn in a tight line.

"Mom died a long time ago. And my dad...well, he never wanted much to do with Mom and me."

"That's rough," said Steve, wincing in sympathy.

Autumn's hands fidgeted. "Yeah."

"I used to whine because my dad was gone all the time. You know, he missed things like my wrestling meets, my violin recitals..."

"Shut up!" she said, playfully punching him in the arm. "The wrestling makes sense with who your dad is, but you don't seem like the classical music type."

"I'm not, but my mother insisted that I get some culture. Pop's kind of a redneck, through and through. I guess she wanted me to be more of a Renaissance man."

They stared at each other, then looked away as they navigated the crowd and found the door leading to their seats.

"What kind of music do you like?" he asked when the silence became unbearable.

"Lady Gaga," she said, ticking off the names on the lithe fingers of one hand, "Justin Bieber, Bruno Mars…"

Steve tried to hide his surprise but largely failed. Autumn suddenly favored him with a wicked grin.

"I'm fucking with you," she said. "I like most anything, really, but I've got a soft spot for The Cure, the Beastie Boys…and I really love metal, especially British metal."

"Really?" he said, blinking in amazement. "Iron Maiden is probably my favorite band."

"Iron Maiden?" She rolled her eyes. "They suck."

Steve's smile dropped off his face.

"I'm fucking with you again," she said, howling with laughter.

chapter 3

"I think these are our seats," said Steve as he pointed to the padded steel chairs almost flush with the metal guardrail encircling the ring.

He moved aside, allowing Autumn to get past. Once she was seated, he situated his tall frame in the chair next to her. The Garden had been curtained in half, the stadium seating forming a rough U shape around them. Throngs of people threaded through the aisles, the multitude of their voices becoming a din. A local radio station played over the sound system, partially masking their conversation. The arena was just a bit shy of being uncomfortably warm, and sweat stood out on his brow.

"I have never been this close before," said Autumn, doffing her coat and letting it drape over her chair back. Steve swallowed hard at the sight of her bare shoulders. A brightly colored tattoo of an oriental dragon was on her right deltoid, while a tribal pattern adorned her left shoulder. There was evidence of more ink, but her forearm-length gloves concealed most of them. He was suddenly, intensely aware of her as a woman, and he was desperate to keep the fact off his face.

"Close enough to get sweat and blood on us. My sister Susie and I used to call it Tetanus Row as a goof."

"You have a sister?" Autumn was craning her neck and scanning the crowd for something.

"Yeah, she just turned nineteen. I think she's the son my dad always wanted; she actually likes wrestling. She's even training to be one."

Autumn fixed him with a somber gaze, chewing her lower lip.

"You don't like wrestling?"

"Not really. Ironic, eh? I guess I just kind of saw how little time Pops got to spend with us, much less time for himself. It's a hard life, there's no benefits package, and you're on the road constantly. Plus, when I watch wrestling, I'm always thinking stuff like 'well, that guy's belly-to-belly suplex could be tighter,' or 'how long you going to work that resthold, fatso? Do some cardio for the love of god,' you know?"

Autumn laughed at his mocking sentiments, clearly delighted with mean-spirited humor.

"Then why did you come?" she asked once she had regained her composure. "Obviously, your dad won't even be able to acknowledge you tonight."

"Well…the company is good."

"Oooh," said Autumn, flinching. Her face broke in a wide grin. "That line's a panty peeler too. Shame that this isn't a date."

He folded his arms over his chest, brow knit with confusion. After a moment he spoke, his voice a bit stiff. "So how come?"

"How come what?"

"How come this isn't one. A date, I mean."

She turned away from him, brown eyes narrowed as she stared intently at the ring. "I don't date. Try not to take it personally, huh?"

"Why don't you date?"

"It's just a waste of time. Mine and theirs."

"Why?"

She shook her head, falling silent for a moment. He formed his hand into a fist, berating himself for bringing it up. He spotted a beer vendor and flagged the man down.

"Thirsty? All they have is beer and soda, I'm afraid."

"I could go for a beer." She was digging in her purse.

"I got it," he said, digging in his own wallet.

"No, you don't. I'm being a total bitch to you, you're *not* paying for my drink."

"Yes, I am. And you're not being a bitch, total or otherwise."

She stopped her hunt for bills, watching as Steve dug out a twenty and handed it to the vendor. Soon they each had a tall plastic cup.

Autumn brought hers to her painted lips and sipped at the foam as it spilled over the edge.

"Most women don't like beer," he said with admiration.

"I don't either, if it's Milwaukee's Best or Keystone."

"Does Keystone even get you drunk? Seems like drinking water. And the Beast tastes like they filtered it through a New York Knick's jock strap."

She laughed, spraying a mouthful of beer over the safety railing to spatter on the rubber mats laid out for the wrestler's protection.

"You made me abuse alcohol," she said, flushing as she tried to mop up the fluid from her chin.

"I liked the sound of that."

She raised an eyebrow at him, a gesture he found both a little goofy and endearing.

"Your laugh…I like it when you laugh."

"Stick around. I find all sorts of inappropriate things funny, so it should be a riot!"

The bell rang loudly three times, eliciting a whoop from the gathered masses. Loud rock music played as the first athlete was announced. Steve watched Autumn as she stood up and leaned on the metal rail, straining to see the distant wrestler. Her brown eyes were shining, and a simple, beautiful smile was on her face. In that moment, she seemed more like an excited child than the caustic young woman she normally appeared to be.

The night's matches passed, and Steve found himself enjoying them in a way he hadn't since he was a child. Autumn whooped and hollered for the wrestlers she liked, booed and hissed the ones she hated, all with great enthusiasm. When a particularly bone-crushing impact occurred, she winced in sympathy and turned to look at him, her mouth an O.

Near the end of the program, the lights dimmed low. A tremendous shout rang out as "Hell's Bells" played over the loudspeaker.

"Here he comes," said Steve, feeling a tinge of pride in his father in spite of himself.

"He always had the best entrance theme," said Autumn, on her feet and staring intently at the curtain wall. Steve couldn't resist watching her rear as she shook from side to side in rhythm with the music.

Steve's father appeared in a cloud of smoke, causing an even more thunderous cheer to rise up and smash against his eardrums. Autumn added her shout to the mix, punctuating it with a shrill whistle. Deathslayer strode purposefully toward the ring.

"I gotta admit, the man has presence."

"Yeah, he's got the 'it' factor," she said with a nod, never taking her eyes off his father. "Some guys don't. I mean, they're athletic and everything, but you just don't care, you know?"

Steve nodded, looking again to his father. The old man had transformed, black eyeliner and mascara creating a creepy look on his visage. He wore a floor-length, black leather cape with a frilled collar, like a twisted Eurotrash count. He stopped, standing still as a stone before the ring, and held his arms out to his sides. The crowd's cheering rose to a frenzy.

"I love this part," said Autumn.

Suddenly, the Deathslayer brought his arms up and then down. A tremendous pyrotechnic burst went off around the ring, startling Steve, even though he was prepared for it. Autumn shouted, waving her arms wildly as the big man finished his entrance ritual. It was subtle, but Steve caught his father nodding slightly in his direction when their eyes met. The Deathslayer's gaze slid over to Autumn, and the tiniest ghost of a smile played over his face. Then it was gone, the Deathslayer from Hell returned, and he rolled his eyes back into his head in an *Exorcist* parody.

"I could never do that," said Steve, shaking his head. "Gives me a headache."

He felt a hard smack on his bicep. He turned his gaze back to Autumn to find her eyes showing nothing but white.

"That's creepy," he said with a laugh.

"What, this isn't creepy." She pawed at his arm, the satiny touch of her gloves light on his skin. "Brains," she said in a guttural voice. "Braaaaaains!!!"

He laughed at her continued antics, which she did not stop until a hard slam from the ring alerted her to the beginning of the action.

Autumn picked at the grilled chicken breast on her plate, tearing off shreds of meat with her fork.

"Is it not good?" Steve's eyes narrowed as he stared across the table at her.

They were seated in a diner several blocks from the Garden, packed with people, most of them having just left the arena themselves. Their ears were still ringing from the sound of the crowd, and he had suggested they get something to eat several times before she had heard him.

"It's fine," she said, pushing the plate away from herself. "I guess I drank too many beers."

"You only had two," he said.

She shook her head, staring at her gloved hands folded on the table.

They sat in relative silence for a time, Steve cutting into his steak and wincing at the scraping sound. He fumbled about in his head for something to say, anything to break the awkward silence. It was Autumn who eventually spoke.

"Are you sure you don't want me to chip in?"

"No, it's fine."

"You must have a good job."

"Yeah, it's all right. I'm a kindergarten teacher at PS 122."

"No way," she said, her mouth flying open in amazement.

"Yes way."

"You don't meet many male kindergarten teachers," she said, taking a sip of her soda.

"Yeah, there are some stereotypes to rail against, to be sure."

"How many people have asked you if you're gay?"

"Less than you might think. I believe people are afraid to ask. If I am, then they've just made an issue out of something society expects you to be cool with. If I'm not, they've probably just offended me."

"Does it bother you that people think that?"

"Not really. I've learned to have fun with it. You know, ham it up in front of parents who clearly think I like dudes." He adopted feminine body language and effected a high-pitched voice. "Oh, little Randall has done so *fabulously* this year!"

She burst out laughing, squirting him with the soda that shot out of her nose.

"Sorry," she said as he grimaced. She quickly took a handful of napkins and dabbed at his face. The touch of her fingers was electric, making his heart race.

"I think I got it all."

He slowly opened his eyes. She was looking at him with a half-lidded gaze, mouth pouty. "What?"

"I said I think I got it all," she said, exaggerating her speech.

"No, I mean what was with that expression you just made?"

"I don't know. I can't see my own face, so I don't know what you're talking about."

"You looked sad, almost jealous, I don't know…"

"Oh." Autumn took her soda cup in both hands and sucked noisily on the straw. "I was just thinking that it's too bad I don't date, because you seem like you might be all right."

Steve could not help the goofy grin that spread over his features.

Autumn rolled her brown eyes. "Oh, stop it! You're acting like I just proposed. Dork."

Much later in the evening, they stood outside her building, the cool breeze playing with Autumn's hair. She had one hand on the smooth metal handle, a foot placed on the single stone step.

"Thanks for sharing that ticket, and feeding me to boot! I had a blast."

"No problem." Steve fidgeted from foot to foot. He tried to make his mouth work, but found his speech had left him.

"So, it's getting late." She turned toward the door. "I should probably head in."

"Hey," he said as she pulled the door open about an inch.

She paused, her manner cool but with a tinge of expectation as well.

He cleared his throat. "Maybe we could do it again sometime? I mean, you know, hang out?"

Autumn gave him a slight smile. "Yeah...yeah, I'd like that."

She waited while he dug out his cell phone, and then they exchanged numbers.

"Call me," he said, seeing that her eyes were shining.

She went into the door just before her smile became a wide grin. He couldn't keep one off his own face, whistling "Hell's Bells" as his eyes searched for a taxi.

"I need a heal!" came the frantic, high-pitched, barely-masculine voice in Phil's ear.

"I'm coming," he said, fingers flashing over his keyboard. The figure on his computer screen, a pointy-eared fellow with baroque armor, was obscured briefly by an open menu. Without really seeing the symbols flashing before him, Phil made a rapid series of commands. When he came back out of the menu, his avatar strolled up to an animated melee. The avatar's hands glowed, and one of the fallen digital warriors was soon back on his feet.

"What took so long?" came the whining voice in his headset.

"You're welcome, Dean." Phil's voice dripped with venom.

"Hey, is that Phillip's voice I hear?" asked a feminine voice through the headset.

"It's me, Crawley. You need a heal?"

Crawley chuckled.

"No, I just thought you had band practice on Saturday nights."

"There is no band right now." Phil's fingers flashed over the keyboard. "Unless we can find another lead guitarist, stat!"

"Who cares about your fucking band?" said Dean. "We're in the middle of a raid here."

"I can carry on a conversation and play, you know." Phil gritted his teeth.

"Then how come my heal was so late?"

"I play guitar," said Crawley's voice.

Phil felt a rush of elation, but he was busy trying to keep Dean off his back. "Uhm, that's great."

"I've been playing since I was eleven! I know there's chicks who embarrass themselves all over the Internet trying to seem artistic, but I can actually play."

"Am I the only one who cares about the Darkstone Legacy Shadow Warriors bearing down upon us?" asked Dean.

"Yes," said Crawley and Phil at the same time, causing them both to burst into laughter.

"I guess you could come out and, I don't know, jam with us or whatever," said Phil, clicking rapidly on his mouse.

"That would be awesome! I used to play a lot with my brother's band, but they broke up when he got deployed to Afghanistan."

Phil allowed himself to be cautiously optimistic.

"What kind of music did they play?"

"Kind of classic rock, but they did a few contemporary songs, like Nickelback."

"Oh, yeah, that's cool."

"If you want to be in this guild, you have to take it seriously!" said Dean.

"Shut up, asshole," said Phil. He winced at his own words. "I was talking to Dean, not you Crawley."

"Yeah, I knew that. You said asshole, so I knew you were talking about Dean."

They both laughed, causing the butt of her joke to sputter.

"I don't need this shit! I'm turning off my headset, so you two can flirt all you want."

"Uh," said Phil.

Crawley's voice giggled in his ear, a girlish sound that made him grin.

"So when are we gonna do this?"

"Uh, I guess tomorrow might be good," he said slowly. "I know Rex is off, and our lead singer never works weekends. Rex will just use it as an excuse to have a barbeque."

"I *love* barbeque! You're still friends with me on Facebook, right?"

"I should be," said Phil, bringing up another window. He looked at a picture quite similar to the video game character she used as an avatar. The name looked a little strange. "Uh, there's an Eleanor Chav Rng Leizl...What is this, Chinese? I can't pronounce it."

Crawley's voice giggled in his ear.

"Tagalog, actually. Crawley is our Anglo approximation. Dad got sick of his mail never coming to the house a few years ago and legally changed it to Crawley. It's close enough and easy to spell. When I started an online account, I thought I'd use the old family name."

"That's cool." Phil felt foolish for mangling the name.

"I'll message you my number...right after this raid."

"Right!" Phil's focus returned to the game.

chapter 4

Susan banged on the thin door of Steve's apartment, raising her voice to be heard above the din she was making.

"Wake up, jerk! It's noon, for God's sake!"

A moment later his face appeared in the doorway, still swollen with sleep. An indentation from his pillow created a comical design across his cheeks, which were covered in fine stubble.

"I don't give a shit what time it is, I'm goddamn tired. What are you doing here?"

"Uh, duh?" She pushed past him into his tiny apartment. "We're having lunch with dad today, remember?"

"Oh, shit...give me a minute?"

"Take two." Susan plopped down on his sofa. She had on tight jeans and a snug-fitting T-shirt, her long, dirty-blond hair cascading down her back. Her painted thumbnail flicked through a dozen channels in a matter of seconds. "Don't you have cable?"

"What's the point?" he shouted from his bathroom. "Anything on cable you can watch on the Internet for free."

"I just like to surf, sometimes. Ugh, *network* television."

Steve rubbed a hand over his stubble, deciding he really didn't have time to shave. He ran a brush through his thick head of hair, growling as he hit snarls.

"You can't surf the web?" he called out.

"Nah, it's just not the same. You have to type in what you're looking for."

Steve laughed as he spritzed on cologne from a small amber bottle. "Oh, poor baby, you have to push a few more buttons than normal."

"I know, it's terrible, right?"

"Where are we going to eat?" Steve rifled through the shirts hanging in the tiny chamber laughingly referred to by his landlord as a closet.

"Applebee's, I think."

"Good!" He grabbed a black T-shirt without taking down the hanger, which bounced crazily in the closet until its momentum played out. "I can dress casual."

"When do you not dress casual? You even wear jeans to work!"

He came out into the living room, now clad in a pair of jeans and an Iron Maiden T-shirt that wasn't too worn.

"Do you know how messy my kids get? 'Dry clean only' just isn't an option in my profession."

The two of them exited the apartment, Steve locking the door behind them. They trod down the noisy hallway as Susie's face scrunched up in disgust.

"Why are you still living in this dump?"

"Rent's cheap. Besides, I always thought…"

They walked down the short flight of narrow stairs, avoiding sticky spots on the railing. When they reached the street level, she turned to regard him.

Her tone bore some annoyance that he had left her hanging. "You always thought what?"

Steve felt quite uncomfortable. Sweat broke out on his forehead and palms, and he pursed his lips as he stared at her lovely face. When he spoke he did not meet her eyes. "I always thought, well, I thought that I'd move once I got married."

"Well, that's logical, at least. Don't give up hope! Dad says he saw you with a date at the match last night. You know, he was really, really happy you showed up."

"Yeah, well, I couldn't keep blowing him off. And it wasn't a date."

"Oh, is she seeing someone else?"

"No, I don't think so."

"And are you seeing someone else?"

"No, you know I'm not."

"Then it was a date." Susan elbowed him in the ribs and gave him a wink.

Steve looked at the busy street before them as vehicles zipped past as quickly as they dared. He grimaced when he didn't spot a taxi.

"How are we getting there? You want to split the fare on a cab?"

"Dad's gonna pick us up on Hudson. He just bought a new Cadillac, and I think he wants to show it off."

"Fine for him. I hate driving in the city."

The siblings walked down the sidewalk, bathed in bright sunlight. Susan seemed to enjoy it immensely, closing her eyes and letting the warmth spread over her face. Steve squinted at the brightness, appearing quite uncomfortable. They stopped at a Kinko's parking lot, Steve leaning against a light pole while Susan fished out her cell.

"Daddy?" she said a few moments after putting it to her ear. "Yeah, we're in the copy shop's parking lot, like you said."

Susan paused for a brief moment, listening to their father. Then a smile spread across her face. "Okay, see you in a few, Daddy!"

She grinned fiercely at Steve. "So, tell me all about this new girl."

"No. All you'll do is make fun of me."

Susan adopted a plaintive posture, her large eyes glistening in the sun. "C'mon, please? Or do you want to hear the most annoying sound in the world?" Susan opened her mouth and a dissonant screech emanated from her oral cavity, causing Steve to wince.

"God, you know I hate that! Fine, what do you want to know?"

"Is she cute?"

Steve smiled, eyes seeming far away. "She's gorgeous."

"How many tattoos does she have? She's got at least one facial piercing, right?"

Steve's smile faded. "Shut up."

"Oh, I'm just messing with you, bro! We all have our types. Is this one at least out of high school?"

Steve shook his head, mouth twisting in a sneer. "One time, one time when I was in college, and you never let me hear the end of it. Besides, they don't count as high school girls when they're eighteen."

"I bet she is younger than you, though."

Steve's head tilted to one side, eyes far away as he pondered something that he hadn't really cared to as of yet. "I don't know. She probably is, but she doesn't seem that young. Kind of jaded, really. Funny, though, in a smart ass kind of way."

He fixed her with a glare. "You'd probably love her."

"I'm sure I will!"

"But we're not dating. She was very adamant about that."

"Play it cool, big bro. Don't try to push her into anything before she's ready."

"Then what should I do?"

"Just be yourself," said Susan, taking his arm in both of her hands. She leaned her head against his shoulder. "You're a sweet guy, Steve. I really hope you find a sweet woman, because otherwise you're in for a lot of heartache."

"I really wouldn't describe her as sweet per se. Yeah, I'm probably in for a bad time."

"But you never know..." Susan released his arm and punched it solidly. "She might be the one."

"I'm not holding my breath." Steve's interest was piqued by a long, royal blue Cadillac pulling into the lot. He saw his father's great shaggy head over the steering wheel, face split in a wide grin of unconstrained pride.

"Great car, Daddy!" said Susan, opening up the passenger side door.

"Thanks, pumpkin!" He accepted her peck on the cheek. "Why don't you get in the back seat, and let us long-legged men have the front?"

"You're so buying me one of these when I graduate," said Susan as she complied.

"You're buying her a car?"

"Maybe. It depends on what her grades are like. If she gets all A's, sure she can have a Caddy. B's, she'll end up with a Lexus. C's, and she'll get a Pontiac."

"What do you think you'll end up driving?" Steve, turned his head to address her in the back seat.

"An old Pinto with a headlight missing," she said, causing all three to laugh.

"A chick?" Rex shook his head incredulously, looking at Phil as if he'd grown a second head.

"Yeah, sort of." Phil scratched the back of his head.

"What do you mean, sort of? Either she is or she isn't, and if she is then there's one simple rule."

They were in Rex's basement, the older man wearing the same sweat pants as the night before. Phil had carefully picked out a pair of dark dress pants and a button-up collared shirt in a complementary shade of light orange. He wore black tennis shoes to complete the ensemble, apparently unaware that one of his laces was untied.

"What rule?" Phil asked.

"Easy! Either she's ugly, in which case she can probably play, or she's cute, in which case she won't be able to play at all."

"Stereotype much?"

"It's true!" Rex was distracted by a knock at the door.

"What's up, faggots?" said Rich from the other side.

"Oh, god," said Phil, taking off his glasses and rubbing his eyes. "Why did you invite him?"

"Our mothers play mah-jongg together," said Rex with a shrug. "Besides, didn't you go to high school with him?"

"Don't remind me."

Rex moved to open the door. Rich appeared in the opening, wearing cargo shorts despite the cold weather. He had on a Jimmy Buffet T-shirt and flip-flops.

Rich grinned as his eyes moved up and down Phil's form. "You dork. It's a fucking *Sunday* for god's sake, you don't have to dress like you're at the office."

"I'm not taking fashion advice from a guy who looks like a homeless person," said Phil.

"Ooooh, look who brought his big boy voice to the basement today!"

"Dumbshit here," said Rex, indicating Phil with a jab of his fat finger, "thinks he's found us a new guitarist. A chick."

"You dumbass," said Rich, laughing.

"Yeah, I was just telling him if she's hot, she won't be able to play."

"Who the hell is it?" Rich asked, sitting down on a battered lounge chair and helping himself to a can of beer.

"Eleanor Crawley," said Phil. "You remember her? We had Chem class together."

Rich burst out laughing, almost dropping the beer he was trying to open.

"Creepy Crawley? Oh my god, Rex, you got nothing to worry about, buddy!"

"Why is that?"

"'Cause Creepy Crawley ain't hot. Far from it!"

"She wasn't that bad looking," said Phil.

"Like you could tell, with those layers of wifey Mormon dresses she always wore! And do you remember her hands? They were as big as a dude's! She could knock out Tyson with one of those things!"

"Could she play?" Rex asked, cautious optimism creeping into his voice.

"I guess so," said Phil with a shrug. "She was always in band all the way through high school."

"Wait a minute," said Rich, his eyes growing thoughtful. "Where did you run into Creepy anyway? Buying razors, Band-Aids, and peroxide?"

Phil stared at him silently, eyes narrowed and brows knit, while Rex burst out laughing. "I don't get it."

"He's trying to insinuate," said Rex, "that your girlfriend cuts herself."

"I'm just trying to *feeeeel* something!" said Rich, pantomiming violent slashes of his thighs.

"God, will you just let it go for a minute? You better not embarrass me when she gets here!"

"Embarrass you? Buddy, I'm just gonna sit back and watch you embarrass yourself!"

"I bet this chick is into you," said Rex with a sly grin.

"Oh god, of course not! I haven't even seen her since high school. We chat on *WoW* sometimes, sure, but—"

"Fuck no," said Rich. "This chick is one of your role-playing geeks? You're gonna spend all night trying to keep her tongue out of your throat!"

"Shut the fuck up!" Phil took a threatening step toward the blond man.

"And then she'll give you a handy j," Rich continued, eyes aglow, "and with her big, manly paws she might pull off your peter!"

Phil seemed on the verge of throttling the man. The veins stuck out near his temples, and his face was flushed. His hands grasped at his sides as his eyes narrowed to slits. Rich was saved a good smack by Phil's phone ringing.

"Asshole!" Phil exited the garage. He stepped carefully past the oil slick and put the phone to his ear. "Hello?"

"Phillip?" came the response.

"Uh huh. Having trouble finding the place?"

"No, I Googled a map. I was just wondering if there was going to be alcohol there."

"Oh…" Phil was taken a bit aback. "Well, Rex likes to drink, and so does my friend Steve, but I don't think there's going to be a bunch of drunks running around."

Her laughter was almost musical in his ear. "No, you dummy. If there's no booze, I was going to buy some."

"Uh, okay. I think there's plenty of beer here."

"I'm not big on beer. I mean, I'll drink it, but only if there's nothing else available."

"Well, if you want to get something, I can chip in on it." Phil dug in his back pocket for his wallet.

"That's all right, I'm not worried about money. I'll see you soon, okay?"

"Okay." Phil wondered why his hands were suddenly so sweaty.

"I'd invite you up," Steve said as his father pulled the Caddy in front of his apartment building, "but there's not much to see."

"Don't sweat it," said the big man. "I'm taking Susie to see some friends of mine."

"You mean wrestling buddies." Steve's blue eyes were narrowed to near slits as he glared at Susan in the back seat. "You really want that kind of life for yourself?"

Susan rolled her eyes. "Pffft."

"What's wrong with the life?" His father's brow came low over his eyes.

"That's not what I meant. It's always the same thing. You two gang up on me and I end up looking like the bad guy."

"No one's ganging up on you," Susan said.

"Then why does it feel like it?" Steve said, getting out of the car. He left the door standing open, both due to his anger and because Susan was switching to the front seat. Deathslayer watched him go, face slack and eyes seeming to be focused on something far away.

Steve fumbled with his keys, dropping them to the hallway floor several times before he managed to jam it into the lock. He shouldered the door open, cursing as it swung open too hard and banged against the wall. His upstairs neighbor stomped hard several times on the floor/ceiling.

"Yeah, yeah, sorry," said Steve in a low growl. "Fucking asshole. I don't complain when you listen to that fucking god-awful rap shit at top volume."

He went to the fridge, jamming his hand up to the elbow inside the Miller Lite box, disgusted when he came back empty-handed. Heaving a sigh, he strode over to his sofa and sat down heavily on it.

Picking up his phone, he opened an app that would let him stream movies onto his TV. In short order he was watching a mindless action movie. His face remained passive as the movie changed from one violent scene to another more violent scene. At length he picked up his phone again and brought up his contacts list. Autumn's name appeared at the top.

He sat still for a moment, finger poised over the screen. The choice was made for him when the screen flashed, heralding an incoming call. For a brief second he thought it might be Autumn, enough that he was disappointed to see Phillip's name come up on the screen.

"Yeah?" he said as salutation, not bothering to keep the annoyance out of his voice.

"Hey, man," said Phil, a little abashed, "is there any way you could come out to Rex's?"

"It's a school night, dude. If I'm late one more time, I'm gonna get my ass chewed."

"You don't have to stay till two a.m.! C'mon man, I need you to do me a solid. That asshole Rich is here, and —"

"The overgrown frat boy?"

"Yeah, in all his aggravating glory. But that's not the worst of it. There's a chick coming here. She's maybe going to play with us, and she, well, she—"

"You know her from somewhere, and she's ugly, and you need me to be a buffer in case she gets clingy."

"How'd you know I was going to—"

"It's hardly the first time. Can you pick 'em, or what?"

"So are you coming over?" Phil's voice had a wheedling tone.

"I'm tired, man. I have to work tomorrow. I was out late last night and had to get up early—"

"Aww, come on, man, didn't you send me a text about some chick you met at the wrestling match? Augusta or something? You could bring her along."

"Autumn. And I probably should wait a day or two before I call her again."

"Why is that? Why can't you call her right now?"

Steve sighed in exasperation. "Phil, I know you're not all that experienced on the dating scene, but if I call her tonight, I'm gonna seem desperate."

"And you aren't?"

Steve choked back an angry retort, stopping himself before he had uttered a single syllable. His eyes narrowed to flinty blue slits, and he hated himself for secretly agreeing with Phil. "No promises, but I will give her a call. Or a text. Do you think I should start with a text?"

"I don't care. Just hurry!"

"We'll see." Steve set down the phone. He again brought up Autumn's name, again poised his finger over the screen. Suddenly he jabbed it down, putting the phone to his ear in a rush.

"No backing out now. Maybe she won't answer. Maybe it'll go to voice mail. Then I can tell Phil to go suck it."

"Hello?" Autumn's voice seemed thick and slow, as if she had been sleeping.

"Hey, uh…Did I wake you up?"

"Kind of…just taking a nap, really. I'm surprised you called me. I mean, aren't you worried about that three-day rule?"

"Rule? Is that a law on the books? Is the NSA gonna bust in my door and put a gun to my head for violating it?"

She giggled, then coughed, making unladylike hacking noises. "Sorry. I should really quit smoking, y'know?"

"I guess I seem kind of desperate right now, violating that three-day rule."

"Don't worry about it. I have trouble following the written rules, let alone the unwritten ones."

Steve chuckled. "I kind of get that impression."

"So what's up? I assume you didn't misdial me and decide to just go with it now."

Steve laughed as much at her easygoing manner as at her quip. "No, no, I meant to call you. Listen, I know it's short notice, but I got a friend of mine having a barbeque-band-practice- hoedown kind of thing."

He winced at his own awkward fumbling of the English language.

"I don't know, are there going to be dangerous people at this barbeque-band-practice-whatever thingie?"

"There might be, but I'm secretly a crack covert operative for the CIA in deep cover. They won't stand a chance."

She laughed again. For some reason, he found himself wanting to make her do it more.

"If you're telling me, does that mean you have to kill me?"

"No, you're the asset I was sent to protect. You have, a, uh, a cipher in your head that unlocks the nuclear launch codes."

"Then I better start getting ready. I'm not safe at home. When are you coming to get me?"

"Twenty minutes," he said, then rubbed his stubbly face. "Make that thirty minutes."

"Okay, give me one ring when you're outside my building. And don't forget—"

"This isn't a date?"

"That, too," she said after a brief pause.

The connection went dead, and he heaved a sigh.

chapter 5

Phil sat in the corner of the basement garage, almost invisible behind the concealment of his keyboard. He looked up with chagrin as Rich related an utterly ludicrous story. He shook his head at the way Rich was able to hold so many people in thrall at once, when he was crude and crass in so many ways. Yet, the gathered crowd (some fifteen people all told) continued to wait on his every word with bated breath.

"…so we finally, *finally* find the address Pedro gave us, which was really hard since none of us spoke Mexican, and we go inside. The first thing we're thinking is what's with all the chickens? Where's the babe? Where's the donkey? Come to find out, it wasn't a donkey show — it was a cock-fighting ring!"

"That wasn't funny," said Phil to himself when the crowded room filled with laughter. Frustrated, he rose to his feet and scooted out from behind the keyboard. He squeezed by two people he had met but whose names he never remembered, and reached the exit. He stepped out into the cool, darkening evening, sighing in relief as Rich's voice was at least partially muffled.

A white Eclipse came rolling up the street. Phil noted with interest that the driver was a young woman, and her slow trajectory down the pavement gave him ample time to see that she was pretty. Unlike most pretty women, she didn't seem to look right past him. In fact, her face split in a cheery grin. She waved enthusiastically at him, parking about three cars away from Rex's house.

He cocked his head to the side and tried to place her as she approached. She was petite and slender, with smooth skin a muted caramel hue. Her long, silky black hair was hanging loose, the bangs kept out of her face by a pink barrette. She was wearing a long-sleeved gray shirt with blue flowers, which hung over the top of her tight blue miniskirt. She wore opaque tights which disappeared into sneakers with an anime theme.

"Phillip!" She approached, beaming at him. He stared at her cute face and found his breathing was getting more rapid. She had dark brown eyes, nearly black, with slight epicanthic folds at the corners. She had a nose that was a bit wide, but did not seem out of place on her visage. Her lips were small but pouty, and coated with a dark red gloss.

"Uh," he said, "can I help you?"

"Phillip," she said, her smile fading, "it's me, Crawley."

He did a double take, eyes growing wide with realization. It *was* Creepy Crawley, but not at all the way he remembered.

"Oh my god! It's been years since high school. I didn't recognize you!"

He gave her a big smile, and was taken aback when she gave him a friendly hug.

"I recognized *you*. I am wearing my hair different now, I guess."

"That must be it," said Phil, eager to move past the awkward moment.

"Should I get my guitar now, or..." She pointed behind herself at the car.

"Yeah, yeah, definitely."

He walked with her to her car, offering to help with her burdens.

"You can carry the amp, but *nobody* touches Molly."

"Molly?"

"Molly Hatchet," she said, slapping the black plastic case.

"You named your guitar. That's cool. I never named my keyboard."

"Well —" Crawley's cheeks flushed red "— I guess it's a girl thing."

"I think it's great!" They walked back to the garage. "My friend Steve named his muscle car. He calls it Black Moon, even though it's kind of a primer color right now."

"Black Moon," giggled Crawley. "That sounds cool."

They passed below a buzzing streetlight, its din drowning out the constant sounds of traffic from Manhattan. He found himself unable to stop staring at her. Her breasts were small, but still bounced nicely with every step she took. Her waist seemed almost impossibly tiny, and her hips flared out to give her a sensuous, womanly appeal.

He opened the door for her, standing aside to let her through.

"It's kind of crowded in here, and you have to watch out for spiders, but…"

"What kinds of spiders?" she asked eagerly.

"Uh, not poisonous ones, I don't think."

"Oh." Crawley's eyes were cast downward for a moment and she seemed disappointed.

Rex's gaze fell on them as they entered, his face breaking into a wide grin. He shouldered past the throng of people listening to Rich's dissertations and reached out to shake her hand eagerly.

"Hey, you must be Eleanor."

"I am," she said, dimpling at him.

"I'm Rex, your drummer and founder of Settle the Score."

"Settle the Score?" said Phil. "I thought we were calling ourselves We Shall Overcome."

"We were." Rex crossed his arms over his barrel chest. "But then your buddy Rich pointed out that sounds like a gay porn movie."

Phil fumed, staring at Rich with eyes narrowed into slits while his hands clenched into fists at his sides. Then the almost musical sound of Crawley's laughter reached his ears.

"You guys are still best friends! That is so great!"

"He's not my—" said Phil.

"Creepy Crawley!" shouted Rich, stopping his story mid-sentence. The crowd parted for him as he traversed the short distance to the front of the garage. "Man, you turned out to be hot!"

"Shut up, asshole!" said Phil in a growl, while Crawley giggled behind her hand.

"You've still got man-hands, though," said Rich.

Phil was shocked. He turned a wide eyed-gaze on Rich, his mouth flying open.

"Dude, that was *not* cool."

"It's all right," said Crawley, smiling at him. She raised one of her hands for his inspection. "I do have boy hands. I bet they're bigger than yours!"

She grabbed his right hand and lifted it, sending a shock through his body at her contact. Placing her palm flat against his, it was evident that her hands were indeed longer and thicker than his own.

"See?" She smiled prettily at him.

"Yeah," he said, a goofy smile on his face.

"She's hot," said Rich, turning to nod at Rex. "That means she can't play for shit, according to your logic."

Rex laughed nervously. "You're such a kidder, Rich," he said through gritted teeth.

Phil cleared his throat.

"She could be hot *and* be able to play." In a split second, concern spread out over his features. "I didn't mean to say you were hot! I mean, I think you are, but I didn't mean to say it out loud. I mean, it's not like I'm sitting here checking you out, it's just that, you know, you're pretty and —"

She put a finger up to his lips and giggled again, mischief flashing in her dark eyes. "You're cute when you're rambling." Abruptly she removed the finger and walked over to the gaming table. She set the case down upon it and flipped open the latches.

"Come to momma," she said softly, carefully taking the guitar out of the case. It was a beautiful Gibson six string, its red body polished to a shine. A medieval battle ax decal was affixed just below the whammy bar. The frets had some wear, indicating that she played the instrument regularly.

"Where can I set up?"

Rex led her over to the power strip on the wall. "I'll show you. You know, I had to rewire the grounds myself..."

As the pair made their way to the power strip, Rich slapped an arm around Phil's shoulders and moved his head in close. "You are about to be given a great responsibility."

"You make my life miserable."

"You," said Rich, as if Phil had not spoken, "are about to begin dating a rock solid ten. Rock. Solid."

"I doubt someone like her would be interested in someone like me. And anyway, why aren't *you* all over her like stink on shit?"

Rich looked at him aghast, releasing his shoulder and standing a few feet away. "Phil, I'm hurt! I'm deeply, deeply hurt by your harsh words! I'd never try to horn in on your territory."

"Why?" Phil was genuinely discombobulated.

"'Cause—" Rich punched him hard in the bicep "—we're broskis. And broskis never rub another broski's rhubarb."

Rich went back to his waiting audience and picked up his story where he had left it. Phil looked past him, to where Crawley was setting up her amp. She seemed confident as her fingers spun the dials on the front of the device. She noticed his attention and gave him a grin.

He returned the smile, not knowing what else to do. A light rap at the door behind him gave him an excuse to break the eye contact, and he hustled to open it. Steve stood outside, towering over him and dressed casually in jeans and a T-shirt. He had a leather jacket on over the shirt, and with his long hair and sullen eyes, he looked the part of a hooligan.

His date was equally off-putting. Phil had never liked women with tattoos, and this one had them all up and down her arms. She had a sleeve design on both of her forearms, while her biceps were more sparsely decorated. She was dressed in a pair of tight black pants with far more straps and buckles than was necessary, her torso adorned in a snug T-shirt. She had a pleather coat over it, but it was unbuttoned, accentuating her bustline. She wore dark purple eye shadow, her lips painted much the same. Her hair was done in pigtails.

"Stop drooling," said Steve, slapping him on the arm. "Phillip, this is Autumn. Autumn, Phillip."

"Nice to meet you," she said in a husky voice that Phil had somehow expected.

"Nice to meet you, too." Phil politely gave her hand a shake. "Come on in. Unfortunately the party is just getting started."

"I wouldn't call this a party," said Autumn, wrinkling her nose. "There's barely a dozen people here."

"Well, we can't all be social butterflies."

"Hey, this is fine," said Autumn defensively. "I kind of didn't mean it as an insult…but I guess I kinda did, too. Told you I was a pain in the ass."

Steve looked at her with a raised eyebrow. "So you keep saying."

They made their way into the garage, Steve introducing her to Rex's wife and other select guests whom he knew well. Autumn smiled broadly at each of them, curbing her normally acerbic tongue and exchanging pleasantries well enough.

In short order, they found the only available seating, a dingy and worn loveseat embroidered with geese. Steve got them both a bottle of Leininkugel, popping off the tops with his thumbs.

"That's a talent! To good times." Autumn clinked her bottle lightly against his own.

"I'll drink to that."

Both took long pulls on their drinks, not breaking eye contact the whole time. They sat staring at each other without speaking for a short while, as Crawley tuned up in the background.

"So…this is nice," said Autumn.

"Yeah."

"Cozy. And everyone seems friendly."

"Yep. It is and they are."

"Wanna get the hell out of here?" Autumn's smile was as fierce as it was sudden.

"Absodamnlutely." Steve rose to his feet and stretched. He held out a hand and assisted Autumn.

"Where are you going?" Rex asked as they headed for the front door.

"Just going to get some fresh air," said Steve.

"If you want some privacy, you can use me and the missus's bedroom."

Autumn tried to stifle her laugh behind a palm as Steve sputtered a response.

"Oh, I'm just kidding," said Rex, giving him a slap on the shoulder. "Have fun."

They exited the building and stood under a starless sky. A fair amount of cloud cover largely concealed the moon as well, though a bit of its cheery silver light could be seen peeking out from time to time.

"Wanna take a walk?" he asked. "This is my old neighborhood. It's pretty safe at night."

"Sure. After all, I have a secret agent for a bodyguard."

They slowly strolled along the sidewalk, Steve pointing out land-marks. "There's where I fell out of a tree." He indicated an empty lot overgrown with vegetation. "Broke my arm and had to have a cast. That used to be Phillip Seymour Hoffman's house, right over there."

"Are you a fan of PSH?"

"Of who?"

"PSH. Phillip Seymour Hoffman."

"Oh, I guess so. *Capote* was pretty good."

"I loved PSH in everything he did. He was like, the brute force and ignorance actor. Not handsome, and not classically trained, but he put so much enthusiasm into his work. Shame he had to go and OD."

Steve nodded.

"Good actors, musicians, they all die young. Fred Durst and Adam Sandler will probably live forever."

She chuckled at his quip, her large brown eyes shining. Then her face fell, a grim specter casting a pall over her pretty face.

"What's wrong?" he asked.

"Nothing. Nothing's wrong. This feels nice. Maybe that's the problem. I'm not used to hanging around people who just let me *be*, you know?"

"I think I understand where you're coming from. A lot of the time, I'm afraid to say what I'm thinking."

"Oh?" she said, playfully elbowing him in the ribs. "Dirty mind?"

"No! No, I just…sooner or later, I seem to rub everyone the wrong way. I don't do it on purpose. It's just, some people are just so damn stupid! They say things like they're speaking with the voice of God, and what comes out of their mouth is just so fucking ignorant that it gives me a stomachache."

"Do I fall into that category? I'll tell you right now, I never gradu-ated from high school, never went to college…"

"No! Of course not. I think you're witty, funny, and smart. A little mean, but funny and smart."

"Mean?" Autumn jabbed her finger in his ribs. "I'll show you mean, you prick!"

Her nail slipped between the soft tissue connecting his ribs.

"Ow! It's like being jabbed with a sword!"

"Big baby." They crossed a road and turned left, putting the Manhattan skyline in their view. The lights shining from the glass towers, the pale yellow from the windows, and the bright red atop the skyscrapers mingled to create an aesthetic portrait.

"Wow," she said, her mouth slightly open. "It's beautiful, at least from a distance."

He looked at her, licking his lips nervously as she peered intently at the city. "Some things are even more beautiful up close."

He reached his hand toward her own, brushing the backs together. She flinched at the contact, jerking her hand away.

"Sorry, I know, it's not a—"

"Your hair tickles, dumbass," she said, glaring at him even as she wrapped her hand around his and gently squeezed it. "It's like holding hands with a gorilla! What did they feed you growing up, whole roast cow?"

Steve laughed, hard enough that his ribs ached. "Ma liked to cook pasta. Spaghetti and meatballs with pickles was my fa—"

"Pickles in spaghetti? Are you fucking kidding me?"

"Don't knock it until you try it. Maybe if you come over some time I can cook it up for you."

Autumn lifted their conjoined hands, bringing them close to her face. "Oh, it has the opposable thumbs necessary for such feats?"

They stopped in the circle of light cast by the buzzing fixture overhead, Steve chuckling as the tattooed young woman examined his hand with great scrutiny.

"Well, it looks like a human hand, but due to the size and hairiness, I'd say we're dealing with a Sasquatch."

Steve stopped laughing, his mouth falling open and blue eyes opening wide. "Sasquatch?"

"Yeah, you know, like the Canadian team, what's it called? *Awful Flight*?"

"She reads comics too. You just keep getting more awesome."

"Shut the fuck up. And I didn't read it, but I was aware of it. I only read *Sandman*, *Preacher*, the more edgy stuff. My boyfriend at the time tried to get me to read the superhero crap."

"I read *Sandman* a little. Pop actually got the Deathslayer idea from some sword and sandal mag back in the day. *Heavy Metal*, I think."

Autumn's eyes narrowed, and her mouth twisted up in a pout. "I hate that fucking magazine. It's cartoon tits. Do people really get off on cartoon tits?"

Steve laughed. He realized his cheeks were hurting, he was doing so much laughing and smiling. It felt good, made him remember his younger days.

"I'm asking you a serious question, Sasquatch." Autumn yanked on his arm until he stopped laughing and met her eyes. "I can tell you right now, that I don't get off on cartoons. I'm sitting on my couch with *Magic Mike* playing on the TV saying PEACE, and LOVE, and —"

Steve was overcome with mirth once more, as much because Autumn was using enthusiastic pantomime to enhance her authentic-seeming facial tics and moans.

"You're terrible! Someone's going to call the cops on us."

"Pffft. Faking an orgasm ain't a crime. It ought to be, but it ain't."

They walked toward the city for a time, until they were at the edge of the subdivision. Her hand felt good in his own, as if he were being charged like a battery. Reluctantly, they turned and headed toward Rex's house, putting the city out of their view.

They walked in silence back to the garage, holding hands the entire way. Steve found himself feeling relaxed and excited all at once, as if he were a child standing in line for a roller coaster ride. At times he would glance over at Autumn and find her soft brown eyes gazing at him. She would look away nervously after a moment, but inevitably the eye contact would resume.

He felt a tinge of regret as Rex's house came back into view. They could hear music playing from within, a melody they both recognized.

"Damn," said Steve, "that little chick can *play*."

"And she's cute as hell." Autumn gave his hand a squeeze.

"I hadn't really noticed," he said nervously.

"Liar!" Autumn pecked him on the cheek. He was startled by the contact, grateful that she kept talking so he would not have to. "Stevie Wonder would notice that she's hot as hell. It's only natural to take an interest, even if you never intend to do anything about it."

"The irony is that I was supposed to be here to be a buffer between her and Phil. I guess that went out the window when she wound up being cute."

She arched her pierced brows at him. "He seems younger than you and Rex. Not that you're old, or anything, but—"

Steve smiled, giving her hand a squeeze back. "We used to run with his big brother, Tyler, and he would just kind of follow us around, you know? Then Tyler...well, he stepped on an IED in Iraq, and that was that. We kind of adopted Phil after that." His lips drew into a thin tight line, his eyes downcast.

"You miss him, don't you?"

"A lot. I try to think back on the good times, try to keep his memory alive, but...I don't know. Over time, I'm not sure if I'm even recalling his face right, or how his voice sounded when he laughed. Death sucks."

"Yeah," said Autumn, pulling her hand out of his grip. "Yeah, it does at that. C'mon, I need another beer."

They re-entered the party, Steve struggling to catch up.

chapter 6

"I don't suppose," said Steve as the taxi pulled up outside his building, "that you'd want to come up for coffee?"

Autumn looked over at him, blinking. She had spent most of the ride staring out the window silently, resisting his attempts at conversation.

"Don't you have to work early?"

"Yeah, but I'll sleep when I'm dead. I'll call you another cab."

"I don't think..." She turned her face toward his, and her eyes met his for a long moment. "All right."

Steve paid the fare, the driver sneering over the meager tip.

"Sorry!" Steve was left in a cloud of exhaust that made him choke.

"He'd just use it to make a bomb or take flying lessons or something," said Autumn, causing him to burst out in laughter.

"Oh," he said, wiping his eyes while willing his ribs to stop aching, "that's *terrible*. I mean, I think he was a Hindu or something..."

"Eh, Vietnamese, Siamese, dirty knees—" she opened up her coat and thrust her chest, breasts straining against the thin fabric "—look at these, Japanese! They're all foreigners who hate America! Fox News told me so!"

Again he was overcome with laughter, while she rubbed her hands together as if she were cold, though the evening was fairly warm for the season.

"Let's get inside before we get mugged," she said.

"Right." Steve extracted his key card out of his wallet and slid it in the reader. The door popped open and he held it for her.

"God," she said with a sheepish grin, "you're such a gentleman!"

"Thanks." He was momentarily distracted by the mound of mail awaiting him in his box.

"It wasn't a compliment, and it's wasted on a mean bitch like me."

"What's wrong with being a gentleman?" They walked up the short flight of stairs to the second floor. "Other than the fact that women like jerks, of course."

"Women do not like jerks!" She punched him in the arm.

"Sure seems like it. Look how those bimbos were swooning over Rich at the party. He's the biggest jerk I know."

"Women don't like jerks. We like guys who kind of *look* dangerous, but don't act like it."

"Really?" Steve fumbled with his door latch. "I always thought you wanted a bad boy you could reform as proof of your feminine wiles."

"You have some strange ideas about women."

He turned toward her with a bit of shame in his eyes as the door swung open. "Uh...it's not much. I always figured I was gonna move when I got married. That was six years ago and counting. But it's clean. No roaches or mice, and rent controlled to boot."

"I'm hardly a snob." She followed him into the apartment. He flipped on the lights and she whistled as she took in the environs. "Of course, I wasn't expecting it to be *this* bad..."

"Ouch," said Steve, lips pouty and trembling in an exaggerated way.

"Oh, I'm fucking with you again. Honestly, how do you do your job? Seems like those kids would eat you alive, you're so easy to mess with."

"It helps that I have a really deep, stern-sounding voice."

"Shut up! Is that really all it takes?"

"Not all. At the end of the day, being a good teacher isn't about how knowledgeable you are about the subject, or how many degrees you have. It's about empathy, understanding what's going on inside their little brains. I guess I'm a bit childish, because I can usually figure out their line of reasoning."

He invited her to sit on the battered sofa while he prepared the coffee. She idly thumbed through the magazines on his ragged coffee table, an amused smile on her face.

"At least you don't keep porn out in the open," she called over her shoulder. "Although this black chick in your *National Geographic* has a nice rack."

He laughed, coming around the couch bearing two steaming cups in his hands, dropping sugar packets and creamer in a line behind him.

"Here. I don't know how you take it, so…"

"I take it black. I'm not a pussy like you who has to drown it in cream."

"I can drink it black."

They sipped their drinks in silence for a time, enjoying each other's company without being overt about it. After a while, Autumn dug her phone out of her purse and stared at it, her eyes going wide.

"Uh, what time do you have to be at work?"

"Eight. Have to be up by six thirty if I want to catch the train on time."

"Well, it's one o'clock, sugar. I think you better get to bed."

"All right. I'll call you a cab."

"Don't waste your money. I could crash here, on your couch, if you don't mind. I can just walk to work in the morning, it's not like it's far."

"Oh," he said, closing his mouth and feeling more than a little nervous. "Well, if you want, I'll sleep on the couch and you can have the bed."

"Like you'd fit! You're so freakishly tall, we'd have to cut off your feet!"

They laughed once more as Steve rose to his feet and rummaged around in his bedroom. He returned shortly with a flat pillow and a worn electric blanket in his arms, as well as a large Garfield T-shirt and a pair of sweat pants.

"Here. You can, uh, change in the bathroom."

"Not necessary." Autumn pulled the blanket over her lap. His eyes went wide as she reached down to the hemline of her shirt and pulled it up and over, revealing a black lace bra. With a grin on her face that said she knew exactly the effect the gesture was having, she slipped on the shirt he had given her. It fit her like a tunic, the neck so large her bra strap was visible.

"It's like putting on a parachute," she said, causing them both to giggle. She squirmed in her seat, and he heard first one boot and then the other thump onto the floor. Soon she was wriggling out of her pants, piling them up on the floor atop her boots. He watched, mesmerized, as she wormed one hand into the sleeve and removed her bra while keeping the shirt on.

"That's a talent."

"Avert your eyes, you perv!" She sent the bra flying across the room. It landed across the arm of one of the kitchen chairs, dangling by the strap.

She stretched out, arranging the pillow so it was under her head. She laid her bare feet across his lap. He fought to keep his arousal in check, but in a moment she was sitting up and glaring with a half-smile on her face.

"Go to bed, Steve," she said, withdrawing her feet and using them to push against his thigh.

"Okay, okay. It is pretty late."

He made his way to the bedroom door, stopping to look over his shoulder.

"I had a good time tonight."

"Yeah, me too." She rolled over on her side and closed her eyes, pulling the bands out of her pigtails as she did so.

He stood staring at her for a moment, then went into the bedroom. He slipped out of his clothes and into a pair of boxer shorts and slid into bed. As soon as his head touched the pillow his eyes opened wide. Heaving an exasperated sigh, he attempted to relax, but sleep was difficult to find.

He tossed and turned for almost an hour, seemingly unable to turn off his mind. He was considering getting up and drinking a shot of whiskey when he heard the door to his room open slightly. Autumn stood in the doorway, his shirt reaching nearly to her knees.

"Hey, your electric blanket doesn't work, and I'm kind of cold. Can I just…?"

Steve blinked at her in silence for a moment, before pulling the covers open for her. "Yeah. Sure."

She slid into bed next to him, snuggling close. Her bare legs felt good against his own skin. One of her hands idly played with his chest hair as her breath came warm against his neck.

"Good night," she said softly.

"Good night." Shortly, both slumbered easily, still wrapped in each other's arms.

"Bro, make a move already," said Rich, smacking Phil hard in his arm.

"Leave me alone! It's none of your business."

They were sitting at the table, watching as Crawley spoke with Rex's wife. Occasionally she would glance over at Phil and smile shyly, then giggle to herself and go back to her conversation.

"This ain't one of your stupid *Dragons and Dungeons* books," said Rich. "She's not just going to swoon and fall into your arms. You need to give her a little push."

"This is the first time we've seen each other since high school." Phil stared darkly at him. "It'd be weird if I hit on her tonight."

"It'd be weird if you didn't! If you don't go over there and ask her out, right this minute, *I'm* going to."

"Don't you fucking dare," said Phil menacingly.

"Then you better go. Because I'm giving you to the count of ten before I go talk to her."

"You're an asshole." Phil pushed up his spectacles and glared at him.

"One," said Rich with exaggerated slowness, "two, three…"

Phil rose to his feet, giving a last withering glare to Rich. He composed himself as best he could, but on the short walk to her side his heart hammered in his chest, and his tongue felt like lead. He managed a weak smile as Crawley looked up at his approach, grinning.

"Hey," she said. "Well, what did you think?"

"You were awesome. I mean, our last guitarist couldn't even play the intro to 'Rock Me Like a Hurricane.' You killed it!"

"Thanks!" Her cheeks turned a shade darker, and she gazed at her feet.

"Uh, listen, I was wondering if maybe you'd like to, I don't know, hang out someti —"

"I'd love to!" she said, beaming at him. The lush, smooth surface of her face stood out to him at that moment, and he longed to run his hand across her perfect cheek. She dug around in her jacket pocket and withdrew her phone. "It's a new phone, and I still don't have the number memorized…"

He produced his own phone.

"Why don't you call mine?"

"Sure!"

He gave her the digits, and soon his phone was ringing. He carefully typed in her name as a new contact, willing his fingers without success to stop shaking.

"Oh my god," she said, glancing at her phone. "It's after midnight! I really need to go home!"

"I should probably head home too. Got to be in the office by eight tomorrow."

Crawley's eyes lit up eagerly. "Do you want a ride?"

"Yeah," he said, pushing his glasses up on his sweaty nose, "that would be great."

After saying his good-byes to Rex and the dwindling guests, they headed for the door. Phil gave one last truly black sneer at Rich, who was smiling with what seemed genuine pleasure. The blond man mouthed a silent *you're welcome* just before the door shut.

The night was cool, but not chilly as they stood below the overcast sky. Crawley dug in her pocket and produced her keys, jangling them merrily.

"So where do you work again?" Phil asked as they walked the brief distance to her car. "I know you work for your dad, but—"

"Oh, we work out of our home. I really could afford to move out, but what's the point? I'd like to save money for my own house, but of course, that's hard to justify when you're living on your own."

They entered the Eclipse, sliding atop the leather bucket seats. Phil was impressed by the numerous lights and displays on the dashboard.

"Nice car. I feel like I'm in a starship."

She giggled sweetly, turning on the radio with her thick finger. "Everybody Wants to Rule the World" thumped out of the swank stereo system.

"You like eighties music?" he asked.

"Is the Pope Catholic? They've been playing this song a lot lately."

"It's a good song."

"Yes, it is. Have you ever listened to the lyrics? They're kind of beautiful and sad."

"Yeah. Kind of like, even though it's Armageddon and the whole world is screwed, at least we're still together."

She beamed at him, briefly turning her attention from the road.

"You get it!"

Phil struggled to come up with small talk, but the fact of the matter was he didn't need to. Crawley kept up a near constant stream of comments and rhetorical questions, jumping from subject to subject as crazily as a bee zigzags through the air in search of pollen. It almost seemed that she was afraid if she stopped talking, he would decide that he didn't like her. Before he knew it, they were pulling up outside his apartment in Queens.

"Nice place," she said, staring at the modern structure looming over them.

"Yeah, but it's kind of pricey."

"You have a good job, though."

"It's not bad. A lot of people find it boring, being an accountant, but I kind of find it soothing. And when I find a mistake and solve it, I don't know, I kind of feel like I'm fulfilling a purpose, I guess."

"That's really deep, hon." She patted his hand.

"I guess I should go in..." He opened the door and got half-way out.

"Aren't you forgetting something?"

He paused halfway out of the vehicle, and fixed her with a blank stare. Remembering what Rich had told him, he slid back into the seat and gave her a quick, light kiss on the lips.

Crawley's astonished gasp and wide-eyed stare made him cringe on the inside, thinking he had gone too far. Then she giggled again, hiding her mouth behind her hand.

"I mean, aren't you forgetting to tell me *when* we're going out?"

"Oh," he said, cheeks reddening. "I-I guess, I, uh, how does Friday night sound?"

"It's a date!" Suddenly she put her hands on his cheeks and kissed him, her tongue slipping into his mouth for just a moment. Then she pushed him away gently and put her hands back on the steering wheel, cheeks flushing red. "Sorry. I'll see you Friday, okay?"

"Okay." Phil stood watching her taillights until they were out of sight.

Steve woke in the pre-dawn hours, lying on his back. Autumn had rolled over onto her stomach but still had an arm flung across his belly. The beer he had drank earlier demanded to be recycled, and he gingerly moved her arm off of himself before heading to the bathroom.

When he came out a few moments later, the toilet still flushing, he noticed her eyes were open. He slid back into bed and their hands clasped.

"What time is it?" he asked.

She glanced at his cell phone, sitting on the nightstand.

"Almost five."

"Shit. I hate waking up an hour before you have to anyway. Not enough time to go back to sleep."

"Sure there is," she said, snuggling up to his side and laying her head on his chest. "Just relax."

"I'll try." Her head rose a few inches as he inhaled deeply, the precursor to a satisfied sigh. They lay like that for several minutes, his hand stroking her hair.

Autumn lifted her head to look him in the eyes. They stared at each other for a long moment, then their lips met, very gently. He put a hand on her cheek, her eyes glistening in the feeble light bleeding through the window.

"I thought that, that you didn't —"

"Shhh…" She silenced him with both her words and her mouth. Gradually, the kisses grew longer, more intimate. He slid his hand down her back, feeling her spine under the thin T-shirt. She grabbed his chest hard with her fingers, kneading the muscle and flesh like a playful cat. Her other hand dropped down below his waist, making her intentions crystal clear.

Steve slid his hand over her cheek, thumb brushing lightly across her soft lips. She opened her mouth, licking and sucking the digit as she added her other hand to her task. He gasped as her efforts raised him to readiness, even as her teeth lightly bit his thumb.

His other hand wormed its way under the shirt, groping for her breast. When he found it, he was surprised by the feeling of smooth metal. He gently explored her nipple piercing, which caused her to smile softly at him.

"Surprise," she said in a low voice. Steve was unable to respond, caught in a moment of ecstasy as her hands slid over his skin, twisting and rubbing his erection expertly.

Autumn let go with one hand and lifted her hips into the air. She gasped, almost as if in pain, as she slid down atop him. Their eyes locked in a moment of primal connection, no words necessary to express the unity they felt as their bodies intertwined.

Autumn closed her eyes, gyrating as tiny cries escaped her lips. He ran his hands over her breasts, gently squeezing the almost impossibly soft flesh. With a sudden half-lidded grin she pulled the shirt off and flung it on the floor. Their bodies arched in unison, and his own moans of ecstasy mingled with hers. Leaning back and bracing her hands on his knees, he could just make out her eyes behind the mounds of her breasts, her eyelashes fluttering like a butterfly's wings.

Later, they lay exhausted in each other's arms, damp with sweat. The alarm on Steve's phone went off, eliciting a groan from both of them.

"There's nothing more horrible than a Monday morning after a great weekend," he said groggily.

She rolled away from him and lay on her side, giving him a pursed lipped glare.

"What?" he asked.

"Now you're gonna think you're my boyfriend."

He chuckled, running a finger gently through her bangs. "You'll never hear it from my lips."

"Good," she said, smiling sleepily.

"I've got to get in the shower."

"I know."

"That was incredible."

"It was pretty good."

"You could join me in the shower," he said, blue eyes shining.

She grinned wryly at him. "You and I both know that if I join you in the shower, you're gonna be late for work."

"I see how you are. Separate showers means my water bill is going up."

"Well," she said, lifting her nude form out of bed and taking him by the hand. "If it's for the environment, I guess I have no choice."

She led him into the shower and closed the door.

chapter 7

"You look tired, Mr. Steve," said Darrien. The boy was sitting on his lap, craning his neck to peer at the dark circles under his teacher's eyes.

"I am." Steve yawned hugely. Despite his weariness, he found the day seeming to fly by. It was nearly lunchtime already, and he idly watched the children roam around the room.

"How come?" asked Darrien. "Couldn't you sleep? My mom makes me warm milk when I can't sleep."

"Just…I'll explain when you turn eighteen, okay?"

"That's a long time, isn't it?"

"Not really," said Steve, gently pushing the child off his lap. "Why, according to the geologic record, that's barely a sneeze."

"The gee oh rocky record? Who are they? Do they play that song with all the whistling in it?"

Steve did not answer, but did give the child's tow head a gentle pat. He rose to his feet and barked orders to clean up the room. The children, seeming to pick up on his renewed energy and drive, obeyed far more readily than normal.

After his children had returned from lunch and been laid down for nap, Steve took out his phone and checked it. He silently cheered Phil's message pertaining to his imminent date. He rolled his eyes at an enthusiastic diatribe from Rex about Crawley's musical prowess.

He ignored a message from his father, instead opening up his contacts list and sending a text to Autumn:

What's up? -S

He set the device down and picked up half a turkey sandwich, noisily masticating. A minute later his phone screen flashed. He checked the reply and couldn't suppress a laugh.

A direction. -A

Will you be able to come over later? -S

A moment later, the response came.

Can't. Sorry. Promised roomie I'd help edit her term paper.
-A

Okay. I'll call you 2 morrow, then. -S

You can call me tonight. –A

A moment later another message followed it.

This will keep you company :) -A

There was a photo attached, and he opened it.

"Jesus Christ, woman," he said in amazement. The photo was a selfie, apparently taken in a bathroom mirror. Autumn had her shirt pulled up and her bra pulled down, the fingers of her free hand idly playing with her nipple piercing. A wide, goofy grin on his face, he typed out another message.

Great. Now I have a boner around a bunch of children and look like a molester. -S

A second later he sent another text:

You're really beautiful :) Thanks for the pic. -S

A moment later the screen again flashed, and he eagerly read her reply:

If that pic ends up on the Internet, I'm going to cut off your balls and mail them to a fertility clinic. -A

I'm not into sharing. -S

Good. Neither am I. -A

"What's up, nerd?" said Rich, slapping Phil hard on the back. "Did you nail that little hottie last night, or what?"

Phil's shoulders grew tense, his face a mask of annoyance. Rich had already violated his personal space by entering the cubicle. To make things worse, his old school mate was speaking loudly about a matter Phil considered to be quite personal.

"Will you shut up? She's not that kind of girl."

"What other kind is there?"

"You're hopeless." Phil tried to return to his spreadsheets, but of course Rich kept talking.

"So says the virgin to the man who got nookie last night, *and* this morning."

"Yeah, well, not everyone is impressed with that."

"*I'm* impressed by it."

"I'm tired, and hung over, and I really need to send this report, so if you could come back and pick on me some other time, that would be great."

"Okay," said Rich, turning to leave, "but women gots *needs*, same as we do. Don't make her wait too long before you slip her the salami."

Phil held his face in his hands, pushing his spectacles up on his forehead first. He cast his sleepy eyes at the ceiling and muttered a question about what he'd ever done in a previous life to warrant such a miserable tagalong.

Stoically, he steeled himself and finished the report. He had long ago designed his own macro keys, far more efficient than the ones pre-installed on his work computer. It did not take him long to send it off to the home office, and he found himself with a spare few minutes.

"Oh, what the hell." He brought up the web browser on his desktop and went to his Facebook account. Clicking on Crawley's name, he brought up her page. A wide grin spread on his face when he read her status update.

Had a blast last night! I joined a band and got asked out by a really cute guy! I can't wait until Friday!

He clicked the "like" button on her comment, considering adding a response but deciding against it. He took out his phone and wondered about the three-day rule.

"Better not." He stuffed it back in his shirt pocket. "I'd probably just screw things up."

He checked his messages, and found that Steve had responded to his earlier text.

As Shakespeare said,
'I had the sweeter rest last night' :) -S

Phil flinched, mouth going slack.

That was fast. -P

Phil put the phone on his desk, surprised when there was a quick response. "Oh, right," he muttered. "Kids are taking a nap this time of day."

He checked the message, grinning at its content.

Just kind of happened.
She still says we're not dating, though. -S

Just go with it and try not to ruin everything
by being you. -P

Asshole :) -S

Phil chuckled and stowed the phone in his shirt pocket. He grabbed his coffee mug, a sleek silver design with his initials monogrammed in red ink. His mood soured as the cold, coffee-ground-infested liquid entered his mouth. Pouring the scant remains into his waste basket, he rose to his feet. He tucked his shirt into his pants and pulled it straight, smoothing out a stray wrinkle on his sleeve. Steve may have been off work, but Phil still had a bit more to do.

Steve trotted down the short flight of chipped concrete stairs, one hand on the cold metal railing while the other gripped his phone. Because he was staring at the device, he nearly walked into his father's blue Cadillac, which was parked right outside the staff entrance.

"Steve!" said Deathslayer at the last moment.

Steve glanced up, startled, then relaxed when he saw who it was. "Hey, Pop!" He leaned low to peer in the open passenger window. "What are you doing here?"

"Thought I'd give you a ride, maybe buy you dinner."

"Uh, I'm supposed to stop by and see someone…"

His father's blue eyes darkened. "You can't blow off one of your stupid friends to spend time with —" he began, then cut himself short. "Wait, is this that new girl you've been seeing?"

"I wouldn't say I'm seeing her yet, but close enough, I guess."

His father's face split in a grin, contrasting sharply with his black facial hair. "Never mind. I'm the Deathslayer, not the Cockblocker!"

"No," said Steve, shaking his head, "it won't take long. She's at work. I was just gonna go through the line, buy a coffee, maybe chat for a minute."

"I'll give you a ride, then we can go grab a bite. How's that sound? I'll stay in the car and everything."

Steve got a calculating gleam in his eyes as he got into the Caddy. Then he chuckled. "No, I think it might be cool if you went with me."

"Really? I really don't want to —"

"She's a huuuuge wrestling fan, Pop. She'll get a kick out of it, trust me!"

"Oh, so in a way, I'll be kind of like you guys' cupid."

"Maybe that can be your new gimmick. You can come out in pink tights, with a little pink bow and arrow…"

Deathslayer laughed, his guffaws filling the car. "You're a lot like your mother," he said, wiping the tears from his eyes. "A smart ass! And Susie, well, she's a lot like me. But that doesn't mean I don't love you both the same."

Steve shifted in his seat uncomfortably. "I know, Pop. Forget what I said the other day. I was just…I don't know."

Deathslayer pursed his lips, deep thoughts churning behind his eyes. When he spoke his voice was soft, almost a whisper. "I know I wasn't always there when you needed me," he said, drawing a sudden glance from Steve, "but I'd like to be there for you now. If you ever want to talk, I always got my cell on me. As long as I'm not in the ring or on camera, you know I'll answer it."

Steve wanted to say something, felt as if he should, but his mind was blank. It had been a long time since his father had been so overtly affectionate with him. He was unable to formulate a response before the Cadillac rolled up in front of the Crafty Colombian. The closest parking spot was halfway down the block.

"Why don't you get out here and I'll park?" asked Deathslayer. "She'll totally freak out if I just walk in all of a sudden."

"Always the showman. Yeah, she's a pain in the ass, she deserves to get messed with."

"A pain in the ass? That's the best kind of woman. Keeps things interesting."

Steve laughed, shook his head helplessly, and closed the car door. He turned toward the café, pushing open the glass door with his palm. Autumn was on the phone when he entered. She was busily restocking condiments on the customer side of the counter with her free hand. She did not notice his approach, so he waited patiently for her to finish.

"Prednisone? No way," she said into the device. There was a pause as the caller responded. "Because it makes you swell up like a blow fish, it wrecks your liver, and—yeah, thanks for the concern, *Mom.*"

Steve's blue eyes narrowed, but he tried not to eavesdrop further. Autumn's eyes flicked up to see his, and then she spoke quickly into the phone. "I have a customer, Sal. Talk at you later, okay?"

Autumn hung up the phone and smiled at Steve. She was wearing the same clothes she'd worn the night before, though she had pulled her hair back into a tight bun at the back of her head. Her brown eyes seemed tired, her skin a bit paler than usual. Still, she smiled widely at him.

"Hey, I'm still working, and I've got to help my roo—"

"Relax. I'm just going to get a coffee, say hey, and then I'll be out of here."

"Okay," she said, adopting an officious sounding voice. "What will you have, sir?"

"I'll have coffee. Large Colombian dark, with *one* sugar and *one* cream."

"Still a pussy drink." She poured the coffee. "Less of a pussy, but still a pussy."

"Here." He handed her a five.

"Nah, it's gratis."

"I thought you said it was coffee?" he said, peering into the cup. "Are you trying to slip me something so you can take advantage of me?"

"You don't need to drug guys to take advantage of them. You're all such horny, horny bastards."

"And the pic you sent has kept me like that all day."

She rolled her eyes and sighed. "I knew that was a mistake as soon as I sent it."

"I can delete it, if you want," said Steve, bringing up his phone.

"It's your pic. Do with it what you want…just be aware of the consequences."

She brandished a pair of shiny scissors, snapping them shut in his face.

He laughed, holding up his hands in mock defense. He heard the door ding behind him, saw Autumn's eyes go wide.

"No. Freakin. Way."

The Deathslayer strode into the small café. He smiled pleasantly and came up to the counter. "Nice to meet you. I'm Bill, Steve's father." He offered her his hand for a shake.

Autumn took it, her slim hand disappearing in his massive paw. She opened her mouth to speak, but nothing came out at first. Then, she said in a rush, "You are a god!"

Steve and his father both had a good laugh at that. He fixed Autumn with a smarmy smirk.

"You're a mark."

"I am not!" she said. "What's a mark?"

"Someone who believes pro wrestling is real," said Steve.

"Pro wrestling *is* real," said the big man. "People are what's fake."

"I didn't mean it that way, Pop."

"Oh my god," said Autumn. "I have to get a picture."

She came out from behind the counter, handing her phone to Steve. "You wanna take our pic?"

"Okay."

She stood next to his father, putting an arm around his waist. He put his arm around her shoulder and smiled. The camera clicked and Steve checked the screen.

"Turned out good," he said, handing her back the device.

"My turn," said his father, taking out his own smart phone. "You two stand together."

"Why do you want *my* picture?" Autumn asked.

"It's normal for a man to want a picture of his son and his girlfriend."

Steve sucked in a sharp intake of breath, looking sheepishly at Autumn. "Actually, Pop, she's—"

"Well, that's understandable," said Autumn, putting an arm around Steve's broad shoulders and pulling him in close.

"C'mon, Steve, quit looking at her and look at me! Now smile!"

The camera clicked, and Steve blew out a sigh of relief. "Are we done?"

"Not quite. Let me get one of you two kissing."

"Pop!" said Steve, his eyes going wide.

"Sure," said Autumn, putting her hand on his cheek and turning it toward her. She stood up on her tiptoes to reach his mouth with hers.

Deathslayer grinned at the photo; Autumn had her eyes closed, while Steve stared down at her in disbelief.

"It's perfect! Well, we should probably let her get back to work. It's only a matter of time till a fan comes in and recognizes me, anyway."

"Yeah," said Steve, still feeling discombobulated.

"Call me," said Autumn, adding a peck on his cheek.

They left the café, Steve giving her one last smile.

chapter 8

Phil's eyes were already open, staring at his bedroom ceiling, when his alarm went off. Reaching over with one hand, he flicked the off button and sat up, rubbing his bloodshot eyes. Slumber had eluded him much of the night. Most of the week had gone by quickly, the anticipation of his date with Crawley making him feel giddy and exited. Up until his head had hit the pillow on Thursday night, when all of the things that could go wrong danced through his head.

He stripped for the shower, examining himself in the mirror. The image reflected did not increase his confidence. At that moment, he really wished he had Rich's handsome features, or Steve's muscular torso and arms.

The pulsating stream of water felt good on his back and neck. He turned to face the spray, closing his eyes and watching the tiny flashes of light as the droplets spattered against his eyelids. Once he had washed the shampoo out of his hair, he used his wet/dry electric razor to trim his sideburns and touch up his shave. He usually only had to shave once every other day, unlike that caveman Steve, who seemed to sprout stubble almost as soon as his razor was set down.

Satisfied that his appearance was at least cursorily acceptable, he dressed in one of his better suits. The body spray he had used seemed quite pungent, and he considered getting back in the shower to wash it off. Glancing at his phone, he realized there was not sufficient time, and he left his apartment.

As he rode in the elevator to the ground floor, he checked his phone for messages. The people crowded in the elevator were the same ones he rode with every day, yet they did not speak to one another. Everyone just stared at the doors or at their own mobile devices. He wondered how many of them were silently battling apprehension, as he was.

The walk to the subway station seemed to take longer than normal, as if the universe itself wanted his misery to linger. One short train ride later, he was walking up to the revolving doors of Vickers and Sons. He walked toward the elevator, then decided to take the stairs to avoid Rich.

He scanned the office floor before exiting the stairwell, searching for the blond man. The coast seemingly clear, he made a break for his cubicle.

"Almost there...Made it!"

He sat down in his rolling chair and turned on the computer. Sighing, he said, "And now for a day of blissful productivity."

"Why the fuck did you take the stairs?" Rich asked, startling Phil with his sudden appearance. "Are you on a health kick?"

"Yeah," said Phil without turning around, "that's it."

"Man, dating a hottie for four days and you're already self-conscious."

"I have work to do, Rich."

"*Das Wunderkind?* You always do a goot job, *ja?*"

"Good-bye, Rich."

"You know," said Rich, his tone somber, "sometimes, the way you talk to me, I don't think you respect me at all."

"Can't imagine why."

Rich's good looks twisted darkly, but then he was distracted by a busty secretary clicking by in her high heels.

"Hey, beautiful," he said, leaving Phil by himself at last. "If I was in charge of the alphabet, I'd put U and I together!"

Phil glanced at the time displayed on his desktop. He slapped himself in the forehead when he realized it was just now eight a.m.

"Come on, four o'clock."

Steve practically ran to the door of his dimly lit apartment, pulling on a shirt over his muscular chest as he did so. The view out his window indicated it was twilight. He opened the door while wiping the sleep out of his eyes.

"Autumn," he said with surprise as she stood in the doorway.

She was dressed in her barista's apron under her long black coat, a white dress shirt and dark pants completing her ensemble. Her shoes were platform black boots, and her hair was pulled back in a ponytail.

"I thought you had to work tonight."

"I did." She came inside and put her purse down on his kitchen table. "They sent me home 'cause I threw up."

"Oh my god! Are you all right? Do you need to go to a —"

"I'm fine," said Autumn quickly. "I just drank too much coffee on an empty stomach."

"Well, I'm glad to see you at any rate."

He stifled a huge yawn.

"Were you asleep?" she asked.

"Taking a little nap."

"At six thirty on a Friday night?"

"Haven't got much sleep, lately," he said with a lascivious grin.

She returned the grin and went to him. They wrapped each other in an embrace. The smell of her hair reminded him of the fiery night they had spent together.

Autumn pulled away from him, a wry smile on her face. "So, what do you want to do?"

"I don't know. We could catch a movie or something."

"Yeah, that sounds like it could be fun."

"We could take one of those cheesy carriage rides through Central Park and make fun of the tourists."

"You know how much I like making fun of people."

They both chuckled, then grew silent, gazing into each other's eyes. Suddenly they were embracing each other again, mouths meeting in a fit of passion. Ignoring the line of drool that briefly spanned their lips, they paused for a moment.

"Or we could stay in," he said.

"Absodamnlutely," she said, mashing her lips against his again.

There were less clothes between them, and she became a few inches shorter as she shed her platform boots. Autumn nibbled at his neck, the bites just near the edge of painful. He responded by putting a hand in the small of her back and crushing her to his chest. She giggled playfully as her feet were lifted off the floor.

"You beast," she said through a sensuous smile, her eyes narrow.

Smiling himself, he turned around in place and sat her on the back of his sofa. They kissed again, their breath hot in each other's mouths. With a grunt he lifted her again and spun her around to face away from him.

"Oh, ho ho ho," she said in mock distress. He stared down at her smooth, round buttocks, sliding his hand over her inked skin. She giggled as he slapped a hand lightly across her cheeks, then caressed the skin.

Her laughter was replaced by a long groan as he slid inside of her, hands gripping her hips tightly. Autumn turned her head to the side, face buried in her own forearm. He reached out and gathered a hand full of her thick locks, tugging carefully but firmly until her mouth was in reach of his own. Steve kissed her forcefully, which she returned in kind. Vigorously, he worked his hips against hers, enjoying every grunt and sigh that escaped from her mouth into his own. The sofa was pushed forward a bit with each shuddering thrust, until it was flush with the entertainment center.

Steve was soon glistening with sweat, as was Autumn. He swiveled his hips, his erection rubbing against the walls of her slick flesh. Their mouths parted when Autumn twisted her head and let out a visceral scream.

When Autumn lurched back over the couch, her head nearly bumped into his flat-screen TV. He struggled not to release until she had reached her own summit, grunts escaping from his clenched teeth. Finally, she ground her backside into his pelvis, and they both gasped in unison.

"Wow," she said, turning around and putting her sweaty arms around his neck, "what got into you?"

"I don't know." He felt more than a little bit embarrassed. "I'm not normally that, uh aggressive."

"It wasn't a complaint," she said, kissing him deeply. "It's not like you broke out floggers and ball gags."

"Not on our...What is this?" His face scrunched up. "Our third date? Fourth?"

"I've kind of lost track. It's been quite a week."

Her brows knit together, fear in her soft brown eyes. "You must think I'm a skank, to just jump in bed with you after one night."

"No," he said, putting a palm against her face, "of course not! I normally don't—don't let things move this fast myself."

Autumn smiled, a satisfied gleam in her eyes. She brushed her soft lips against his neck, teasing him with her tongue.

"How many condoms do you have left?" she whispered in his ear.

"Plenty," he said, a bit nervously, "but I'm not...ready yet."

A cunning glint came into her eyes. She pushed him away from herself, holding him at arm's length.

"I bet I can help with that." Softly she trailed kisses down his chest. Slowly, she worked her way down to his navel, then lower, and lower still.

"God," he said, putting a hand gently on the back of her head and gasping.

"Let me know," she said for a brief moment when her mouth was unoccupied. Autumn had a way of looking up at him from her ostensibly subservient position with a smirking glint in her soft brown eyes, as if to say *I'm still the one in charge*. For some reason it made it all the more thrilling, that he was the star of his own adult movie, minus the bad music in the background.

She recognized the way he tugged at her head gently as a warning, and quickly employed her hand upon his slick erection as soon as her lips slipped off of him. Steve's legs went rubbery, his head tilted back so he could see the ceiling vibrate as his neighbor pounded on it.

"Sorry," he said. When he glanced down at her, a dreamy smile on his face, he noted that he had spilled himself along her shoulder and back.

Autumn was wiping away at it with her hand, but didn't appear to be horrified or even disgusted. "It happens. Not like I want you to drench my face with it, but it's the inevitable consequence of what we do, right?"

"Yeah." He tossed her a damp paper towel. He had trouble meeting her eyes, feeling somewhat guilty about his thoughts earlier. She was a real woman, not a djinn conjured from the Internet that could be dismissed as easily as wiping away a stain.

"What's wrong?" Autumn asked, chuckling at his trepidation.

"Nothing," he said, smiling nervously.

"It's waaay too late to be bashful, sugar," said Autumn with a snicker.

"It's not that..." Steve paused, unable to find the right words to express what he was feeling. He stumbled forward regardless. "It's just...you're a great gal, and I want to...that is, well..."

Steve's jaw suddenly set hard, and he put his arms akimbo. The gesture was somewhat comical as he was in the nude, and Autumn giggled.

"What's so funny? You know what, never mind, I need to say this...I'm starting to care about you, Autumn. A lot."

Autumn cast her gaze briefly downward, seeming small and vulnerable in spite of her fearsome tattoos as she knelt nude on his carpet,.

"I know, Steve. You think I don't care about you? Because I do, you know. I'm just not the girlfriend type, you know? I have rough edges that will never, ever be smoothed out."

"Hey, it's not like I want to propose or anything. I just kind of need to know, is this just a physical thing, or is it something more? Because at the risk of putting myself at your mercy, I really, really, hope it's more."

Autumn stared up at him, and for a moment her lovely umber eyes were free of conflict. "It's more. It's so much more it scares me. Now stop being cute and let's get back to the physical side of our... relationship, or whatever."

It wasn't long before they had retired to the bedroom, and he repaid her in kind. Steve laid her on her back and kissed her, very slowly and gently. Gradually, their mutual passion caused the kiss to grow more intimate. He kept her lower lip in his mouth for a moment, tugging it very gently with his teeth before he released the pliant flesh. She gasped as he trailed kisses down her neck, moving his hips to the side so he could continue his ministrations. When his soft lips touched her nipple, she abruptly slapped her hand on the back of his head. Taking her gesture as an invitation to be more dominant in his explorations, he roughly took the dark brown flesh in his mouth. Animalistic grunts escaped his mouth in the brief moment he was not using it to maul her supple skin.

When he got to her belly, she giggled as he discovered a few ticklish spots. He paused as he got to her smoothly waxed labia, marveling in her scent and her undeniable sexiness. Very gently, he used his tongue to tease her outer lips, and the sudden, vigorous way they quivered made him forge forward with confidence. He used his long arm to reach up and cup one of her breasts, while he used his other hand to spread her wide. Finding her "little man in the boat" was easy, as she had pierced the outer hood. She used her own fingers, black with nail polish, to tug gently up on the ring, allowing him access. As she gasped, her hands clamped down on the back of his head, crushing his mouth into her soft flesh. Her nails dug into the back of his head so tightly he felt as if she would rip his hair out by the root. He persevered through the rough treatment, face buried in against her clit, until her voice raised loud in a passionate scream.

They both laughed a moment later when his upstairs neighbor banged on the floor/ceiling.

"Guess we need some cover noise," she said as he crawled back up her body, lying next to her.

"Fuck him," he said with a sneer.

"I don't think I'm tight enough to fuck anything right now. Whew. You sure know how to speak in tongues."

He gave her a shy smile, stroking her hair with his large hand.

"Oh, good lord," she said, rolling her eyes. "When you guys are with each other, it's 'cock' this and 'pussy' that, but when your girlfriend does a little dirty talk you all turn into bashful little boys."

He laughed helplessly. "It comes from watching porn when we're fourteen. We all know how cheesy the dialogue is, so I guess that makes us feel cheesy when we talk dirty."

"Dirty talk is so much fun, though," she said, cuddling up to him and putting her hand to work.

"Again?" he asked.

Phil stood outside his building, peering intently down the street in an attempt to spot Crawley's white car. With nervously shaking hands, he withdrew the phone from his pocket and checked the time. It was eight thirty, making her half an hour late.

He was just about to call her when he heard the sound of a car horn. He glanced up to see Crawley waving enthusiastically from the passenger side of a large white van.

"Hello," he said, his brow furrowing in confusion. "I was looking for your other car…"

"Oh, sorry," she said, a wide smile on her face. She had her hair drawn back in a ponytail and wore little makeup. She was dressed in black pants and a modest button-down shirt. Crawley leaned back in her seat so he had a view of the driver. "Me and my dad had to finish up a few errands."

The driver was an older man, clearly of Pacific Asian descent. He had narrowed, dark eyes that seemed to pierce right through Phil. A closely cropped head of raven black hair sat atop his head. Thick, dun-colored lips parted in a smile, but it did not seem to reach all the way to his eyes.

"Nice to meet you, Phillip," said her father.

"Nice to meet you, sir," Phil replied, swallowing hard.

"Why don't you jump in back," said Crawley. "You can ride with us back to our house and we can pick up my car there."

"Okay," said Phil, taken aback by the change in plans. He gripped the cool metal of the door handle, trying to yank it open. It took several tries, and advice from Crawley, to get it to budge. When the door slid open at last, he was greeted with the sight of dozens of clear plastic tubs filled with tiny white Styrofoam cups. He couldn't tell what was in the cups, due to the low level of light in the van. He took one of the unoccupied seats and closed the door.

"Buckle up," said her father from the front seat, and he hastened to comply.

The van lurched forward, swerving in front of a large pickup. The sound of a blaring horn ripped through the night, eliciting a stream of cursing from Crawley's father.

"You stupid motherfucker!" he shouted, leaning his head out of the window and peering back. Phil was horrified at the cavalier way the man took his eyes off the road. The van began to drift into the oncoming lane.

"Fuck you, Beaner!" came the response from the truck driver.

"Beaner?" shouted her father. "Beaner? I'm Filipino, you dumbass!"

"Uh, Mr. Crawley, you're in the wrong lane," said Phil.

"Daddy…" said Crawley, her eyes going wide.

Adding one last stream of cursing at the driver behind them, her father jerked on the steering wheel and righted their course. The containers were jostled, causing one of the cups to fall on its side.

"So, Phillip," said her father as he wove between slower moving cars, "Ellie tells me you're an accountant."

"Yes, sir."

"How's that working out for you?" he asked.

"I can't complain," said Phil. "The work is satisfying."

"It's good to find satisfaction in your work," said her father, nodding. "Something I've tried but largely failed to impart to my daughter."

"Daddy," said Crawley, a note of anger creeping into her voice.

"If she cared more about her work, and less about her silly rock music and *Dungeons and Dragons* crap—"

"*World of Warcraft*, Daddy," said Crawley. "It's where Phil and I met. Well, sort of."

"Oh," said her father, taking his eyes off the road to stare back at Phil. "You do that stupid computer crap too? Well, if somebody smart enough to have a good career trajectory like yourself is into that nonsense, I guess it can't be all bad." Ahead of them the light changed to yellow, then red, and still her father did not turn around but continued to smile at Phil.

"The light, Daddy," said Crawley.

He turned around and slammed his foot on the brake. All three lurched forward, restrained by their seat belts, as the van screeched to a halt.

As the ride continued, Phil was troubled by two things. One was the noticeable tension between Crawley and her father. It seemed to go to a level beyond the normal parental criticism, and it pained him to see the hurt in Crawley's eyes.

The second was the occupants of the little containers. He was pretty sure they were too small to hold snakes, or anything dangerous, but they still weighed heavily on his mind in the brief moments he wasn't trying to fend off an argument between Crawley and her father.

The van crossed the river and headed to Manhattan. Soon they were pulling up outside a modest two-story brick house. It had a shaded porch with a well-maintained swing dangling by four stout chains. Nicely trimmed evergreen bushes flanked either side of the short flight of stone steps at the end of the sidewalk.

"Could you give us a hand, Phil?" her father asked.

"Sure," he said.

The three of them each took a plastic tub. They were not heavy, but due to the unsecured cups within they had to be carried carefully. Soon they were standing on the porch as her father thumped on the bottom of the door with his foot.

"Honey!" he shouted through the door, "come open the door. We have our hands full with the specimens!"

"Specimens?" said Phil, turning to Crawley. "What's in the cups, seedlings or —"

"Spiders," said Crawley, smiling prettily at him.

"Spiders?" Phil asked, turning white as a sheet.

"Black widows, to be precise," said her father.

"Black widows," said Phil, his stomach dropping out.

"Don't worry," said Crawley, giving him a reassuring nod. "They can't get out of the containers. And even if they did, their bite usually isn't lethal."

"Usually," said Phil.

The door opened and a middle-aged Caucasian woman answered the door. She was short, barely over five feet tall, and slightly overweight, with a thick crop of curly, dirty blond hair. She smiled warmly at Phil.

"Oh, Tran, how could you put this nice young man to work? Shame on you."

She stepped out onto the porch, and Phil gratefully handed her his arachnid burden.

He followed the trio into the interior of the house. The living room was on the other side of the front door. A large flat-screen TV hung flush against the wall to his left. A comfortable-looking leather couch was adjacent, its back against the wall adjoining the living room to the dining area. A matching recliner took up most of the remaining space, along with a tall floor lamp that spread a surprising amount of light off the high ceiling to illuminate the room brightly.

"Have a seat on the couch," said Tran as he headed for a door in the dining room, "while we stow these safely in the basement."

"Thanks." Phil shuffled into the living room. He sat down on the couch and found it to be quite cozy. He leaned back and stroked the smooth, soft surface with his fingers. He idly scanned the decorations on the wall. There was a large family portrait, taken fairly recently, hanging on the wall directly across from him. Knick knacks sat on a darkly stained wooden shelf, just below what he took to be a clock with a starburst design.

He had turned his attention to the stack of magazines on the glass top of the end table near his elbow when something caught his eye. The dinner-plate-sized clock on the wall seemed to have moved. Squinting his eyes behind the spectacles, he leaned forward a bit and scrutinized it further. The clock appeared to be spider-shaped, incredibly realistic in design except for its impossible size. His brow furrowed at the apparent lack of numbers or hands on its surface.

"How do you tell time on this thing?" he asked, getting to his feet. "Sure is creepy." He walked over the nicely polished hardwood floor to stand a foot below the object. He blew out a sigh, which caused the clock to move. With a sudden, terrifying moment of clarity, Phil realized that the clock was not a clock at all, but an actual living arachnid. A *huge* arachnid, one far larger than he had ever thought possible.

He would have screamed if he had been able. Instead, his breath seemed to catch in his throat, and all he could do was make a tiny strangled noise. He found himself standing on the couch, back plastered against the wall, trying to find his voice.

The spider, a dark gray furry thing with a leg span over a foot wide, moved at a quick clip toward the corner nearest the TV. The uncanny speed at which it was able to move despite its size caused him to find his voice at last.

"Help!" he called out. "Help!"

The sound of feet dashing up stairs heralded the arrival of the Crawley family. Her father stared at him suspiciously, while Crawley and her mother appeared concerned.

"There's a spider," he said, pointing in the corner frantically. "There's a spider that got loose!"

"Oh," said Tran with a grin, "so *that's* where the Sri Lankan Huntsman got off too. Help me catch it, Ellie."

"I'll just be on the porch," said Phil, dashing out the door.

Crawley's mother followed him out, her face warm with sympathy.

"It's all right, honey. That would be enough to scare anyone, especially if you're not ready for it!"

"What's with all the spiders?" Phil asked, flabbergasted.

"We harvest their venom for use in the medical field. You know, antivenin, pharmaceuticals."

"Oh. Uh, that's actually a pretty neat job."

"If you can get used to the spiders. It took me years before I could stand to touch one. But Eleanor takes after her father."

As if on cue, the gorgeous young woman stuck her head and shoulder out the front door, an amused smile on her face.

"It's safe now," she said with a giggle.

Soon they were riding in Crawley's Eclipse, slipping beneath the city lights.

"Sorry if I freaked out," he said, unable to meet her eyes. "I've kind of got this thing about spiders, and that thing was huge..."

"Oh, don't worry about it, hon. If it means anything, the Giant Huntsmen aren't dangerous to humans. He was probably more scared of you than you were of him."

"Impossible," said Phil with conviction. They both laughed, their eyes meeting briefly.

"Thanks for asking me out," she said, turning her gaze back to peer out the windshield. Her fingers tapped rapidly against the wheel.

"Thanks for saying yes," he said with a chuckle.

"You know...I kind of had a crush on you in high school."

"Really? No way!"

"Oh, yes way! You were smart, and good-looking, and really good at drawing...but you never talked to me. You never much talked to anyone except your BFF Rich."

Phil caught the mild note of admonishment in her tone. He cleared his throat before speaking. "I was kind of shy in high school. Never had a date until I was in college."

"No way! I didn't either."

"Why not?"

"My daddy wouldn't let me. He's kind of conservative. His mother came from the Philippines, and there's a lot of Roman Catholics there."

"I see."

"The last thing he told me before I left the house was to be a lady." She shot him a grin full of mischief.

He smiled back weakly. "I'll always treat you like a lady."

"I know you will," she said with a shy smile. "You're a good guy. I can tell."

He smiled back, relaxing a bit against the cool leather seat.

chapter 9

"Hey there, Steve," said Miss Stone, catching him by surprise both with her presence and her polite tone.

"Hello." He wasn't sure what his staff supervisor was doing in his room about two minutes before he was about to head home.

"I can see you're about to go home, so I won't keep you long. I just wanted to make sure you were getting ready for the Christmas play."

"Oh, yeah. We've been practicing 'Jingle Bells' every morning and afternoon. I think we'll be ready."

"Excellent." She stared at him for a moment, and he could almost feel the wheels turning in her mind. "Miss Gallo says she saw you at Applebee's last weekend with a young woman."

Steve's blue eyes narrowed. "I've been dating her for almost two months now. Is that a crime?"

"No, not at all. I think it's great, personally. I mean, there are certain...stereotypes...about men who teach primary grades."

"Not that there's anything wrong with that, of course."

"No, of course not. But you have to admit, it makes you look more normal."

"I am normal," said Steve.

Miss Stone chuckled, then turned on her heel and left. Steve thrust out his tongue at her retreating back and then turned to glance at the clock. Way past time he should be leaving.

Steve practically ran down the hall and burst out the heavy metal doors leading to the parking lot. His breath caused streams of steam in the cold air, and he wrapped his black trench coat more tightly about his large frame. Once he was sitting warmly on the train, he dug out his phone. He pursed his lips as he scanned his missed calls and messages. Autumn had called twice, which was unusual since she knew he tended to keep his phone off in the classroom. She had not left a voice mail, and was not responding to his texts, causing his brow to furrow. He jogged the short distance from the underground station to his building, stopping when he saw Autumn cast in a pool of radiance from the nearby streetlight.

She was sitting on a black vinyl suitcase, two bulging trash bags next to her on the sidewalk. When she turned at the sound of his feet and their eyes met, he saw that hers were bloodshot and limned in red, dark circles lurking beneath. Her hair was hidden beneath a thick wool cap with ear flaps, though a few dark bangs could be seen sticking out near her forehead. A black overcoat was wrapped around her, and her arms were crossed over her chest to ward off the cold.

"Autumn," he said, confusion evident in his tone as he trotted up. "Why are you sitting out here? Didn't I give you a spare key the other day? It's freezing!"

"Hey," she said, sniffling. He took her hands in his, rubbing them vigorously.

"Your hands are like ice! What's wrong? What's all this?"

He looked toward the bags sitting near their feet.

"Um…about that…"

"C'mon, you can tell me."

"I kind of need a place to stay." Her bottom lip quivered slightly, tears welling up in her eyes.

"What?"

"We got kicked out of our apartment today," she said through her tears. "My stupid cunt of a roommate was taking my half of the rent and using it to pay her fucking meth-head boyfriend's bookie off. She hasn't paid the rent in over six months, and they changed the locks and threw my stuff on the street and I've got nowhere else to go and nobody but you and…"

"Shh," he said, taking her in his arms. She put her head against his chest, sobbing softly. He stroked the back of her head, squeezing her tight in his arms. "Of course you can stay with me. You spend the night here all the time; it won't be much different."

"Yes it will," she said, her voice muffled by his chest. "It's always different."

"Different isn't always bad."

"Most of the time," she said, pushing away slightly to look in his eyes. She had stopped crying, smiling sadly up at him. "Why are you so good to me?"

"Because..." Steve put his hand on her cheek. "Because..."

He took a deep breath and spoke in a rush. "Because I love you," he said, stroking her cheek gently with his thumb.

Autumn was weeping again.

"Oh no. I knew it was too soon to say that. I'm sorry, you don't have to say it ba —"

"You're so fucking stupid!" she said, smiling through her tears. "So fucking stupid..."

He kissed her, unmindful of the dampness on his face from her tears and mucus. She wrapped her arms around his neck and clung to him like a rock in the storm tossed sea.

"Let's get your stuff inside," he said, pulling away and snatching up both trash bags. He slung them over his shoulder using the yellow handle ties.

"I could barely lift those, you ape," she said with a smile.

They made their way up the narrow stairs.

"This can't be all your stuff."

"Most of it. I had a nice little nineteen-inch flat-screen that got stolen, but otherwise this is the sum total of my life's possessions."

"Jesus. I'm sorry."

Soon they had deposited the trash bags on his bed. Steve wiped the sweat from his brow, flexing his sore fingers. Autumn plopped down on the end of the bed and slipped off her boots. She held her socked feet next to the heat register, sighing in satisfaction.

"Man, I need to be Doctor Who to get all this stuff in here," he said, clearing room in his tiny closet for her clothes.

"Doctor Who? Is that like Dr. Seuss or whatever?"

"Uh, no," he said, hanging a pair of her dark work pants on the scratched aluminum bar. "British Sci-Fi hero. He had a phone booth that was a lot bigger than it looked on the outside."

Autumn leaned back on the bed, looking at him upside down. "You're a nerd, but I'm glad you're my nerd," she said with a self-satisfied smile.

He turned toward her, a bundle of her clothes in his hands. A shadow crossed his features even as he tried to smile.

"What's wrong?" Autumn's smile faded. "Me moving in...It's a little fast, isn't it?"

"No!" Steve shook his head. "It's not fast enough! It's just that..." He sat down on the bed, shoving the bags out of his way.

She took his hand in hers, stroking it gently. "You can talk to me. I promise not to make fun of you for five whole minutes."

He grinned, gave a weak chuckle. "Five whole minutes? My lucky day! Don't think I'll need that long, though."

"Hon, the clock's ticking."

"Right. I'm just scared that, well, that you're going to get bored with me."

"What?" she said with a laugh.

"Seriously. I'm not a musician like Phil, or a tattoo artist like your ex, or a wrestler like my father. I'm just a plain old, boring kindergarten teacher. And you're so, well, you're creative, and funny, and beautiful, and you could have anyone you want. I guess I can't believe that you want me."

She sat up on the bed and pulled her knees under her. Her still cool hand caressed his cheek, her thumb brushing his bottom lip. "You're not as boring as you think," she said, giving him a quick kiss. "And you're really sweet, and supportive, and you put up with my smart mouth, and my bitchiness, and..." She suddenly sneered at him, punched him in the chest.

"Ow!"

"You can disagree with me anytime, jerk!"

"About what?"

"About my being a bitch, my smart ass."

"Who says I disagree?" he said, furrowing his brow in mock con-sideration.

"Now you're getting your ass kicked," she said, pummeling him lightly with the bottom of her fists.

He grabbed her wrists and flipped her onto her back, pinning her to the bed.

"You're not a bitch," he said once their laughter subsided. "You're... opinionated."

"Opinionated," she said with a giggle. "I like that, but I think you're being generous."

He gazed at her with half-lidded eyes, released one of her wrists to gently stroke her jet black hair. He moved his face close to hers, eyes closing as his mouth opened.

"Wait." Autumn put her hand on his chest when their lips were scant inches apart. He felt her warm breath on his skin. "I...I love you."

He stared at her for a long moment, eyes shining. Then their lips met in a lingering, passionate kiss. When he pulled away from her, his face was solemn.

"That's all I need. That's all I need in the world, to hear you say that."

"God," she said teasingly, though the adoration in her eyes did not lessen. "You're such a pussy..."

He mashed his mouth atop hers, eliciting an exited squeal from her. They rolled about on the mattress, knocking the bags to the floor as she ended up on top. Her painted nails picked at the front of his shirt, undoing the buttons. She grinned as the fabric peeled back to reveal several dark circles on his muscular chest.

"Got a little carried away the other day." She kissed the spots gently. "Sorry."

Steve grinned. "They don't hurt, they just look awful."

"At least I don't leave them where they show," she said, nibbling on his flesh.

"It's fine, it makes me think, 'wow, I must be some stud.'"

She laughed, moving her head sinuously upward so their lips could meet. He fondled her breasts, toying with the buttons on her shirt which seemed tiny in his large fingers. A hard knock at his door startled them. He slapped his head as he recalled that he had been expecting company.

"Totally forgot that I'm supposed to help my sister with her laptop."

"It's all right," she said, getting up off of him. "I'll be around."

"Yes," he said, suddenly rising to his knees and wrapping her in a hug, "yes, you will be."

They kissed again, his hand slipping down her spine to caress her rear. The smacking of their lips was interrupted by another, harder knock. Autumn giggled as he cursed, stomping toward the front door.

Susan was standing with her arms crossed over her chest, tapping her foot as he swung the door open. She was dressed in a thick pink coat, a maroon scarf wrapped around her neck. Pushing past him, she placed a leather case on his kitchen table.

"What took you so long?" she asked, eyes scanning his partially exposed chest. "And what happened to you?"

He glanced down, embarrassed at the sight of the monkey bites. He fumbled with the buttons as his cheeks reddened.

"That was my fault," said Autumn, coming out of the bedroom while fixing the top button on her own garment. "Hey, Susan."

"Hey," said Susan with a touch of coldness. "Steve didn't say you were gonna be here."

"She's kind of living here now," said Steve, unzipping Susan's computer case and taking the laptop out.

"Really?" Susan asked, turning to look at Autumn. "That's great! Things are moving really, really fast for you two."

Her face seemed to contradict the warmth of her words, as her smile was forced and her eyes cold.

Steve grunted, not truly paying attention, as he hit the power button to the computer. "You say it comes on, but after you put in your password it goes to blank screen?"

"Yeah," said Susan, still trying to smile at Autumn, "can't figure out why."

"Probably an update to Flash or some bullshit."

"So what do you think? Can it be fixed?"

"I think I got it. Yeah, it was an update that didn't install right. Had to restart it in safe mode and re-run the program."

"Great," she said, checking the device. "Haven't been able to check my mail in days. Let me pay you back. I'll take you guys out to eat, my treat."

"That sounds awesome," said Steve, his stomach rumbling. He looked over at Autumn, who seemed ambivalent. "What do you think?"

"I don't know. I'm a little tired. I might just stay here and take a nap."

"Are you sure?"

"I'm sure. I ate before I left work. It's fine. Go spend some time with your sister."

She moved up to him, kissing him lightly on the cheek. "I'll be wide awake when you get back," she whispered in his ear.

Steve's cheeks reddened as she giggled. He missed Susan's rueful head shake at the gesture.

"C'mon, bro," she said, tugging on his arm, "let's try and beat the dinner rush."

"Be back soon," said Steve as he was about to shut the door. "I love you."

Autumn sighed and sat down heavily on a kitchen chair, staring into her folded hands.

Steve and his sister rode in relative silence, the neon lights of the city slipping past them, painting their somber faces with pastels that belied the dark turmoil boiling beneath the surface. The interior of the cab had a strange energy, like the air just before a thunderstorm.

They were seated by a stout, acne-plagued young woman once they reached the restaurant. Steve asked for a seat near the bar, drawing a narrow-eyed glare from Susan.

"So," he said after they had sat on the comfortable vinyl seats, "alone at last. Are you ready to give me a hard time about Autumn or would you like to wait until after the appetizer?"

She glared at him, taking her water glass in both hands. After taking a long sip she composed herself, setting the glass down with a heavy *thunk*.

"I'm not allowed to care about my brother?"

Steve sat back against the cushion and sighed. "Of course you are."

"Well," said Susan, twirling the cubes in her glass around idly, "part of caring about someone is telling them when they're making a mistake. And you're making a big mistake, bro."

"Oh, come on." Steve leaned forward on his elbows and fixed his blue eyes squarely on her. "You barely know Autumn."

"I know her type. You're a nice guy, Steve, and women like her can tell that. She needs someone to take care of her—"

Steve rolled his eyes and threw his hands in the air.

"—and for a little while, that somebody is gonna be you," she continued despite his display. "But only for a little while, Steve. Sooner or later she'll find a guy who plays guitar, or deals heroin, or runs in a biker gang, and she'll be gone. Just like that."

"I didn't know you could tell the future. If you're that clairvoyant, why not tell me the lottery numbers for tomorrow?"

"She's already moved in," said Susan with vehemence. "How long have you been dating? Two months, tops?"

"She got kicked out of her place," Steve said wearily. "Her roommate was a dipshit."

"Did you ever *see* this 'roommate' of hers? Because if you didn't, it was probably her boyfriend."

Steve stood up, startling the waitress who was coming by for their order. He headed for the exit, past happy couples, boisterous families, and busy servers.

Susan ran after him, pulling on his arm as he strode angrily down the sidewalk. "Steve, wait! I'm sorry."

He stopped, but did not look at her. Instead he stared hard at the cracked concrete at his feet.

"I shouldn't have shot my mouth off like that."

"You're wrong about her," said Steve with tight lips that trembled slightly when he spoke.

"Steve, she's hiding something. I don't know what, but she's hiding something."

"I know. I get that feeling too, but…"

"But you love her," said Susan, rubbing his shoulder.

He nodded, blinking rapidly. "She makes me feel okay about being me. And I'd like to think I make her feel okay about being her. Isn't that what love is? Accepting someone for what they are, then standing by them no matter what? Because if it's not, then I'm not sure I would want anything to do with it."

"Oh, come on, Steve, you think you love her because you're lonely. What do you really have in common with this woman?"

"We laugh a lot," he said, his eyes growing narrow as his mouth twitched. "Neither one of us is big on going out on the town, we'd rather just…*be*. I can't explain it in a way you'd understand."

"You sound like a fresh-on-the-rag suburban princess writing a letter to *Seventeen*."

"You know what?" he said indignantly, drawing himself up to his full height, "you might be right. Maybe she just wants to be with me because I have a decent job and a place to live. Isn't that what women do? Don't they look for someone to be the breadwinner? That's just a feminine instinct, like hating your best friend."

"That's a load of shit," she said, her eyes narrowing dangerously.

"Oh, is it? Then why are women always going on about landing a doctor? What is it you posted on Facebook about that Daniel guy who was so into you? 'I don't want no broke-ass motherfucker'? I do believe that was the precise phrasing you used."

"That was just a goof."

"So what if my job, if my position in the social-economic strata has something to do with her attraction to me? That can't be all there is to it. Autumn is hot as hell. She could go wiggle her big tits at some investment banker who's into goth and emo chicks and have a free ride. But she chose *me*. Seven billion motherfuckers on this planet, and she chose me. That's got to count for something."

"Where are you going?" Susan asked as he turned away from her.

"I'm going home. I don't have an appetite anymore."

"Steve," said Susan plaintively. "Steve..."

He waved his arm at a passing taxi, boarding without a backward glance.

When he slid his key into the door of his apartment, it opened up unbidden. Autumn stood in the door, a prickly grin on her lovely face. She opened the door and moved aside, revealing that his apartment was in the process of being cleaned. His haphazardly arranged kitchen gear was now neatly shelved, the counters bare and clean. The vacuum sat on the rug, its cord dragged out over the floor.

"Wow," he said, his dark mood partially dismissed.

"Wow, nothing. I barely had time to get started."

"Why did you do this?"

"I wanted to earn my keep." Autumn chewed on her lower lip. "Sorry it's not done yet."

"You didn't have to do this." Steve shut the door and locked it.

"So," said Autumn as he turned around, "did your sister tell you I was just using you, or did she bring out the big guns and call me a whore?"

Steve sighed, walked over to one of the wooden chairs and sat down in it, holding his head in his hands. "I don't want you two to hate each other, but if she asks me to choose, she's going to be very disappointed."

"Don't say that. I don't want to get between you and your sister. I'm not worth all that."

He reached out, awkwardly grasping with his hand. She took it in her own and squeezed it.

"You are worth all that," he said, kissing her hand. "I love you."

She leaned in close to him, putting his head against her belly. Her fingers stroked his long hair as he felt her breathing and heartbeat warm against his ear.

"I love you. Very much. The worst thing about getting kicked out of my apartment is that now you're going to doubt that."

He pulled away slightly, so he could look up into her large eyes. Steve wasn't sure if he could believe in souls, but the warmth, the depth of character that seemed reflected in her soft brown orbs made him feel luminous in spirit.

"I don't doubt it, and I'm secretly really, really happy that you got kicked out. Don't take that the wrong way."

She smiled, holding his head to her stomach again. She leaned her head forward and kissed him softly on top of his head.

"I'm going to order some Jimmy John's," she said into his hair, "because I can hear your belly rumbling, and open up a bottle of champagne that my roommate seems to have misplaced—"

He chuckled, the vibrations tickling her belly.

"—and then we're going to bed," she said, stroking both hands through his hair.

"Are you tired?" He ran his palm along the small of her back.

"Nope. Not a bit."

chapter 10

P hil sat with his chin cupped in one hand, eyes struggling to stay open. He was seated near the front end of the long meeting table, meaning he was unable to pass the time by sketching as he so often did. His boss continued to drone on cheerfully, seemingly unaware of the numerous glassy stares pointed in his direction.

He lazily raised his gaze to the sleek clock hung on the wall. It was half past four, long past the meeting's supposed end time of three forty-five. He sighed and straightened up in his padded seat, actually tuning in his boss's voice in hopes of discovering the end was near.

"…and I hope that on this winter holiday, you'll remember those Vickers and Sons' employees who regrettably lost their positions due to restructuring and give generously to the Salvation Army and other charities," he said with what he probably thought of as a sad smile on his face. To Phil, it seemed more like a smirk. "Now, if there's no other business?"

Phil felt as if he would jump up and throttle anyone who dared to raise their voice, but the other people in the room seemed just as grateful to be done with the whole affair.

"No? Very well, I wish you and yours a very Merry Christmas."

"Merry Christmas," said Phil and the half dozen other coworkers who had retained their consciousness. The meeting room was suddenly abuzz with noise and activity as people gathered their things and prepared to leave for the long weekend. Phil noticed Rich's approach and managed to smile at the man, so glad was he to be done with the meeting.

"Sup, loser?" he said, punching Phil in the arm.

"What's up, Rich?" Phil rubbed his arm.

"You ever tag that sweet half-Asian ass?"

"Why do you care so much?"

"That's a no. C'mon, what's the deal?"

"We're both busy." Phil walked toward his cubicle. Rich followed unbidden. "I'm here forty-five to fifty hours every week, on Saturdays we game, and then have band practice. On Sundays, her family lays claim to her on account of them being über-religious."

"You need to make time. Nasty time. You ever consider playing nookie-hookie?"

Phil rolled his eyes. "I'm afraid of the answer I'll get, but what is that?"

"It's when you blow off work so you can get blown. Call off so you can get off. Tell your boss to suck it and Ellie the same thing!"

Phil sighed in exasperation as he gathered up a stack of folders and secured them in his briefcase. "Tonight's only the fourth time we've officially gone out on a date."

Rich's eyes went wide, and he clapped Phil hard on the shoulder. "No fucking way. Then you better stop for some rubbers."

"Why?" Phil walked away from his cubicle and Rich.

The other man jogged to catch up with him. "Don't you know the cardinal rules of dating? No matter what, the fourth date ends in sex!"

"An irrefutable fact, no doubt."

The two of them waited for the elevator to arrive.

Rich shrugged innocently. "I don't write the rules."

"What about those hyper-Christian people, the ones with purity rings?"

Rich's brow furrowed and he let out a snort. "They still have sex, just up the poop chute."

"Then what about Steve and Autumn? They sealed the deal, as you put it, after just one night."

"Autumn's kind of a slut."

"You'd better watch your mouth around Steve. Besides, you're just mad because she blew you off when you tried hitting on her."

Rich's face was covered with a grin, but his eyes mocked Phil. "I'm not scared of a man whose daddy is a fake wrestler, and I wasn't really hitting on her. I was just checking to see if she was gonna be loyal to Steve."

"And when she was, you got butt hurt. And Steve's dad might engage in fake fighting, but Steve has had to fight his whole life."

"Why is that?"

The elevator arrived at the ground floor and the metallic doors slid open. They exited the car and headed for the street.

"Because everyone was always giving him shit about his dad being a phony. Plus, he's two of you, as far as size goes."

"Eh, the bigger they are..."

"The harder they hit. If you doubt me, try and mess with him some time. You'll see."

The two men parted company at the front door, Phil turning toward Grand Central, while Rich made his way to the company parking garage. While he was waiting for a train, Phil withdrew his smart phone from his jacket pocket. The night was chilly, but he had found a good spot next to a heat register, the warm wind tousling his hair. When his fingers had stopped shivering he sent a text to Crawley.

Looking forward to tonight. -P

Her response came almost immediately.

Me 2. Want to come by here first? -C

Phil winced, images of giant, hairy legs and multiple eyes rising up in his mind.

Okay. –P

His stomach flipped and flopped at the prospect of another close encounter of the arachnid kind.

Awesome :) -C

Phil sighed and held his head in his hands. When he had told Rex and Steve of his adventure in the Crawley living room, they had been predictably snide about it. Steve refused to take it seriously, while Rex thought shock therapy might be useful and had dropped a live, tiny spider on Phil's head.

Though he was afraid of the eight-legged denizens of the Crawley household, he found that his excitement was greater. He tried to ignore the comments Rich had made, but he found himself wondering whether it had some kernel of truth to it. Certainly, he and Crawley had engaged in spirited make-out sessions in her car, in the elevator to his building, and the sofa in her parents' house. He couldn't help but wonder if she thought he was weird because he had not tried to take things further.

He spent most of the ride home worrying about it. It did not help that his one prior sexual experience was some seven years past, when he had been a senior in high school. Despite an eager and willing young woman who had consented to be his prom date, he found himself unable to perform. She had been nice about it, not plastering his name all over social media, but often a gaggle of girls had see him in the hallway and giggle, and his blood had boiled with utter certainty that everyone secretly knew of his failure as a man.

After he arrived home, he went through the motions of preparing for the date. He felt ridiculous, as if all the hair gel and cologne in the world could not erase his shame. Nevertheless, he presented a dapper image when he exited his apartment a short while later. He had chosen a dark brown pair of dress pants, nearly black. A long-sleeved, peach button-down shirt was tucked neatly into his trousers.

Crawley's house was not far from the nearest train station, but he still found himself chilled to the bone by the time he rapped upon her white-washed door. In a moment the peephole darkened, heralding the door opening.

"Phillip," said Crawley, a wide smile on her face. "Come on in, you must be cold!"

He entered the living room, carefully wiping his feet first. Crawley's fingers moved gently along his sleeve, helping him take off is coat. She was wearing a pair of jeans so tight Phil wondered if she would be able to bend her knees in them. A V-neck sweater was worn over a white embroidered camisole, showing a small amount of her modest cleavage. Her hair had been brushed out straight and cascaded down her back like a silk blanket. Light red lipstick was complimented by blush and smoky eye shadow. A pair of earrings in the shape of spiders dangled from her ear lobes.

"You look beautiful."

"Thanks." Crawley gazed at her feet and blushed, making his heart dance in his chest.

"Where are your mom and dad?" Phil scanned the house for them with narrowed eyes.

"They're off at some Christmas party." Her voice was muffled as she went into a closet to put away Phil's coat.

"Oh," said Phil, as his heart seemed to skip a beat.

"Yeah," she said, coming out of the closet, "we have the whole house to ourselves, at least until midnight or so."

She went up to him and put her arms around his neck. Their lips met with a moist smacking sound. Remembering Rich's words, Phil ran his hand down her spine, caressing lower, and lower, until he was cupping her shapely buttocks with his palm.

He thought he had been too bold when she stiffened a bit, pulling away to look at him with wide eyes. Then she favored him with a smile, and they kissed deeply once more. Her tongue was agile inside his mouth, stealing his breath. He ran his hand over her firm buttocks, amazed at how good it felt to touch her.

She broke the contact, stepping away from him. With a wordless smile, she took his hand and pulled him toward the wide stairs leading to her room. He followed, heart hammering in his chest, as the door to her bedroom opened. It appeared to have been recently cleaned, and was surprisingly Spartan for the room of a young woman. There was a poster of a large orb weaver spider on one wall, a few paintings that looked as if Crawley had done them some time ago, and a flat-screen TV flush against the wall. Her full-sized bed had a white bedspread with little flowers embroidered upon it. She tugged him until he was sitting next to her on it.

He could almost hear Rich screaming at him to stop being a pussy, so he took her in his arms awkwardly and kissed her again. She leaned back, pulling him with her so that her torso was under his own, their legs still half off the bed.

In the heat of the moment, their teeth banged together, but it created only a momentary pause in their passion. Gradually, their kisses became slower, more mediated. Her breath, minty from a recent brushing, felt cool in his mouth. He ran a hand through her silky hair and nibbled on her neck.

"Oh, god..." she said as a shudder went through her.

"What's wrong?" he asked, stopping for a moment, concern in his eyes.

"Nothing. Don't stop! Lick me…lick me all over."

Her eyes were tightly shut, her cheeks flush. When his fingers, shaking with nerves, fumbled with the buttons to her sweater, she reached down to her waist and yanked it off over her shoulders. He gently took down the spaghetti strap of the camisole, trailing kisses down her smooth brown shoulder. The sounds she kept making were confusing him, as they sounded halfway between pleasure and pain, but the soft smile on her face encouraged him to proceed.

He hooked his hands in the narrow space between her toned belly and the jeans. With difficulty, he undid the snap and tugged them off. A rush went through his body as her shapely legs were revealed, and he tossed the pants behind him on the floor inside out.

"Wait," she said as he gently fingered the waistband of her tiny pink panties. "Rip them off."

"What?"

"Rip them off!" she said with a moan.

He got a firm grip on the translucent satin material, gathering it up in his fist. She shuddered again as the fabric slipped up inside her. With a sudden jerk of his elbow, the panties tore off easily. Crawley gasped as her labia were exposed. Phil was shocked by the intense aroma emanating from her body. There was a tuft of black hair in a neat line above her smoothly shaven lips.

"Hurry," she said, prompting him from his reverie. Not knowing what else to do, he buried his face in her crotch, working his tongue inside her. She gasped as he went about the ministrations, hands stroking his hair.

"Here," she said, moving his head up for a moment. She used her own fingers to manipulate her slippery flesh. "Right there. Lick right—"

He complied, and her grip on his head suddenly became tight and fierce.

"Oh, god!" she screamed, pounding one hand against her headboard. "Don't stop! Don't—"

Phil felt her legs quivering, the soft flesh his face was buried in shudder. Suddenly his face, moist with her passion, was drenched as she climaxed. He blinked in confusion, wiping the sticky fluid from his eyes.

"Sorry," she said, though a wide smile was on her face.

"It's okay." Phil didn't even like for his fingers to be sticky, would go to great lengths to keep them clean, but for some reason he did not feel soiled by her ejaculation. Rather, he felt as if he had been anointed somehow.

"Looks like you're ready…" She was eying his crotch.

He was amazed to find that he was fully erect, straining against his pants. Moving quickly in case his body decided to betray him again, he slipped off the garment, taking his boxers down at the same time.

"I don't," he said as he crawled atop her half-dressed form. "I don't have any—"

"I'm on the pill," she said, pulling him down with a hand on the back of his head. Their mouths met once more, and Phil awkwardly tried to insert himself.

"Here." She reached her hand between them and provided him with assistance. Suddenly she gasped as he slid inside her, the grip on his hair growing painful. He struggled to last, to grind against her hips until she climaxed, but within three minutes he could no longer hold back. He grunted as he filled up her belly with his seed, lost in ecstasy. She hooked one of her legs over his calf, pulled his head back into her chest when he tried to rise.

"You're not done already, are you tiger?" she asked, practically purring.

Phil swallowed hard. His back and calves were screaming in pain, unused to the strange positions he was contorting them into. Worse, his body, long used to quick browses of the web to facilitate satisfaction, had betrayed him by going flaccid.

"Oh, Phil," she said with a smile, "this was your first time, wasn't it?"

He raised his head off of her chest, but was unable to meet her eyes. Phil's head nodded slightly, eliciting a sympathetic *aawh* from Crawley.

"Don't worry about it, you did fine. Cuddling is almost as good as sex anyway."

Then they were lying next to each other on her bed, hands clasped as they stared in exhaustion at the ceiling. Crawley raised her sweaty head off the mattress and laid it over her arm, smiling at him.

"Oh, Phil," she said with a giggle. "I haven't been with anyone in over a year."

Phil smiled sheepishly, squeezing her hand.

"I don't mean that I've done it with a lot of people," she said, face falling as she misinterpreted his silence.

"It's all right," said Phil, "that really doesn't bother me."

Yeah right, he thought to himself, *and cuddling's just as good as sex.*

A twinge beneath his abdomen gave him hope that his body was about to rise to the occasion again. He rubbed his hand over her smooth thigh, caressing it gently. She took his hand and put it below her waist, rubbing his fingers.

"See what you've done?" she said softly. "I'm all wet again…"

Phil raised his torso up and kissed her, hoping the rest of his body would do the same.

Steam billowed out of a manhole cover, creating a curtain of fog that was dashed apart as Steve and Autumn ran through it. They were still partially in the intersection when the light changed, causing angry motorists to blare their horns.

"Eat shit and die, asshole!" said Autumn, turning toward a green Pontiac and flipping twin birds.

"Autumn, c'mon," said Steve, trying to pull her onto the curb.

"Fuck these dickweeds! The fucking light *just* changed, how impatient can you be?"

"C'mon, killer," he said, as he finally pulled her up on the curb. Her booted heel stomped down hard, as if she were imagining it was the motorist's face and not concrete she were stepping on.

They walked, hand in hand, up a sidewalk jam packed with pedestrians despite the cold. Loud music poured out of doorways, occasionally growing in volume as a patron would swing the door open. All about them the New York nightlife was in full swing. Autumn was wearing her long black coat, concealing her leather bodice and mini skirt.

He had gone with a black polo shirt and dark jeans which were slightly baggy. His hair had been brushed back and gathered in a ponytail, and his shave was impeccably close. Autumn ran a gloved hand over his cheek as they circled a gaggle of black teenagers.

"What? Did I miss a spot?"

"No. I just like touching you."

He didn't know how to respond to that, so he just grinned and put an arm around her shoulder. They stopped in front of a particularly raucous establishment, its sign proclaiming it to be Manhattan Knights. After showing their IDs to the bouncer, who was a head shorter than Steve and visibly upset by it, they entered the crowded bar.

Steve whistled in appreciation because the bar was bigger than the outside would suggest. A large dance floor was arranged in front of a full-sized stage, on which an amateur rock band was performing. Eight or so tables sat in a crude U-shape flanking the dance floor, while a balcony area featured a dozen more above them. Autumn, apparently having been there before, led him up a flight of stairs behind the bar to the balcony, choosing an open table with a decent view. They sat down and were almost immediately beset by a busty waitress in a short skirt. Steve ordered his favorite imported beer, while Autumn had an amaretto sour. They sipped at their drinks and watched the band play in silence for a while.

"Christmas is in two days," said Steve at length, his blue eyes peering across the table at her.

"Yeah, so what?" said Autumn with a sneer.

"Not a fan of Christmas, I take it?"

"Why should I be? I'm not a Christian, and I'm way too old for Santa Claus."

"Christmas is fun. It doesn't have to be about religion."

"Originally, Christmas was a big gay orgy held at the end of December. The Christians couldn't stop the partying, so they just changed the name of the holiday."

Steve laughed, taking a long pull on his beer. "I've heard something like that before, but Christmas is about friends, family."

"Ha! Christmas is about retailers and manufacturers getting people to go into debt buying presents for relatives they can't stand."

Steve shook his head sadly. "Sometimes, you're really negative. You don't talk about your family much, I mean, I know your mom passed away."

"At Christmas," said Autumn, staring down into her glass.

"What?"

"At Christmas. My mom died around Christmas, all right?"

Steve's mouth turned into a thin line. "I'm sorry. I didn't know."

She stirred her drink idly with the tiny red plastic straw in her fingers. When she spoke, she did not look up at him. "Mom was depressed. My Dad ran out on us not six months before, and it broke her heart. I found her face down in the bathroom, a needle sticking from her arm."

Steve blinked back tears, his voice breaking when he tried to speak.

"That's awful," he said, putting a hand atop hers. "How...how old were you?"

"Sixteen," she said, looking up at last. A joyless smile was on her face, her brown eyes more profoundly sad than he had ever seen.

"Sixteen...and there was no one to take care of you?"

"My grandma. But she was eighty at the time, and it wasn't long before I was burying her too."

"What about your dad?"

"That son of a bitch knew better than to talk to me, or I'd have ripped his fucking head off."

"But he's your dad," said Steve, brows coming low over his blue eyes. "As much of a pain in the ass that Pop can be, I still —"

"You don't know what my dad did. You wouldn't be so quick to defend him otherwise."

Steve squeezed her hand. "I'm not defending him."

She yanked her hand out of his grasp. "It sure sounds like it."

"Look, forget I mentioned Christmas. Let's just relax and have a good time, okay?"

She sighed, peered out over the bar below them. "Okay," she said, a ghost of a smile playing across her lips. She looked back to him, almost apologetic in her behavior. "Told you I was a pain in the ass."

"You're not a pain in the ass."

Autumn did not speak, just arched her pierced eyebrow.

"Okay," he said, laughing helplessly. "You can be a bit...persnickety."

"Persnickety? Is that just another synonym for bitchy?"

"I think I should shut up now while I'm ahead," he said, holding up his palms.

"Who says you're ahead? You're way *behind*, sugar."

They laughed, gradually winding down to stare into each other's eyes. The waitress came by, took Steve's empty bottle and replaced it with a new one. Despite the server's flirty nature and the brevity of her garments, Steve kept his focus almost entirely on Autumn.

"You know," she said as the waitress walked away from them, her brown eyes on the woman's shapely rear, "I think that waitress wants to bang you."

"I think that waitress wants a tip."

"We could bring her back with us," said Autumn wistfully. "She looks like she knows things."

"Uh," said Steve, his jaw going slack.

Autumn's face broke into a wicked smile, and she pounded the table in mirth. "If you could see your face," she said between giggles.

"Not funny."

"I beg to differ." She glanced at him, a calculating gleam in her eyes. "Why did you throw your invitation to that Christmas party in the trash?"

"Oh," said Steve, his face scrunching up, "I didn't think that you'd want to go to that."

"Why not?" Autumn straightened up and crossed her arms over her chest. Steve took a long swallow of beer, not quite able to meet her eyes.

"Because...I just, you know, it's a bunch of stuffed shirts, people that Phil works with at the office. It's not really your scene, I guess is what I'm getting at."

"I see," said Autumn, her face growing cold. "You don't want your uneducated, tattooed and pierced girlfriend embarrassing you."

Steve looked down at the table, chewing on his lower lip. "It's not that you embarrass me. Not at all. I...used to date a woman Phil works with, and now she's the big, successful exec and I'm still teaching. I guess I don't want her to gloat."

"Bull. You just don't want this girl to see you with *me* because you obviously still have feelings for her."

"If you want to go, we'll go. You don't have to be nasty about it."

"Now you just want to go because I'm mad," she said after draining her glass.

"Then what do you want?"

"I want you to *want* to take me."

"I *do* want to take you," he said in exasperation.

"Then why did you throw the invitation in the trash?"

"To avoid this conversation," said Steve through his teeth.

"What?" Autumn asked, a dangerous note creeping into her voice.

Steve glared at her angrily. "You know what? We're going, period."

"Just because you say so?" she said incredulously. "And I don't have anything to wear to something formal like that."

"I'll buy you a dress," said Steve, pounding his fist on the table so hard their glassware jumped.

"A nice one?"

"As long as I don't dip into rent money, fine, if that's what you want."

"I guess I could go and hide in the corner so I don't make you look bad."

"You don't have to hide in the corner."

"Are you sure? After all, we wouldn't want to tarnish your reputation."

"I'll show you off! I happen to not give a fuck what Cathy thinks about any of it."

Autumn smiled, trying to sip at her glass but finding it empty. "You're very passionate," she said, a small smile on her painted lips. "But you're afraid to show it. You don't have to be afraid when you're with me."

She clasped his large hand in her smaller ones, rubbing the tiny hairs on its surface with her gloved fingers.

"All right," he said, giving her hands a squeeze. "First thing when we get up, we'll go shopping."

"Don't you have your stupid *Lord of the Rings* crap going on tomorrow?"

"*Dungeons and Dragons*, and I don't need fantasy when mine has already come true."

She smiled again, almost shyly, and her tone belied the harshness of her words when she spoke. "You're such a pussy."

chapter 11

Steve shuffled into his bathroom, yawning cavernously. His bare-chested reflection stared back at him briefly before he swung open the attached door, revealing his medicine cabinet. He rolled his eyes at the proliferation of products that Autumn had crammed into it. In just a short week she had taken over most of the space that had once been exclusively his own. Now, his deodorant and razor were packed in next to bundles of cotton swabs, nail polish, tampons, Q-tips, and hair bands. That wasn't even taking into account the lipstick, eye shadow, compacts, and waxes laid out around the circumference of the sink. Gingerly, he tried to ease his deodorant out of the cabinet but wound up dislodging a miniature avalanche of feminine accoutrements.

Hastily, he gathered them up from where they had fallen in the sink, hoping that Autumn had not heard the spill. She was banging about in his kitchen, under the pretense of making him breakfast. So far he had seen her prepare Jiffy Pop and toaster pastries, so he was a bit dubious about her promise of pancakes and sausage.

He lifted a spongy mass of hair curlers restrained by a rubber band out of the sink. He cursed as he spotted another item he had missed. Picking up the small brown bottle, he saw it was a prescription of some sort. It bore Autumn's name and old address, and was nearly empty, containing only two pills. He read the label, seeing a name that he did not recognize. As Steve had to administer medicine to his young charges at times, he thought he was pretty familiar with pharmaceuticals.

Hearing Autumn curse, he headed quickly for the kitchen, the bottle largely forgotten in his hands. He came around the corner to find her lifting a huge griddle cake out of a sea of foamy hot grease. She plopped it on a plate, crying out as a bit of hot grease flew from the skillet to land on her bare foot.

"Are you all right?" he asked, smirking at her ineptitude.

"Shut up or I'll mix arsenic with your syrup." She poured more of the thick batter into the skillet. As soon as the batter was sizzling in the grease, she glanced up at him. Her playful smile faded when she saw the bottle in his hand.

"You can throw that away." She waved her hand dismissively.

"What was it for?" Steve asked, again staring at the label. "I've never heard of this stuff."

"It's for female problems, all right?" She reached out and snatched the bottle from his hand and tossed it into the trash can near the stove. "Do you like butter, or are you one of those weirdos who likes to put grape jelly on their pancakes?"

"Actually, I'm one of those weirdos who like to eat peanut butter on my pancakes."

"Instead of syrup?" she asked, aghast.

"No, *with* syrup."

"You are such a giant toddler," she said, laughing at him. "You like your sugar, sugar! My grandma was from Germany, and they eat jelly on everything, and I do mean *everything*. She even ate it on bologna!"

"Eww," said Steve, wrinkling his nose. Autumn bade him sit at the kitchen table, and shoved the mass of pancakes across the table at him. He raised an eyebrow at their unusual appearance; Autumn had difficulty getting them out of the skillet, and they were shredded badly. Also, the color was dark caramel, and strange bubbles appeared in the finished product.

Nevertheless, he swathed it in peanut butter and added a dollop of syrup, determined to reserve judgment. However, when his knife and fork made a crunching noise as he attempted to slice the haphazard stack into more manageable bites, he had to grin.

"Are pancakes supposed to be crispy?"

"Shut up," she said, trying to prepare her own meal.

Steve put them in his mouth and chewed. The taste was not horrible, but the greasy yet crunchy consistency was rather unpalatable. He forged on, finishing most of his plate before she sat down with her own food.

"How are they?" she asked, her fork poised near her chin.

"Uhm, they taste just fine." Steve washed down the questionable meal with a cold glass of milk.

He quickly rose to his feet and cleaned his plate at the sink. Autumn lifted the bite to her mouth and carefully took it off of her fork. She chewed once, twice, and then spat it back onto her plate.

"LIAR!" she shouted, as he had already disappeared into the bedroom. "These taste like shit!"

Phil stared up at the magnificent chandelier, a touch of pink tinging the light it spread about the vaulted ceiling. The hotel had a nice ballroom, he had to admit, as he drew his gaze back to floor level. Wooden tiles with elaborate patterns that appeared three dimensional beneath a glaze of wax formed the dance floor, which would have been a generous size even for a club. Sconces in the wall held electric lights shaped to appear as candles, their tapered stems colored red, green, and white. A towering Christmas tree, nearly twenty feet tall, dominated the far wall, the red skirt at the bottom largely concealed by faux presents. A Christmas carol wafted over the room from the DJ's turntable, providing background music for the guests who alternately danced and feasted at the long buffet tables.

"Wow," said Crawley, "this is nice!"

He turned to regard her, a smile on his face. She had her dark tresses put up, some length cascading down her back. A dark burgundy sleeveless dress fitted to her form, hitting just above her knees. The satiny material felt good under his hand as he stood with an arm around her waist. He himself was dressed in a nice tuxedo that he pretty much wore once a year, usually to this particular party.

"Vickers pulls out all the stops," he said with a nod. "There's caviar on the buffet line, if you can believe that. Used to be an open bar, too, until a few guys got too drunk and ruined it for us, but I think they still have free champagne if you can stand to wait in line."

"Sometimes," said Crawley, peering about the room intently, "I kind of regret working for my father. I mean, the work is fine, I enjoy what I do, but it gets awfully lonely sometimes. I don't…"

"What?"

Crawley heaved a heavy sigh.

"I don't have a lot of friends, Phillip." Her eyes seemed far away, and her nostrils flared slightly.

"What are you talking about? I mean, you have all kinds of friends on Facebook."

"Those don't really count. I mean, real friends, you know? Most of the people I hung out with in high school, they all moved on."

The two of them joined the long lines at the buffet tables.

"Didn't you have friends in college?"

"Sure, but they were never really close friends, you know what I mean? Other girls don't seem to like me much, and guys, well, most of them are only interested in one thing."

"I like you," said Phil with vehemence, squeezing her arm.

"Do you?" Crawley stared at him with half lidded eyes, biting her bottom lip. "I hope so, because I like you, too."

Their lips briefly met in a kiss. Phil felt conflicted, at once desiring her and dreading another intimate encounter that he might fail. Despite what Crawley had said, he was aware of how much more experienced she was in the bedroom, and he was worried that his lack of prowess would be the undoing of their burgeoning relationship.

He forced such worries aside as Crawley smiled at him, dark eyes shining. Phil thought about her confession, that she had few friends besides the band. He had always been the first one to roll his eyes at the way beautiful young women would complain about their lot, but he supposed that just being attractive didn't solve all one's problems.

He did wish that they were more on the same level with regard to sex, though. Either he could have been more experienced, or she could have been less, and it would have worked out fine. But he could not help thinking that she must have been comparing him with every other lover she had ever had, and seeing how she trashed newbs on WoW he had little doubt she preferred experience.

"Hello, Phillip," came a woman's voice to their left. Standing there, bearing a clear plate laden with hors d'oeuvres, was a large-busted woman with striking red hair. Her mascara was heavy, but she wore a light foundation so as not to hide her numerous freckles. A floor-length pale blue gown adorned her voluptuous figure, a single shoulder strap leaving much of her back bare.

"Hey, Catherine," said Phil. "Ellie, this is Catherine Snyder, our regional PR director. Cathy, this is Ellie, my girlfriend."

"Girlfriend?" Cathy asked, taking Crawley's hand and pumping it.

"Uh, well," said Phil, glancing nervously at Crawley, "we're dating, anyway."

"Nice to meet you," said Crawley, shaking Cathy's hand and smiling at her.

"I don't suppose Steve's going to come tonight?" Cathy asked, glancing around the crowded room.

"Uh, you know Steve," said Phil. "He's not really into this kind of party."

"Oh," said Cathy. It seemed to Phil that she was a bit disappointed. "Yeah, probably not."

"Oh, Steve's coming," said Crawley. "Autumn sent me a photo of the dress she picked out."

"Autumn?" Cathy's eyes narrowed.

"Autumn texts you?" Phil asked.

"Uh, sort of," said Crawley. "She doesn't always respond. I think… I think I kind of annoy her, like everyone else."

"Who's Autumn?" Cathy asked.

"Steve's new girlfriend," said Phil a bit eagerly, happy to cause his friend's tormentor a bit of jealousy. "She just moved in with him, actually."

"Oh," said Cathy, her eyes narrowing just a bit, "so she's someone he met at work, or what?"

"Uh," said Phil, "I don't think so, but you can ask him yourself. They just walked in the door."

Cathy followed his pointing finger to where Autumn and Steve stood in line waiting to present their invitations.

"They look so cute together," said Crawley with a sigh.

Over at the door, Steve adjusted his bow tie, put out. "This thing is strangling me."

"I tied it three times," said Autumn, smiling at him. "Get used to it."

She was wearing bright ruby lipstick, heavy eyeliner, and mascara. The dress she had chosen, a black as midnight number that hugged her generous curves well, displayed a good expanse of her shapely legs and bust. The light glinted off her painted lips, the golden hoops of her earrings (seven in each ear), and the silver heart pendant which hung around her neck. She idly toyed with the new bauble as she giggled at his continued antics.

"I can't breathe."

"Bullshit," she said softly in his ear, then more loudly. "If you were choking you'd be going *ack! Uck!*" She grabbed her own throat and rolled her eyes back into her head.

"Come on, zombie princess." Steve tugged gently on her elbow. "Let's go mingle, maybe get some of that champagne."

He led her around the room, introducing her to the few people he remembered from years past. They had nearly done a complete circuit when Autumn spotted Crawley and Phil.

"I guess we should go say hello." Her nostrils flared, and her brow came low over her eyes. Steve chuckled.

"You don't like Crawley much, do you?"

"She's not a bad person, or anything. She's just kind of annoying, you know? Like everything she says is designed to get you to pay attention to or be impressed with her."

"She might come across as conceited, but people who fish for approval like that usually have low self-esteem. Hell, that's why she dresses in those tight clothes, so people will pay attention to her."

"Oh, so you noticed her tight clothes?"

"Uh, not *noticed* noticed, but I noticed, yeah."

"Calm down, sugar," said Autumn, elbowing him in the ribs playfully. "You're not on the witness stand. We have to go say hi now, they just spotted us."

"Ugh, do we have to? That woman they're talking to is my ex."

"That's Cathy? You didn't say that she had such big knockers."

"Autumn!" hissed Steve, glancing around them. "Not so loud!"

"What, knockers isn't a bad word."

To Steve's horror, she tugged on an elderly man's sleeve and got his attention. "Excuse me, sir, is knockers a bad word?"

"Uh, no," said the man, unable to keep a smile off his wizened face.

"See?" said Autumn, turning back to Steve, who had slapped a palm over his face. "Now, let's go make your ex jealous so you can feel better."

"I'd rather not talk to her at all."

"Too bad," said Autumn, pulling on his arm. "We're going in!"

He had to laugh at her Vietnam-era chopper pilot sounds as they navigated their way through the milling throng to reach Phil and Crawley's side.

"Oh no!" said Autumn, pretending to lock sights on Crawley. "It's one of the yellow commies right there! Fire all weapons!"

Steve winced as she pantomimed firing a machine gun, complete with sound effects and vigorous jumping of her arms. Crawley seemed to take it in good humor, even narrowing her eyes comically and joining in.

"I get revenge, you western devil!" She emulated a stereotypical Asian accent while shaking her fist. "Some morning you wake up, there land mine under your head!"

Steve smiled apologetically at Phil. "They're going to get us thrown out."

"Hey, Steven," said Cathy, tugging on Steve's sleeve.

Steve turned to face her, carefully keeping his face a mask of neutrality. "Hello, Cathy. How've you been?"

"Busy, of course," she said, shaking his hand. "Who's your friend?"

"Girlfriend, actually," said Autumn, taking her hand and smiling sweetly. "Nice to meet you."

"I love your tattoos," said Cathy, eying Autumn's form. "I have a couple myself."

"Oh, really? I've done some ink before, do you care if I see them?"

"Oh, I couldn't do that here," said Cathy, a cross between a sneer and a smile on her face. "But Steve can tell you all about them."

"Steve's never mentioned you, actually," said Autumn, her voice pleasant but a bit of an edge creeping into her brown eyes.

"Let's go get some champagne, babe," said Steve, practically dragging Autumn away. When his back was turned Autumn stuck her tongue out at Cathy, then turned around and smacked a firm hand over Steve's buttocks.

"What was that for?" Steve was rubbing his rump though he was laughing.

"Just marking my territory."

"You don't have to do that. Cathy doesn't compare to you."

"Oh, bull. She's got a great rack, and her red hair is really pretty."

"Yeah, but she's more concerned about the way things look, or should be, than how they are. Might come from working in the PR field, but she never took my profession seriously. Used to call me 'her boyfriend, the babysitter.'"

"Ouch." Autumn squeezed his shoulder in sympathy. "I can see why you guys broke up, then. I know how hard you work, sugar. Some nights you just collapse into bed after a couple of beers."

"Yeah." Steve gratefully took two glasses of champagne from a passing waiter. "Sorry about that."

"Oh, don't worry about it. It's not like we're old marrieds yet."

"If I was going to marry anyone, it'd have to be you."

Autumn smiled, but there was a sad light in her eyes that seemed to belie it.

"What's wrong?"

"Nothing," she said, draining most of her glass in one go.

Steve pulled her toward the dance floor as a Frank Sinatra tune played over the speakers.

"No!" she said, literally dragging her heels. "I don't dance to this kind of music!"

"Just one song." He kept the pressure up until he finally pulled her along with him.

"Just one," she said, allowing herself to be tugged in tight against his body. After some initial awkwardness, due to their difference in height, they were soon slowly sashaying around the wooden tiled floor. His hand was warm on her bare back, caressing the curve of her spine. She kneaded the muscles in his arm slightly, squishing around a big vein that was invisible under his sleeve.

"You know," she said into his ear, "you're not the type of man I thought I'd end up with."

He smiled, pulling her more tightly against him. "What kind of man *did* you think you'd end up with?"

She laughed softly. "A jerk. You're way too tall, and entirely too sensitive for your own good, but you're definitely not a jerk."

"Gee," he said with mock indignation, "thanks."

"I shouldn't…I shouldn't be with you."

Steve stopped dancing to stare her in the eye. "What's that supposed to mean?"

"Don't get all jealous," she said, putting her head on his shoulder. "I don't mean what you think I mean."

"So explain," he said as they began to dance once more.

She stiffened against him, the muscles in her back taut under his hand. "I can't, not right now, not here. Let's just dance, and forget about it, all right?"

"Does this have anything to do with that bottle I threw away?" Steve frowned slightly, his eyes staring starkly ahead as they continued to dance.

She made no verbal reply, just wrapped her arms around him more tightly and leaned her face against his chest.

"Take me home," she said, patting his chest. "If you think I look good in this dress, wait till you see what's underneath…"

"What's underneath?"

"Something that cost waaay too much for less cotton than you'll find in an aspirin bottle…"

On the cab ride home, they could barely keep their hands off each other. Her clandestine behavior, and the intangible pall it cast over them, seemed to demand an equal and opposite response. If it were possible to smolder her trepidation away with passion, Steve would surely have done it. By the time they had made it up to his apartment door, both were glassy eyed and breathing hard.

As soon as the door had shut behind them they embraced, mouths exploring each other as tiny cries and grunts escaped their throats. With a sudden, mischievous grin, Autumn put a palm to his chest and shoved him back onto a chair. He plopped down heavily, taken aback by the gesture. She sauntered over to his stereo, grinning over her shoulder as she put on music. She turned toward him and undid the string at the back of her neck. Steve watched with shining eyes and a slightly shy smile as she slowly peeled the silk away from her skin. She stepped out of the garment and let it fall to the floor, revealing a skimpy lace bustier and garter belt, matching her dark stockings. No panties blocked his view of her smoothly shaven nether region, and he found his body responding vigorously.

"Do you like it?" she asked sensuously.

"I love it." He buried his face in her breasts, kissing them firmly but gently. Her hands teased his hair, nails scraping across his scalp in her vigor. Seizing her leg under the knee, he brought it up over his shoulder and dipped his head low.

"You're so bad," she said as his tongue wormed its way into her. "So baaaaad!"

Steve buried his face into her labia, rutting his mouth in to bask in her scent. Very gently, his tongue flicked over the ring in her quivering hood. She tilted her head back and gasped, nearly toppling both of them over as a wave of ecstasy washed over her.

"You like that, huh?" he said in a whisper, briefly pulling his moist face free.

"God, yes," she said, hands encouraging him to return to his task.

Using his tongue, he hooked under the ring pierced through her flesh and pulled, gently at first and then more firmly. Her clit bulged against his lips, and he took it in his mouth like a fish taking bait. When he added suction, she nearly tore strands of his hair out as she was hit with a wave of contractions. All thoughts of her standoffish, enigmatic behavior left him as he concentrated solely on pleasing his woman. One hand curved around her buttocks, partially holding her steady, while his other kneaded a generous handful of her large bosom.

"That's—" Autumn gasped "—that's really nice…"

Steve kneaded the flesh of her buttocks as he redoubled his efforts. His fingers slid along her sweaty skin, arcing to the middle of her cheeks. Just the tip of his pinky touched the tight ring of muscle there, and he took her satisfied sigh as an indication that he had not crossed a line. Slowly, he worked his finger into the orifice, acting in concert with his tongue to drive her wild. He became lost in her body's reactions, the wooden chair creaking dangerously under their combined weight as she lost control and let loose a scream that was sure to have his neighbor riled up.

"I need to sit down —" she gently pushed his head away "—while my legs still work."

Sit down she did, carefully straddling his lap. As their bodies interlocked she gasped, eyes tightly shut.

"Are you okay?" He was trying to sound concerned though he was obviously distracted.

"I'm fine. It always kind of hurts going in…you're *huge*."

He tried to shrug in mock arrogance, but her suddenly swiveling hips caused him to gasp instead. Their hands clasped together as she leaned on him for support, grinding her sweaty pelvis against his. Their cries grew louder, drowning out the furious stomping from the upstairs apartment. Autumn let loose a scream that would have been blood-curdling under other circumstances, collapsing against him. With a loud snap, the chair finally gave up its fight. They ended up sitting on the floor, the remains of the chair still under his bare bottom. After a brief moment of shock they both laughed, Autumn putting her forehead against his chest.

"That chair was ugly anyway," said Steve, before carefully extricating their tangled limbs and rising from the shattered ruins.

chapter 12

"Good news!" said Autumn as she opened the door to their apartment and came inside. Steve glanced up from the stack of papers he was working on and smiled. "I don't have to work tomorrow after all!"

"Did Tammy switch with you again?"

"No, I got another job!"

"Oh yeah? At PetSmart?"

"No," said Autumn, wrinkling her nose. "Sal just opened a tattoo parlor right on the river, and he said I can start the day after tomorrow!"

Steve's smile faded and his lips pursed in a pout. "Sal? The ex-boyfriend Sal?"

Autumn put her hands on her hips and glared at him. "Yes, we used to date. So what?"

"So you'll be working for your ex."

"Oh my god," she said, shaking her head, "you're jealous. I can't believe that you of all people are going to get jealous of—"

"And how am I supposed to feel about it?"

"I don't know, you could try and feel happy for me that I'll be doing something I love, rather than asking some dipshit if he wants fries with his Big Mac."

Steve sighed, rubbed his eyes. "I trust you, I just don't trust *him*."

Autumn rolled her almond shaped eyes, then sat down heavily in one of the surviving chairs. "Trust me, he's not going to force himself on me, or anything like that. Sal's a sweet guy, he just…"

"He just what?"

"Never mind. What are you working on?"

"Just some stuff," he said, dragging the papers into a stack.

Autumn snagged a yellow sheet and peered at it. She set the paper back on the table and stared him squarely in the eye. "You're paying bills. Let me help." She dug in her purse for her billfold.

Steve put a hand on her wrist, stopping her. "I can take care of it. You make minimum wage."

"I *used* to make minimum wage. Now I get ten bucks an hour, plus commission."

"That's very generous of Sal," he said, unable to keep the grimace off his face.

"You want me to fucking quit?" Autumn leaned forward, slapping her palms on the table on either side of her purse. "I'll fucking quit. I'll just keep pouring coffee and smiling at every mouth breather who says 'hey baby, do the tattoos go all the way down?' I'll keep the miserable fucking job I have now so you won't have your manhood threatened."

"I don't want you to quit."

"Yes, you do. It's written all over your square-jawed face!"

"Maybe I do want you to quit, but that doesn't mean I think you *should*."

Autumn stood up and angrily snapped her purse shut. She stalked toward the door, limbs stiff and eyes narrowed to slits.

"Where are you going?" he asked.

"Out for a walk, if that's all right with my master…I mean my boyfriend."

Steve winced as the door slammed with a shuddering impact. He held his face in his hands and sighed.

"Was I out of line, Ma?" Steve asked into his phone as he ate beans right out of the can. "Am I a jealous asshole boyfriend?"

"You'll have to decide that for yourself," said the warm, if a bit world-weary voice in his ear. "It's up to you if you trust her or not."

"Yeah, I thought you'd say something like that. Thanks for nothing."

"Oh, Steven. Your father says Autumn seems like a nice girl. Try not to run her off like the last one, okay?"

"I didn't run Cathy off. She dumped me because I wasn't 'mature' enough for her."

His mother chuckled softly into his ear. "Don't you think your own fear of being abandoned is clouding your judgment? Either you trust her and she cheats or doesn't, or you don't and she cheats or doesn't. All you're doing is working yourself up and creating drama where there isn't any."

"Then what should I do?" he asked around a mouthful of masticated legumes.

"Go and meet this Sal. You might be surprised."

"Bah," said Steve, sending bean juice out to spatter on the floor. "That sounds like a waste of time."

"Steve, you're six and a half feet tall and more burly than your father. If nothing else, see it as a way to scare the hell out of him."

"Now you're speaking my language!"

"Try and be patient. The course of true love never did run smoothly."

"No, no, it does not."

"What's wrong, honey?"

"Nothing, and everything. I just realized I've been acting like a jerk, when Autumn's got her own problems to work out."

"All right, dear, I have to go. It's very late here."

"I know, Ma, and thanks for listening. I love you."

"And I love you."

He set his phone down and sighed. He glanced at the muted television weather report, noted that the temperature was in the single digits. Suddenly sick with worry, he grabbed his coat and left the apartment, donning the garment as he rapidly descended the stairs. On the way he checked to see if any of his half dozen texts had been answered, grumbling when he saw that they hadn't. He burst out the door at street level just as a highly polished red BMW pulled up to the curb, streetlights reflecting off its surface. Steve's brow knitted as he recognized Crawley in the back seat, and even more so when Autumn got out on the opposite side.

"Hey," she said in a subdued tone.

"Hey," he said, hands jammed in his pockets due to the cold.

"Just a second." She ducked her head back into the car to say her farewells. When she rose back up, a slight smile was on her face. She stepped up onto the curb and went to him, wrapping her arms around his torso in a tight hug. He returned the embrace, laying his cheek next to hers.

"I'm sorry," they both said at once, eliciting a burst of nervous laughter.

"I'm sorry," said Steve, hand on the back of her head stroking her long hair. "I should have been more trusting."

"Oh, whatever, I'd be pretty jealous too, if you started working for one of your exes. I'm just made of bitch."

Steve pulled back from the embrace to look her in the eyes. "Don't say that. I can be a pain in the ass sometimes, too."

They went back into the apartment, her leaning heavily on his shoulder.

"So, how come the Crawleys were giving you a ride?"

"Oh, they found me at a diner down the road and fed me. I think I know why Creepy has so many problems."

"Oh," said Steve, fumbling with his keys, "why is that?"

"Her father is a tool."

Steve arched an eyebrow and clucked his tongue.

"Well, he is. Not only does he think that the world is only six thousand years old, he wants Ellie to date a nice Catholic boy and squeeze out a half dozen puppies for him to dote on. And don't get me started on what he thinks of a woman's right to choose."

"You left him breathing, right?"

"He's in one piece," she said, kissing him on the cheek. "Mostly!"

Crawley's long, muscular fingers flew rapidly over Molly's strings, a veneer of intense concentration on her fine features. Occasionally, she would make a mistake, and an odd note would cause her face to crinkle up. Despite her own harsh criticism of herself, the faces of her bandmates were pleased.

Phil, seated in his corner of Rex's garage, had a wide-eyed smile on his face as his girlfriend shredded through "Freebird." Rex, hidden behind his drum kit, was fiercely pleased with her performance, causing his own to be more vigorous.

The lead singer was nodding his head and holding up a lit lighter. He was tall and lanky, his tow head nearly brushing the low ceiling. His Slavic features, a long wide nose and decidedly pointed chin, made him look a bit silly, but nobody would never mock his powerful singing voice.

Blinking the sweat out of her eyes, she ground through the outro.

When they were finished, Sven clapped his hands and whooped. "That was awesome, *ja?*"

"Oh, *ja*," said Rex, standing up and clapping himself.

"I think we're ready," said Phil.

"Honestly," said Crawley, though she beamed from the praise, "I think Rex shouldn't be allowed to have any caffeine. He keeps speeding up when he gets excited."

"Don't be worrying," said Sven, "the beer will counteract the effects, *ja?*"

"Yeah," said Phil. "We took a road trip up to Maine and Rex showed up with his only suitcase full of beer."

They had a laugh at Rex's expense, though he seemed not to be too terribly offended.

"Explain to me again," said Phil, coming over to speak with Rex while Sven tuned his bass guitar with Crawley's assistance, "why we have to work on a night when everyone else is partying?"

"Exposure," said Rex with a grin on his homely face. "This party is probably going to be huge. Chet has a six-car garage, and it was *packed* with people last New Year's. Eve I told Chet he should have a live band next time, and he asked me if I knew any, and here we are."

"Yeah," said Phil, glancing nervously at Crawley, "but I've never had a girlfriend on New Year's Eve before. I was kind of looking forward to—"

"You can play 'hide the salami' after our last set," said Rex with a shrug. "Besides, look how excited she is. You know how much of a thrill it is to play for a live audience the first time, even if you're not getting paid to do it."

"We're not getting paid?" Phil asked in alarm.

"A little bit," said Rex, his eyes narrowing. "Three hundred in cash, plus we get to drink for free."

"Guess it's too late to back out now," said Phil, running a hand over the peach fuzz he no doubt thought of as a mustache.

"Glad you see it my way," said Rex. "Now shave that pathetic cunt hair off of your face!"

"Stop it," said Autumn harshly, glaring at Steve on the sofa.

"Stop what?"

"Ever since you found that stupid bottle, you wince whenever I sneeze, groan, or fart. It's annoying as hell, so stop it."

"I hadn't realized," said Steve, chewing his lower lip.

"Well, it's stupid and unnecessary, so stop it."

Steve sighed, rubbed his fingers along the bridge of his nose, and then gave her a small smile. "I'll try to keep it in check."

"You'd better," she said, kissing him on the cheek. "I never want you to treat me like a porcelain doll. Hell, you know how much I love it when you throw me around."

Steve shook his head and smiled a bit bashfully.

"Oh, there he is again." She leaned forward and put her hands on his face. "Your inner Puritan is back!"

Steve took her hands in his and gently kissed them. "I so don't have an inner Puritan."

"Yes you do," she said, kissing him. "It's one of the things that I like about you. I get to corrupt that god fearin' little shit right out of you!"

"Corrupt this!" Steve suddenly tickled her in the ribcage.

"Stop!" she said through peals of laughter. "Don't...Stop it!"

"Don't stop it? Whatever you say."

"Can't…breathe…" said Autumn, tears rolling down her smiling face.

Steve stopped, and she gasped on the couch for a moment, trying to compose herself.

"That was dirty, getting me in my weak spot."

"I can think of more delicate areas." Steve pretended to be thoughtful with a finger pressed up to his lips.

"That's not a weak spot; it can grab hold of you and give you a decent hump, can't it?"

"I'd say more than decent," said Steve, running his hand over her black sweat pants.

"At some point we have to start getting ready for this party."

"Sun's not even all the way down yet." Steve began kissing her on the neck. He left a tender trail down to her shoulder, exposed due to the wide neck T-shirt of his she was wearing. Hooking his hands on the collar of the shirt, he jerked his arms back and ripped the garment in half. Autumn gasped, her toes curling in her Hello Kitty socks.

chapter 13

"I guess we're setting up over there." Rex pointed across the already crowded garage. His tone seemed to indicate he was less than pleased.

"Only place there's room," said Phil, ducking around a greasy engine clock suspended from a thick chain.

Crawley maneuvered Molly's case around the same obstacle, wide eyes taking in the crowd. She licked her lips as she scanned to and fro.

"There's a lot of people here." She was growing a bit pale.

While the male band members were dressed casually, Crawley had dressed in style. She wore a short skirt with a leopard pattern, held up by a wide leather belt with a profusion of dull metal spikes. A dark pair of fishnets covered her legs below the skirt, until they reached the tops of her patent leather, calf-high boots. The heels were delicate and tapered, and Crawley was nearly Phil's height in them. Her hair was done with a side part swept into a high ponytail, held in place by a pin designed to resemble a black widow spider. Dark red lipstick stained her mouth, and her eye shadow was far more dramatic and heavy than normal. Underneath it all, though, she still seemed like a scared girl. Phil took her free hand in his own and squeezed.

"It's just a little stage fright, Ellie. I thought I was gonna pee my pants the first time we played live."

"*Ja*," said Sven, "except that the difference is Phil is peeing his pants all the time."

"Fuck you, you overgrown strudel muncher!" said Phil, face flushing red as Crawley giggled behind her hand.

"Set up first, bicker and argue second," said Rex in mock seriousness.

They threaded their way through the mingling mob of humanity, trying not to knock over any of the myriad drinks being held or sitting on the concrete floor of the garage. The ceiling was surprisingly high, nearly twenty feet at its apex. Fluorescent light fixtures buzzed above their heads, providing ample illumination.

"Hey!" said Crawley, turning around sharply. "Someone just grabbed my ass!"

"Sorry," said a seated man, bulging with muscle that was quite visible under his thin T-shirt. He grinned at her with glassy eyes that said he had been celebrating the New Year a little early. A dark mohawk decorated his scalp, and numerous tattoos could be seen on his arms and neck. "It was an accident!" His peal of raucous laughter indicated that it was probably not an accident.

Phil stepped up to the man, put a hand on his shoulder and tightened his grip. "That wasn't a very heartfelt apology," he said harshly.

The man slowly stood up, a smile on his face saying that he had gotten exactly what he wanted. He rose to tower over Phil, the smaller man disappearing from Crawley's sight behind his massive frame.

"Too fucking bad," said the mohawked man, jabbing his finger in Phil's chest.

"Just let it go, honey," said Crawley, seizing Phil's bicep and dragging him away. "He's just jealous 'cause you're in the band."

"Yeah, Train," said a man nearly as inebriated as his robust friend, "don't start a fight with the band."

"You're lucky," said Train, turning around and returning to his conversation at high volume. "Did you see that guy? What a little pussy, won't even stand up for his woman."

Crawley hooked her arm in Phil's and dragged him toward the staging area. "Ignore him, honey," said Crawley, using her calloused fingers to pull his face back around when he seethed at the comment. "I'm going home with you tonight, because you're more of a man than that alpha male creep will ever be."

Her words helped, but still Phil felt as if the only balm for his soul was the sweet crack of knuckles on the jaw of someone who desperately deserved it.

They finally got over to where Rex and Sven were talking and laughing with their apparent employer. He was about the same age as Rex, maybe a bit older, with a handlebar mustache peppered with gray. He wore a sleeveless T-shirt, a Confederate flag tattooed on his right arm, while an American flag graced his left. He was spotted with freckles and possessed a tan complexion that spoke of many hours in the sun. His thickly calloused palms, almost painful on Phil's hand when he shook it, seemed to confirm that he was a laborer of some sort.

"Howdy! I think we might have met once or twice at Rex's place, but I'm Chet."

"Nice to meet you. I'm Phil."

"And who is this vision of loveliness?" Chet asked, playfully taking Crawley's hand and kissing it, causing her to giggle.

"Our new guitarist, and my girlfriend, Eleanor Crawley."

Chet raised an eyebrow at the declaration but smiled easily enough. "Hope you're as good as Rex here says you are. I happen to love the Scorpions, and if you don't nail the solo there might be a riot."

"Then I'd better get it right!" said Crawley, beginning the arduous task of setting up and tuning Molly.

Phil busied himself with carrying in the components for his keyboard. He was careful not to pass too close to Train and his entourage, and was able to avoid another incident. He was puzzled by the addition of a saxophone in the trailer bearing their gear.

"Hey, Rex," he said, coming up to the older man with the instrument still in its black plastic case. "How come you brought a sax? I thought we dropped 'Who Can it Be Now?'"

"We *did*," said Rex with a grin, "because you couldn't handle the bass so Sven could play the sax. But Steve is gonna be here, so..."

"Dude," said Phil, shaking his head, "don't put him on the spot."

"Oh, he'll love it."

Phil sighed, feeling outranked by Rex as always.

"The ball drops at midnight, hon," said Steve, sitting on the sofa and seeming quite bored. "You going to be ready sometime before then?"

"Shut up and wait!" Autumn's voice came teasingly from the bathroom. "Girls like to dress up on New Year's Eve."

"I just don't want to get there after they start their second set. Rex was real specific about that."

"Oh, it'll be fine. I'm almost ready."

"Said that half an hour ago," muttered Steve under his breath. Dress shoes with a fresh shine tapped impatiently as the minutes stretched on. He had gotten a haircut earlier in the day, his locks now shorn to shoulder length. His face was impeccably shaved, the skin shining with a healthy glow. A black dress shirt which he had not buttoned was worn over a gray T-shirt. He had chosen a pair of his better black dress pants, and was wearing some fruity foreign cologne that Autumn had gotten him.

At last, he heard the bathroom door open. He rose to his feet as Autumn's heels clicked on the floor. His eyes went wide as he ran his gaze lingeringly up and down her feminine form. She had styled her hair into two mini buns a few inches behind and above her ears, from which trailed short braided pigtails, just brushing the top of her nearly bare shoulders. Silver lipstick matched her shimmering, short mini dress, which was held up in a seemingly precarious fashion by two nearly invisible straps. Her legs were adorned in the black garters he had become familiar with at the Christmas party, but she now wore dark blue suede boots that reached just above her knees. She had silver bracelets on both her wrists in a pattern that seemed haphazard but aesthetic. Smoky blue eye shadow made her lovely brown eyes stand out dramatically.

She did a little pirouette, smiling prettily as he basked in her beauty. "You like? Worth the wait, right?"

"You are amazingly, incredibly beautiful," he said, rising to his feet and giving her light applause.

"Oh, stop," she said, picking up her long black overcoat and wrapping herself in it snugly.

"Not for a minute."

The ride out to Long Island was relatively silent, as they both stared out the window at the numerous flashing lights and opulent decorations on the route. They stared out different sides of the cab, but their hands remained locked together on the seat between them.

When they arrived, Steve got out first and went to Autumn's side, opening the door and offering a hand.

"Oh, such a gentleman," she said with a giggle.

"At least you didn't call me a pussy."

They walked up the long blacktop driveway to Chet's garage. The air was chilly, but there were small clusters of party guests huddled against the structure, engaged in the smoking of tobacco and other plants.

"Pussy," she said, turning her smiling face toward him. The warmth of her tone, and the soft kiss she planted on his cheek belied the term. She giggled when she realized that a lipstick mark was left on his cheek.

"What?"

"Nothing." She grinned and adjusted his collar a bit to hide a large dark spot on his neck. "Got to hide your hickeys, that's all."

The pair entered the garage, carefully navigating the mass of humanity. Over against the north wall, Rex and the band were pounding out "We're Not Gonna Take It" to the delight of the enthusiastic crowd.

"Lot of people here," said Steve.

"I don't like crowds." Autumn's brown eyes narrowed beneath her lowered brows.

"Me neither." He gave her hand a squeeze. "If you want, we can bail after the second set that Rex insisted we see."

"Depends on how good the booze is."

"Probably a couple different types of beer in kegs, not to mention the champagne Rex brought."

They found a spot near the stage, Steve feeling familiar enough with the environs to move a box full of auto parts off of a workout bench. As they watched the band play, Autumn leaned her head on Steve's shoulder. He put an arm around her, gently squeezing her bare shoulder with his large hand.

"Autumn!" came a voice, straining to be heard over the music. "Hey, Autumn!"

Sidling up to the two of them was Train, a beer sloshing in his hand. Autumn straightened her posture, but kept her hand on Steve's thigh.

"Hey, Stan," she said, a trace of impatience in her voice, as if she were addressing an annoying child. "Been a while."

"Don't you know it," he said, eyes running up and down her scantily clad form. "You look hotter than shit."

Steve shifted a bit, drawing a panicked glance from Autumn.

"Have you met my boyfriend, Steve?" she said, turning to smile at him.

"No," said Train, his face falling a bit. "I haven't."

A new grin broke out on his face, and he clapped Steve hard on his free shoulder. "You're a lucky dude, Steve," he said, walking away from them and draining his cup.

"Don't I know it," said Steve, turning back to Autumn and raising an eyebrow. "Another ex, I take it?"

"Yeah. My least favorite mistake. I was in one of those dangerous-guy phases."

"I'm not dangerous?"

"Only to furniture," she said, kissing him on the cheek again.

"You're cheerful tonight."

"It's a party, isn't it? What's not to be happy about? I'm young, cute, and with the absolute best man in New York."

Steve was taken aback by her words, cheeks flushing as he stammered. "I'm nowhere near the best man in the city. I'm probably not even the best man in the Bronx."

"Oh, bull," she said, eyes shining. "I say you're the best. Are you going to dare to argue with me? I'll kick your ass, you know."

"Yeah, all hundred twenty pounds of you."

"Hundred and sixteen, jerk!" she said, jabbing him in the ribs with her silver painted nails.

"Oww. Is this how you treat the best man in New York?"

"Aaaaaand it's already gone to your head," she said. "It's okay, you can feel like that just for tonight."

They watched the rest of the set with Autumn resting her head on his arm. At one point she inhaled deeply, enjoying his scent, with a soft smile on her face. Steve drank several beers in quick succession, trying to catch up with the rest of the revelers.

Rex, Phil, and Crawley stopped by to chat for a moment, the young woman mopping sweat from her brow.

"Yo, Rex," said Steve, "is there a port-a-potty this year, or are we allowed to go in the house?"

"The band's allowed to go in the house. You know what, we're heading that way. You can help us carry the Jell-O shots back out."

"Cool. My bladder's about to burst." He kissed Autumn on the lips before rising to his feet. Their hands stayed linked as long as possible without stopping his momentum.

Steve went into the house, burdening himself with two trays filled to capacity with colorful cups of alcohol-laced gelatin. After placing them carefully near the stage, he went back to his seat. His eyebrow arched as he noticed Crawley and Autumn speaking with their heads very close together. They both glanced at him, then turned back to each other and giggled like schoolgirls. Crawley nodded at him as she gave up her seat, eyes lingering on his chest and arms.

"What was that all about?" Steve asked, as the trio returned to their instruments.

"Phil is a lucky man. I get the feeling that girl is a *freak*."

Steve laughed, drowned out as the band tuned up. "You know what they say about Catholic girls."

"What?" Autumn put her arms akimbo, beautiful face lit up with faux anger. "You know I was a Catholic girl, right?"

"No way!"

They both laughed at his incredulity.

"Yes way. Right after I got my first tattoo, my mom enrolled me at St. Augustine's."

Steve jutted his teeth out as if he were buck-toothed and assumed a nebbish lilt to his speech. "You still have the uniform?" he asked, punctuating his question with a nerdy snort.

"Oh, stop! I think I burned it, actually. Fit of teenage rebellion and all that."

"Now that sounds like you, refusing to conform down to the last."

"Damn right!"

"It wasn't a complaint," he said, squeezing her knee.

Their attention was drawn to the stage as Rex spoke. "How's everybody doing tonight?"

The crowd roared, Steve and Autumn adding their own voices to the mix.

"Everybody who attends tonight gets a free piece of ass in a glass," he said, causing a ripple of laughter. "We are Settle the Score, and we are here to rock this beeeeyoooootch!"

The crowd cheered again, and they began their second set with "Rock Star."

"I can't believe that Swedish Neanderthal sings so beautifully in English," said Autumn.

"I know, and you can barely understand him when he talks. Go figure."

They applauded at the end of the song. Sven took the microphone off the stand and walked to the edge of the staging area.

"Are you ready to open up a can of ass whip on this mother?" he asked, prompting as many laughs as cheers. Rex set up another microphone on the stage as Sven worked the crowd. "We're going to be needing ze hand from a goot friend in the crowd for zis next one."

"Oh, no," said Steve, laughing as he slapped a palm over his face. "I should have seen this coming."

"Seen what coming?" Realization dawned in her magnificent eyes, and she giggled. "Oh my god, he's talking about you. I didn't even know you played anything! Wait, what do you play?"

She tugged playfully on his arm, causing him to grin.

"You'll see." He rose to his feet, limbs shaking from alcohol as well as fear.

"Steve!" said Sven, repeating it. "Steve, Steve, Steve…"

The crowd chanted with him, causing Steve to redden as he walked up to Rex and accepted the shiny sax in his hands.

"I'm going to fuck up all over the place," said Steve.

"Nobody's gonna care," said Rex. "They're all too drunk!"

Steve was a bit tipsy himself, and was way out of practice. No one seemed to mind his missed notes, however, and soon he was able to relax and enjoy himself. He tried scanning the crowd for Autumn to gauge her reaction, but the bright lights shining on him cut his visual range to about ten feet from the stage. Assuming that she was at least somewhat impressed, he carried on with his performance despite his frequent errors.

The crowd cheered at the end of the song, and Steve was high-fiving Rex and Sven. Crawley elected to give him a hug, which he awkwardly returned, patting her on the back.

When he returned to Autumn, his spot was occupied by Train. The man was leaning forward with his elbows across his tree trunk thighs, a broad grin upon his bleary eyed face.

"C'mon, Autumn, you can't tell me you don't miss me a little."

"I don't miss you at all," she said with a grumble. She rose to her feet and kissed Steve passionately as he returned.

Train's eyes to narrow to mere slits. "Hey, you mind taking a hike? Autumn and I were having a private conversation."

"Seriously?" said Steve, his brow coming low over his ice blue eyes.

"Why don't we go?" said Autumn. She tugged on Steve's arm, and something about the urgency of her voice made him comply. He followed her outside into the chilly night air.

"I'm not scared of that ass clown. You didn't have to 'rescue' me."

"I think I did, sugar." Autumn sighed and cast her gaze skyward, shaking her head as Train came out the door behind them. "Oh, balls."

"You don't just walk away from me, bitch," said Train, stepping toward her.

Steve blocked his path. He wasn't quite as tall as the body builder, but he seemed broader, stockier. Even in his inebriated state Train allowed his progress to be halted.

"Piss off, asshole, your tattoos and beach muscles don't mean shit to me." Steve stepped closer.

"Steve," said Autumn, tugging on his arm.

"You think you're a bad ass?" Train asked, jabbing a finger in the air at Steve.

"Badder than you—" Steve said, halting his speech as Autumn stepped in front of him.

"Go away, Roidzilla," she said. "Or *I'm* going to kick your ass."

"Let's see you do it, sugarlips," said Train. His mocking laughter changed to an agonized scream as Autumn slammed her foot down hard on his, striking a toe joint. Her hard spiked heel focused all the energy on a tiny point of impact, and her sudden vicious twist at the end of the attack audibly snapped a few digits unbroken by the initial stomp.

"What did you do?" Steve asked as Train dropped to his butt, holding his foot and hollering.

"You broke my foot! Fucking bitch broke my foot, and I have a match next week!"

"Match?" Steve asked.

"He's an MMA fighter, sugar," said Autumn. "You were gonna get your ass kicked."

"I'm calling the fucking police," said Train. "Vinny! VINNY! Bring me my phone so I can call the cops on that bitch. This is fucking assault."

"Are you kidding me?" said Steve as Train made good on his threat.

"Oh well," said Autumn, putting her arm around his waist and leaning on him. "It's not a party until someone goes to jail!"

chapter 14

"Of course, back in those days, they hated you more for being black than being on the outs," said the yellow-toothed elderly man sitting next to Steve. He cackled at his own jest, his brown face wrinkling merrily.

"Damn," said Steve, chuckling, "it must have been the battle of the stereotypes."

They were both seated in the crowded lobby of Long Island Precinct 14. It being New Year's Eve, there were plenty of people who needed bailing out. Occasionally, the sleepy-eyed female officer at the desk would call someone's name, and that person would nervously shuffle up to the counter and speak in low tones to the woman. Sometimes money was given, sometimes not, but the one constant was how abysmally slow the proceedings were.

He had been chatting with the elderly transient, who had identified himself as Sam, for over an hour. Steve found the old timer's company soothing, like putting on a pair of comfortable shoes.

"Yeah," said Sam, coughing a bit, which drew concern from Steve. "Those were the good old days. Enlisted in the corps, because I figured if white people were gonna bust my ass I might as well get paid for it."

"You were military?"

"Yup," said Sam showed his worn dog tags. "Fought in Korea. Our platoon got pinned down by a bunch of 'volunteers' from China."

"How'd you know they were from China?"

"Koreans is pretty damn small, but them Chinese fellas, they can grow big. When a six-foot-two-inch Asian is trying to hide in a foxhole dug for someone a foot shorter, it kind of shows. It's also real easy to splatter their brains with a round."

Steve laughed obligingly, then sighed, staring at the display on his phone. It was nearly two in the morning.

"I hope Autumn's all right," he said.

"Borgia, Steven," said the chubby officer.

"Got to go," said Steve. Snatching a piece of paper from the table at his side, he scribbled on it briefly. "This has the number of a guy I know who runs a gym. It'd be sweeping up floors and taking out the trash, but I think he needs somebody. Give him a call. I'll put in a good word for you."

"Thanks," said Sam, cautious optimism dawning on his wizened face.

"Borgia, Steven!" said the woman more loudly, her face sneering.

"Here," said Steve, coming up to the counter.

"Ms. Winter's bail is set at one thousand dollars."

"One thousand?" said Steve, jaw agape. "Why so much?"

"Aggravated assault is a serious charge."

"But it was a load of bull! It's just her ex-boyfriend trying to fuck with her life."

"That don't confront me, honey. All I know is you need one thousand dollars in cash to bail her out."

Steve opened his wallet, eyes scanning the scant bills within. "I don't have that much on me. Is there an ATM around here?"

"You passed one in our foyer," said the officer, setting his paper-work aside. "I'll keep you at the top of the queue."

"Thanks. Figures they'd have a fucking ATM on sight. This is usury!"

After calling his bank to get a maximum withdrawal override, Steve finally had fifty crisp twenties. He ruefully checked his balance. "Gonna have to pull some out of my savings—again."

He returned to the desk, waiting with as much patience as he could muster as the slow-moving officer dealt with another annoyed patron. After paying her and signing about two dozen forms he finally was told to return to his seat.

Twenty minutes later, Autumn appeared, escorted by an elderly cop. He buzzed her out a stout glass door, and she walked up to Steve, unable to meet his eyes.

"How much did you have to pay?" she asked.

"Not that much." He wrapped her in a fierce hug that elicited a surprised grunt. "Let's go home."

"Bullshit, you've got sticker shock written all over your face. How much?"

"A thousand," said Steve, trying to sound casual. "Not that much in the grand scheme of things."

"Oh my god," she said, slapping an arm over her eyes. "I am the worst girlfriend ever."

"You must be the best girlfriend ever. I just paid one K to get you out of jail!"

She leaned on him as they walked down the concrete stairs leading to the parking lot. Steve pulled a set of keys out of his pocket and made a beeline toward a muscle car coated with primer.

"Whose car is this?" Autumn asked with a raised brow.

"Mine," said Steve, opening the door for her.

"No way! Where has it been all this time?"

"At Chet's. I'm surprised the damn thing is even running. I don't have a muffler for it, so it's going to be loud."

"Why not just take a cab?"

"I had no idea how much running around I was going to have to do in order to bail you out." He turned the key and the engine roared to life, rattling their very bones with its power.

"You're full of surprises, sugar."

"Yeah," he said as he pulled slowly out of the spot. "Look, next time would you let me fight my own battles?"

"Steve, that guy was a trained fighter. I've seen him beat down men a lot bigger than you."

"I've got news for you, beautiful. I'm regarded as something of a bad ass myself."

Autumn gave him a smile with her eyes half closed. "You called me beautiful."

"Sorry. I know you don't like pet names."

"When did I say I didn't like pet names?"

"But you said—"

"I don't like being called babe, sweetcakes, or darling. But beautiful is just fine."

"Okay," said Steve, a warm smile on his face. It fell quickly, replaced by a half-hearted glower. "But I'm still mad at you. I think I could have taken that guy."

"I'm sure you could have, sugar, but I reaaaaally didn't want anything to get in the way of our post-party sex-a-thon." She dropped her hand to his lap, while her gaze remained on his face.

He grinned and put a hand atop hers. "And you say *I'm* bad."

"Oh, ho ho, if there wasn't a shifter in the way, I'd show you how *bad* I can be!"

"It's probably for the best that this is a manual then, because I really don't want to wreck it."

"Playing it safe is going to get you nowhere," she said, giving him a peck on the cheek.

They rode the rest of the way in silence, due to the motor becoming deafening on the highway. When they finally parked behind Steve's building, their ears were ringing and their bottoms were numb.

"You have got to get a muffler for this thing. But it's still a sweet ride. I can't wait to drive it…"

Steve laughed, patting the steel colored hood with his palm. "Do you even have a license?"

"Maybe…" she said, locking hands with him and intertwining their fingers.

Once they had gotten up the steps, Steve fumbled with his keys as Autumn busied her hands below his belt.

"That's very distracting," he said, though there was a smile on his face.

"Too bad. Seeing Phil's girlfriend rub her cootchie all over you on stage has me wanting to mark my territory."

"When did that happen?" Steve asked with a laugh. "Honestly, I had my eyes closed. I felt someone lean up against me, but Sven does that sometimes during the solo."

"Well, she wants to jump your bones," said Autumn as the door popped open at last. "Probably mine too…"

"What?" he asked, though her only answer was to mash her lips against his. He moved backward, heading for the bedroom.

"Wait." Autumn stepped away from him, laying a restraining hand across his chest. She hooked her thumbs in the thin straps of her shimmering dress and slid them away from her smooth, decorated shoulders. With a half-lidded smile, she let the dress drop to the floor. Underneath she wore only stockings and a garter belt.

"Wait," she said, still holding him at arm's length.

"This is torture!"

She started to step out of her boots, then grinned and kept them on.

"Come and get it," she said, dropping her arm down.

Steve seized her in a powerful grip around the waist, lifting her from the floor and putting her over his shoulder. He took her into the bedroom and flopped her down on the matress using a wrestling-style slam. She bounced with a grunt, and may have bounced right off the bed if he hadn't followed her down, pinning her torso under his.

"Am I in trouble?" she asked with slightly parted lips.

"*Huge* trouble," he said with a smile, eyes half lidded. "Sooo much trouble."

"Do I get a spanking?"

"I think you'd like that too much."

Gently, he nibbled on her neck. She caressed his hair as he trailed hot, warm kisses down to her chest. He took her pierced nipple gently in his teeth, putting just enough pressure to stretch the pale brown flesh. With a sudden, calculating wink he pulled back ever so slightly, rising to a kneeling position. Autumn went along with the game, allowing herself to be raised up by her shiny nipple ring.

"What are you going to do now?" she asked as he settled into a cross-legged position.

"Someone needs a spanking." He guided her across his lap by pulling her hair.

"Oh, no," she said with a giggle.

He stared at her shapely rear, tantalizingly close. There was a heart tattoo on her left cheek, which he put his mouth on and bit gently. Then, he raised his hand into the air and brought it back down in a firm smack.

"Oh," said Autumn softly with each impact. "Oh, you can do it harder."

He complied, her cheeks beginning to grow red. Steve's grin was a mile wide as Autumn gasped, wriggled, and sighed as he "disciplined" her. Suddenly she shuddered, her rear quivering like a bowl of jelly.

"Did you just…?"

"I just got warmed up!" She pulled herself into a sitting position and practically attacked him with a passionate kiss. Soon he was the one pinned under Autumn, her hot breath on his chest. He put his hand on the back of her head as she left lingering kisses on his belly, moving ever lower.

"You're so beautiful," he breathed.

If Autumn heard, she gave no sign, just continued on her inexorable path. She peered at him with arched brows before opening her silver-painted lips to take in his length. The wet, sucking sounds she made mingled with his own soft cries as he stroked her hair. In short order he gasped, hand forming into a fist in her hair.

"I'm ready," he said, trying to move her head. Stubbornly she stayed where she was, accepting the results of her efforts. She subtly discarded the liquid cargo in one of Steve's old shirts, her face split with a devious, delighted grin when she turned back to him.

"I felt like being bad," she said with a giggle.

He chuckled a bit himself as he raised himself up on his hands until their lips met. He rolled Autumn over to her back. His tongue slid over the smooth flesh of her neck, tracing a path down her sternum and over her soft belly.

"No! You bailed me out, it's your night."

"And this," he said when his soft lips weren't pressed against her flesh, "is what I want to do with it."

"You're so bad…"

Steve kissed the inside of her thighs, licking the flesh near her hosiery. The slick feeling of the material was thrilling as it slid over his shoulders. Soon he was kneeling on the floor, her knees bent over his large shoulders as he was plying his mouth to the purpose of pleasure. Autumn tore the sheets off of the mattress as she writhed, eyes fluttering back into her head. Steve traced intricate designs with his tongue mashed firmly upon her clit, going through the alphabet, both lower case and upper. When he was halfway finished with the cursive variation, Autumn let out a long moan and her legs quivered violently on his back.

Steve dragged himself onto the bed, traveling up the length of her body until he lay on his side. Their hands met and tangled together, eyes locked in a deep connection that required neither words nor speech.

A few hours prior, Rex, Sven, and Crawley watched ruefully as Autumn was put in the back of a squad car. Steve was soon charging off in his incredibly loud, horrible primer-colored muscle car, intent on getting her out as quickly as possible.

"What a bunch of bullshit," said Rex, glaring at Train where he sat with his foot in a cooler full of icy water. "He's not even going to the hospital."

"Guys can be such assholes," said Crawley. "Having your ex arrested!"

"Anybody seen Phil?" Sven asked, scanning around the party for him. The excitement out front had done little to diminish the guest's enthusiasm, and the bespectacled man was nowhere in sight.

"Uh-uh," said Rex.

"He said he was going to try and find some witnesses," said Crawley, "in case it actually goes to a trial."

As if on cue, Phil came out of the throng, a wide smile on his face. He carried his smart phone in his hand triumphantly, as if it were the severed head of a fallen gladiator.

"Did you find someone?" Crawley asked as he approached.

"Better," said Phil with a grin. "Where's that protein-guzzling douchebag at? Did he go to the hospital?"

"No," said Rex derisively, pointing his hairy arm at Train. The man was being attended by two men nearly as imposing as himself, who were bringing him a steady supply of fresh beer and snacks. "Motherfucker is sitting over there, looking like the cat who ate the canary."

"Great," said Phil, walking purposefully toward the trio.

"Uh, Phillip," said Crawley, catching his arm, "are you nuts? He might have a broken foot, but his buddies are about as big as river barges."

Phil smiled at her, patting her thick hand. "I'll be fine," he said, not a trace of bravado in his tone.

He pulled out of her grasp, and Crawley put her hand in front of her mouth and chewed her finger fretfully.

"Hope he knows what he's doing," said Rex.

"Hey," said Phil. "Train, was it?"

"What do you want, you fucking loser?" said Train, sneering. "Come to try and start shit 'cause my leg is fucked up? Think that makes it a fair fight?"

"I'm not here to start anything," said Phil with a grin. "I'm here to *finish* it."

"Watch your mouth," said one of the towering behemoths flanking Train.

"You professional fighters," said Phil, "seems to me like your reputation is pretty important, right?"

"Yeah, and my rep is all about busting people's heads!" Train's words elicited raucous laughter from his compatriots.

"Well," said Phil, turning his phone so the screen was facing Train, "think of what your rep is gonna be like after this gets posted on the net."

A short video played. The sound was choppy, but it could be clearly seen that Train went down screaming after Autumn stomped on his foot.

"Good luck getting Dana White to sign you once this hits the web," said Phil, pocketing the phone. "Of course, I could just delete it, if you drop the charges against Autumn."

Train shot a panicked glance at one of his friends. "Get that phone!"

His friend grinned, displaying a grill of platinum teeth.

"Hand it over, toothpick," said the man, holding out a massive paw, "or I'm gonna have to not ask so nice."

"Don't try it," said Phil, slipping his hands into his pockets.

"Come on, pencil neck. Just what do you do for a living?"

"I'm an accountant," said Phil with a shrug.

All three men laughed, his current aggressor the loudest of all. "Fucking nerd," he said, face growing angry. "Give it to me, right now!"

"Boy, was that an unfortunate way to word it," said Phil. He withdrew a small device which was contoured to fit his palm like an electric razor. He pointed it at Train's champion and depressed a tiny button. Twin metal barbs shot out too fast for the eye to follow, trailing wires. The man stiffened up, his mouth open but no sound escaping it. He teetered for a moment on stiff limbs before hitting the cold concrete of the garage floor with a hard crack.

"The thing about us nerds," said Phil as he yanked the barbs out of the man's massive chest, "is that we're really good with technology. Like this Taser, for example."

"So what if he posts that shit?" said Train's still standing companion. "No one's gonna see it anyway, with all the other shit going on."

"I have five thousand Facebook friends," said Phil with a smile. "How many do you have?"

"Okay," said Train, "first thing in the morning, I'll go down to the police station—"

"You'll go now, and if I don't get a phone call from Autumn in the morning saying that she's free and clear, you can bet your sweet ass this will be all over the world by tomorrow night."

Phil turned around and left the men, accepting high-fives and a drink from party goers fed up with Train's friends and their antics.

Crawley threw her arms around him in a tight hug, her body soft and warm against his. "Phillip, that was awesome!"

"Ja," said Sven, clapping him on the arm. "You opened up the can of ass whip!"

"Whoop ass, Sven," said Rex, laughing. "Whoop ass."

"That is what I said," said Sven, seeming miffed.

Steve and Autumn lay on their bellies, his form partially draped over hers. They both breathed heavily, a sheen of sweat glazing their nude bodies. Steve ran a hand over the tattoo on her lower back, a tribal sun design.

"So," he said, still a bit breathless, "which one is your first one? The little rose on your ankle?"

She grunted. "You're heavy."

He grinned and rolled off of her. She turned to lie on her side, resting her head on her arm. "You might think that, since it's so faded. But it's actually this one." She pointed to a small demonic skull, done in a simple outline a few inches above her right knee.

"Looks like a prison tat," he said with a chuckle.

"It should. I did it myself."

"No way, really?"

"Yup. My friend had a kit, and I asked her if I could use it."

"Why didn't you just have her do it? I mean, it looks cool, but… giving yourself a tattoo? Doesn't it hurt?"

"Pffft. It don't hurt that much. Besides, I said she had a kit, not that she actually knew what the fuck she was doing."

Steve chuckled softly, running his hand along the artful sleeves on her forearms. "I think I like this one." His finger traced a butterfly with stylized fiery wings.

"Sal did that one for me. He's really talented."

Steve's brow furrowed a bit at the mention of Sal. Autumn slammed a pillow across his face.

"What was that for?" Steve couldn't help but laugh at the nude Autumn gripping the pillow like a martial arts master.

"I was trying to wipe the jealous look off your face."

"Well—"

She walloped him again. "No jealous face!" she said, straddling him across the torso and raising the pillow menacingly.

Steve held up his arms in mock surrender.

"Okay, okay!"

She dropped the pillow, grinned and lowered herself until they were locked in an embrace.

"You should get a tattoo," she said, her voice vibrating his chest.

"I always kind of wanted one. But I'm not a fan of needles. Pop has like fifty tats."

She raised her head to give him a playful grin. "Quit being a pussy. Why don't we go to the shop tomorrow?"

"Sal's open on New Year's Day?"

"Oh yeah. Do you know how many people make a New Year's resolution to finally get that tattoo they always wanted? *Lots.*"

"Maybe I could get your name on my—"

"No!" Autumn punctuated her disapproval by smacking his cheek gently. "Never, never, *never* get someone's name tattooed on you. Not even mine. Your first tattoo should be something personal, something that has a lot of deep meaning."

"One condition: You do the work yourself."

She kissed him on the cheek, snuggling close. "Like I'd let anyone else touch you."

chapter 15

The first vestiges of dawn could be seen outside of Phil's bedroom window, tickling the horizon with pink. The street sounds wafted faintly through the thick glass, easily drowned out by his and Crawley's cries of passion.

She had nearly attacked him as soon as they had entered his apartment, and a string of their clothing littered the floor on the way to his bedroom. As usual, Phil had found himself awkwardly fumbling through their intimate moments. He tried being on top, but after a few moments of jangly limbed thrusting, she had pushed him away and gently rolled him onto his back.

Once again, she ended up on top. Not that Phil minded, as the view was fantastic, and the feeling of her slick flesh upon him was nothing short of amazing. The problem was his own efforts weren't up to par, and the more experienced Crawley had taken charge. Again.

Later, they lay sweating in each other's arms, Crawley tracing her hand along his smoothly shaven chest. Her body was cuddled close to his own, the warmth of her sweaty skin reassuring though he still had his doubts about performance.

"Was it good?" he dared to ask when he noticed that her dark eyes were still open.

"It was great," she purred, snuggling up to him even tighter.

"Really? You didn't, I mean, there wasn't a…you know, a flood…"

"Oh, that?" said Crawley with a giggle. "That doesn't happen every time. Like I said, it had been a year."

"Yeah, but, I want you to, you know, get there…"

"Orgasm. You can say it. You want to give me orgasms!"

Phil swallowed hard. "I—Yes."

Crawley giggled, covering her full lips with her hand. "Well… there's always *mechanical* assistance."

She kissed him on the cheek, then rolled over on her side and dug around in her purse. A moment later she had taken out a small, pink plastic egg-shaped item. A pink wire trailed from it, terminating in a small box with a dial on it. Phil was not sure what to make of the strange device.

"What's that?"

Crawley's brows arched, and her mouth opened in a slight gasp. "It's a vibrator, silly. You've seen them before, right?"

"Uh, yeah. I thought they were bigger, and uh, shaped like a, a—"

"That would be a vibrating dildo, sweetheart. If you don't want to use it, it's all right."

"No, I'm game if you are."

Crawley showed him how to turn the device on, and the different settings. At her direction, he slathered it in a bit of saliva before applying it to the outside of her nether lips. He swept it around her smoothly shaven skin, taking a great deal of care to be gentle. Crawley giggled, causing him to pause.

"What's wrong?"

"You don't have to be so careful. It's not going to bite me, or you for that matter."

She used her painted nails to spread her outer lips, pointing out her clit with her pinky. "Try rubbing it over little Ellie."

Phil erupted in spontaneous laughter. "Little Ellie?"

"Shut up! I dated a guy named Taltos in college who used to call his pecker 'Vlad the Impaler.'"

Phil pushed the device onto her flesh, gingerly at first and then more firmly when she pressed her hand down atop of his. Slowly, he began to feel a bit more adept with it. He would have guessed that she liked it when he just held it tight against her skin, but Crawley seemed to prefer slow circles against the soft flesh beneath her hood.

The vibrator buzzed merrily in concert with Crawley's moans and sighs, creating a symphony that had him feeling mystified and intimidated and powerful all at once.

When she came, it was a long, slow shudder that crept up the length of her body. Her eyes and lips fluttered like the wings of a moth too close to an open flame, and he was afraid for a moment that he'd gone too far. Then her dark eyes opened, and she reached up to caress his hair gently.

"Was that better?" he asked.

Crawley closed her eyes and nodded, her cheeks flushed and breathing heavy.

"Better. You're getting so good at this, babe."

Phil smiled, but once again he felt himself inwardly cringe at the thought that even with a mechanical aid he was not performing as well as he should.

"This ain't so bad," said Steve, grinning at the bloody work Autumn was doing on his large shoulder.

"Told you." Autumn paused for a moment and made eye contact, her smile hidden by the white filter mask she was wearing. She ran the needle over his skin, making it burn hot as she touched up details on the colorful picture she was making. It was a copy of the cover art from an early edition of *War of the Worlds*, where a tripod was vanquishing the Thunder Child with a heat beam. Autumn was adding detail to the waves that rose up in peaks around the legs of the alien craft.

Steve was seated in a comfortable chair in the back room of Sal's tattoo parlor. The owner was not in that day, it being a holiday, but Autumn had introduced him to her friends and coworkers. Steve felt a little uncomfortable, his clean-cut appearance seeming out of place with the others, but they quickly put his mind at ease by being warm and considerate.

Autumn glanced back at the image on Steve's laptop, squinting at the fine details on the screen and mimicking them on Steve's skin. She dabbed at his arm with a white cloth, and it came away red with blood.

"How come there's no ink on that?"

"Because the ink goes in deep. It has to push some blood out of the way, of course."

"I don't mind. Hell, Pop used to come back from Japan with more stitches than a quilting factory."

"I can't believe he did that hardcore crap." Autumn's eyes narrowed over the mask.

"You don't like hardcore wrestling? I would have figured you'd be all for it."

"No. Those guys do awful things to their bodies for less money than a fry cook earns. It shortens their careers and probably their lives."

"I couldn't agree more." Steve winced as she drove the needle a bit deeper.

"Quit flinching," said Autumn, tightening her grip on his bicep.

"Sorry."

Nearly three hours later, they walked out of the parlor, Steve gingerly moving his bandaged arm.

Autumn noticed, and favored him with a wide grin. "Aww, does it hurt?" she asked.

"Not so much. I just don't want it to smear or anything."

"As long as you don't scratch it, and you keep it out of the sun for a few days it should be fine. It's gonna itch tomorrow, sugar."

"Great. And I won't be able to scratch."

"You have to slap it." She pantomimed the motion on her own arm.

"Does that work?"

"Not much, but it kind of helps."

They returned Steve's car to Chet's garage, learning of Phil's triumph the previous evening. Steve spent most of the cab ride home on the phone, trying to confirm that the charges had indeed been dropped. With a frustrated snarl, he turned off his phone and jammed it back in his coat pocket.

"Well?" said Autumn, raising an eyebrow.

"Train sure took his sweet time, the fucking prick. Oh, the charges got dropped, all right, but I have to wait six to eight weeks to get my money back. Fucking government."

Autumn bit her lower lip, eyes going glassy and unfocused. "Sorry."

"Don't worry about it." Steve squeezed her knee. "Just means I have to wait a little longer to get my car finished."

"Why do you put up with me?"

He smiled at her, stroking her silky hair. "You know why."

"No, I don't." Autumn turned away from him, stared out the window. "I'm mean, and bitchy, and I make fun of you all the time, and you're always blowing your money on me. Are you *sure* you don't want a nice, rich girl like Eleanor?"

Steve's brow furrowed, and his tone held a note of confusion. "Crawley? No, not really my type."

"Oh, come on, she's a little hottie! You're real subtle about it, but I've caught you sneaking glances at her."

"I don't love Crawley. I love you."

She smiled shyly at him, then leaned her head on his chest, mindful of his new ink.

"I love you more than I thought I could love anyone," he said, seeming to be amazed at his own words. "I don't want you to leave, ever…"

"Okay," she said, patting his belly. "I'm right here."

"Marry me," he blurted, suddenly shaking with nervousness.

"What?" she said, eyes going wide. Her voice trembled slightly when she spoke. "Can you repeat that, please?"

"Marry me," he said more softly, stroking her hair. "I don't have a ring yet, but I'll get one right this second and go down on one knee if that's what you want."

"Why?"

"For all the reasons everyone gets married. You know, tax loopholes, someone to watch for the cable guy when I'm at work…"

She laughed, though it was through a sniffle. "No," she said, voice thick with emotion, "why do you want to marry *me?*"

"That's easy. You're smart, funny, beautiful, and for some reason you seem to like hanging out with my dumb ass."

She laughed again, though it soon turned to sobs. The driver glanced nervously in the rear view, uncomfortable with the display. "Okay," she said, wiping her face with a skull emblazoned handkerchief. "Okay."

"Why are you crying?"

"Because shut up."

They kissed tenderly, their lips lingering for long moments.

When they broke the contact, Autumn's tears had stopped flowing. She looked him deeply in the eyes, put her hands on either side of his cheeks. "I don't want this moment to end. Can't we just ride around in this cab for the rest of our lives?"

He smiled, not knowing what else to say. Her sentiment echoed the one in his own heart so closely that words seemed unnecessary. Autumn spent the rest of the ride home with her head on his shoulder, eyes closed while she felt the rhythm of his heart with her hand. He kept one hand around her, stroking her ebony hair softly.

"Congratulations," said the driver as Steve gave him a modest tip.

"Huh?" said Steve.

"On your impending marriage."

"Oh...thanks!"

When they arrived at his door, Autumn opened it with her key, giving him a warm and loving smile. Very slowly, she pulled him inside by hooking her fingers into his belt. Once the door shut behind him she purposefully undid the buckle. There was something different to her movements, not the frantic rush they were usually in. The gravity of the cab ride home seemed to require a slow, steady release of tension.

They made it as far as the sofa, where Steve tripped over his own pants that had pooled around his ankles and fell down hard on his bare rump. Autumn laughed gently, offering her inked hand to help him up. Steve did not move when she tugged, instead pulling her down atop him. Her smooth flesh slid against his own until their faces were inches apart. He slipped a palm behind her head and pulled her in closer until their mouths met in a smoldering kiss.

Autumn raised her hips, then slid slowly down on him. She ran her nails down his hairy chest, her eyes half closed and lips slightly parted. Her soft breasts were being firmly massaged by Steve's warm palms, and she grabbed his wrists in a sudden tight grip. Rather than pulling his hands away, she held them more tightly to herself and continued the swiveling of their hips.

Autumn's toes dug into the carpet, giving her purchase for her inspired gyrations. Steve moved his hips in concert with hers, finding a rhythm they were both comfortable with. Autumn leaned forward, supported by his hands as they intertwined with her own. Their faces were just inches apart, eyes locked in a gaze that was profoundly intimate. Steve added a bit more English to his own movements, causing her eyes to flutter closed. Her chin brushed against his shoulder as her head dipped low. He gasped as her teeth nibbled his neck, running the razor's edge between pain and ecstasy.

Gently, Steve pushed her back until she was upright, then further still until her hair brushed the top of his knees. Putting one leg over her torso, he rocked his hips back and forth. Autumn gasped, putting her hands on his foot but making no attempt to move it. The added pressure of his leg across her belly had its desired effect, pushing her soft flesh harder into the head of his penis, until a long, soft moan escaped from her ruby lips.

"Whew," she said, pulling her damp hair back from her sweaty face. She straightened up, putting her palms on his thighs to support herself, bodies still interlocked. Steve gently massaged her leg.

"It's never been this easy. With anyone else, I mean."

"It's never been this good." Her mischievous eyes glanced back down at him. "With anyone else, I mean."

He laughed, then moaned as she suddenly slid her hips forward.

"Don't get lazy now," she said, hands behind her head.

"Show you lazy." He hooked his pinky into her nipple ring. Gently but insistently he pulled until the pink flesh had stretched as far as was comfortable. She followed the tug, an excited smile on her face.

"Oh, no…"

Once her torso was within inches of his own he released her ring and instead wrapped his arms around her sweaty back. He crushed her to him while his mouth covered her own. He rolled her onto her back, still clinging tightly to her body. She gasped as he nibbled and licked her neck, her painted fingernails digging furrows in the carpet. He worked his way up to her metal-adorned ear, blowing in it lightly before taking the spongy lobe between his teeth and applying gentle pressure.

He grimaced a bit as her nails scraped down his shoulder blades, the flesh growing wet from freely running blood. He used the impetus to thrust more powerfully, until Autumn's lusty voice nearly rattled the windows. Spent, he collapsed atop her, and they lay panting in a sweaty pile.

"No," she said as he moved to roll off of her, "let's stay like this awhile."

"I'm not too heavy, am I?"

"Maybe roll on your back."

He did so, and she kept their bodies pressed close together during the motion. She laid her head on his slightly rising chest and sighed, fingers idly playing with his chest hair.

"Never shave this off," she said, her voice tickling his sternum. He chuckled, hand stroking down her spine.

"I manscape it sometimes, but one of the reasons I'm not a wrestler is because I don't like having to shave it smooth. Makes me feel like a little kid."

"I like hairy chests. You said *one* of the reasons. Why didn't you follow in your father's footsteps?"

She felt him take in a large breath, his chest rising, and blow it out in a sigh.

"For one thing, I don't like being hurt all the time — and Pop was hurt literally all the time. If it wasn't a broken toe or finger, it was a sprained wrist, or a groin pull, or stitches in his forehead. Turns out getting slammed six nights a week by three-hundred-pound men takes its toll, even if it's been scripted out in advance."

"A lot of athletes have to work injured," said Autumn, a note of understanding in her voice. "That's why I'm not one."

He grinned, stroked her hair softly. "I'm not much for being on the road, either. I like sleeping in my own bed, and besides, what is your wife doing while you're out on the road?"

Autumn shifted her position so she could look him in the eyes. Her gaze was intent, mouth a thin line. "You think your mom may have cheated?"

"No! I mean, at least, I hope not. I don't think so. But a lot of the boys in the back have had two, three marriages and counting."

"Not to mention all the wrestling groupies," she said, putting her head back on his chest.

"Ring Rats. Dad always called them Ring Rats."

"Ewwww, that's not nice!"

They both laughed, until Autumn stiffened up a bit, her hand becoming still.

"What's wrong?" Steve asked.

"I'm scared. I'm scared to get married."

"Why? If you're not ready, we—"

"No, I didn't say I'm not ready. I said I'm scared."

"Is there anything I can do?"

"Not really. It's my own mind trying to sabotage itself. I'm actually really good at doing that. Screwing up a good thing."

"You're not going to screw things up," said Steve, as if the notion were ridiculous.

"I almost always do, though. I'm just not allowed to be happy. The universe says, 'nope, uh-uh,' and everything realigns and I'm back to being miserable again."

"Have you…do you want to talk about it?"

"There's not much to tell," she said, raising her head off his chest once more. "I've dated some losers, and I've dated a couple of winners, but it's usually been my fault when things have fallen apart."

"Is that what happened with Sal?" Steve asked, trying without success to keep the undertones of jealousy from his voice.

"No," she said, a trace of annoyance in her own tone, "that bastard starts every day with a good whiskey buzz. He was never abusive, but he'd be brain dead by five o'clock. It was like living alone, really."

"I see," said Steve, mouth a thin line. Autumn suddenly kissed him, her lips lingering for a long moment as their tongues explored each other.

"Get that jealous look off your face. Get it off, I said…"

She used her tongue for more than just speaking, her lusty exhalations filling his mouth. He sat up, not breaking the lip lock, and gathered her legs under one arm.

"What are you doing?" she asked with a giggle as he rose to his feet while cradling her in his arms.

"Taking you to bed. I have rug burn in places no one should ever have rug burn."

"Oh, man up!" She threw her arms around his neck and kissed him on the cheek.

Phil sat in his soft brown leather recliner, clad only in his boxers. Despite the late afternoon sun filtering in his large windows, he still had stubble on his chin, his hair remaining in the bedraggled state slumber had put it in. His fifty-two-inch plasma-screen TV was on, but he only paid attention to the mobile device in his hand as he sent a text to Crawley.

Love to see you again tonight -P

He glanced idly up at the TV, his distracted mind barely acknowledging the Sean Connery 007 movie displayed upon it. A moment later his phone beeped, and he eagerly checked the message.

Can't. :(Mom and Dad are trying to act cool, but they're not happy about me being out till six this morning. I think I better stay home tonight. -C

What about tomorrow? -P

Maybe I could stay the weekend? ;) Mom and Dad are going upstate for a fishing trip, and I'm going to be awful lonely :) -C

Phil nearly dropped the phone, so eager was he to type in an affirmative response. All his trembling fingers were able to muster was:

Yes. -P

Cool, have to go now. Dinner time. Miss U. -C

He put the phone down, heart hammering in his chest. There had been precious few opportunities for him and Crawley to be intimate. He worked Monday through Friday at the firm, while her weekends were usually taken up by her father's business. Phil was painfully aware that his awkwardness in the bedroom was not helping the matter. His excitement was tempered with apprehension, the conflict making his stomach turn more than the hangover he had been suffering.

He stripped off the shorts and took a shower, letting the hot water cascade down his aching back. The stool provided by Chet at the gig the night before had lacked any back support, and the strain of holding up his torso all night had left him with fires and sharp needles in the muscles near his spine.

Upon exiting the shower he got dressed and tried to play *World of Warcraft*, but found that his heart was not in it. He considered starting a new character, realized that was a temporary fix to the problem and just turned the game off.

He wound up checking his various social media accounts, changing his status from "single" to "in a relationship"—something he had been afraid to do in case Crawley saw it. Now he wanted her to take notice, because he wasn't certain how to move their relationship forward.

He idly chatted with Steve, who was posting stupid memes while Autumn was out with a pair of girlfriends. The big man dropped a bombshell, saying that he had proposed to Autumn and she had accepted.

What are you always telling me about buying the cow? -P

He got the expected reply:

Fuck off. -S

**Seriously, though. I'm happy for you.
Wish I could move things along a little faster with Eleanor. -P**

Do you love her? -S

Don't know. Really like her, though. -P

**Come on, dude. She's your first real girlfriend.
You're in love. -S**

Maybe. I kind of think I'm not good enough for her. -P

**What? You have a great job,
you're thin, single, and neat. -S**

I mean in the bedroom, asshole. -P

**Lol. Crawley's a bit more experienced than you,
I take it? -S**

All that Phil had the gumption to type was:

Yes. -P

**You're scared of her, and of your own sexuality.
You need to let loose and just be your beastly self. -S**

**Easy for you to say.
You didn't have conservative Jewish parents!
Remember the first time I spent the night at your house,
and I whispered the whole evening? -P**

I remember. You're going to have to get over it, though.
Women like it MORE than we do, dude.
Have you talked to her about it? -S

A little. -P

Did she have an O? -S

Says she does every time. -P

He paused, fingers hovering over the keyboard, then wrote in a rush:

I don't think I've been doing very well, though. -P

Try, try again. -S

Phil sighed.

Thanks for nothing. -P

He signed out of the site. Within a few minutes he was doing a web search for sex advice.

"Guess I'll have to solve this like a nerd."

chapter 16

Steve stared down at the mutilated, glue-sodden mass of paper on the low yellow table before him. All around, his children zipped from one play center to another while a group of four sat across the table from him. Scissors, glue bottles, and scraps of red and pink paper were scattered across the surface, some being used by the children.

"What is this?" he asked, raising a bushy brow at the messy artifact.

"That's for you, Mr. Steve," said a brightly smiling little girl. "It's a valentine!"

"Thank you, sweetie." Steve got to his feet. He walked a short distance to his desk and used a homemade magnet constructed from a clothespin to affix it to his metal cabinet. It joined several other cards of a similar haphazard design.

When he came back to the table, he noticed Darrien was having a mock sword fight with another child, using pencils as sword surrogates. Steve sat down and watched the proceedings, picking up a thicker red painted pencil.

"Have at thee!" Steve zestfully added his own wooden weapon to the mix. The boys were nearly overcome with delighted laughter, growing more zealous in their motions. He was laughing himself, a sound which died in his throat as he heard his classroom door open. Ms. Stone stood in the doorway, a cold narrow-eyed stare plastered across her wrinkled visage.

"What can I do for you?" he asked after leaving the table and his dueling opponents behind.

"You can stop letting five-year-olds play with pencils. Do you want them to lose an eye?"

Steve's smile faded. "Sorry."

"Why do they have adult-sized pencils, anyway? For twenty years I taught kindergarten, and my children always had the bigger pencils...like that one."

She pointed at the implement in his hand, causing him to shake his head. "This is too big."

"Their motor skills aren't so good yet. The larger size is easier for them to grip."

"To grip, yes, but to write with? That would be like you or I using a broom handle for a pencil. Their handwriting is a lot better when they learn using the normal number two pencils."

Ms. Stone put her hands on her hips and let out a long sigh. "Be that as it may, I actually came to see if you're willing to be on the textbook selection committee this summer."

"Uh, sure, I can do that. No problem." Steve cursed inwardly at the loss of free time due to the long, dull procedure involved in picking new books for the school.

"Thank you," said Ms. Stone, seeming almost sincere for a moment, which Steve figured must have been quite painful for her.

She turned on her heel, but not before glancing pointedly at the two boys continuing their pencil duel. Steve sighed as soon as the door shut and walked back to his table and took his seat. The two boys stopped fencing, turning their wide-eyed gazes upon his narrowed blue eyes.

When Steve spoke, his voice was heavy with admonishment. "I hope you two got your projects done!"

The two boys looked at each other and swallowed hard.

The sun had just dipped below the horizon when Steve trotted down the short steps leading to the staff parking lot. He walked over to his GTO, now bearing black paint upon its metal hide. Once he turned the key, the engine roared to life. It was still loud, but the shiny new muffler underneath kept the noise at a tolerable level.

"Wish the radio worked," he grumbled as he put the car in drive. The rush hour traffic had mostly subsided, meaning it only took him marginally longer to get home than it would have on the train. He pulled up in the lot behind his building and suddenly swore as his phone beeped.

"What now?" He checked the message on his phone and cursed again. Roughly, he put the car back in drive and pulled back into traffic.

After waiting in a gridlock for nearly thirty minutes, he finally made it to a grocery store lot. He returned to the car about ten minutes later, a pair of plastic bags hanging from his hands. He hopped back in the driver's seat and made his way back home.

His phone told him it was nearly eight o'clock when he finally got to his apartment door. Loud music blared from inside, muffled by the wooden obstacle. He tried the door, found it locked, then angrily dragged out his keys and jammed them in the lock.

When the door opened he saw Autumn sitting on the sofa, sketching on a drawing pad. "Hey." She did not glance toward him as he entered.

He did not reply, wordlessly putting the bags on the table. He took some aspirin down from a shelf near head height perched over the sink, the tiny white bottle disappearing in his large hand. When he tried to pop the cap off he spilled half the contents on the floor. Swearing, he gathered up most of them and jammed them back inside. He put three of the tablets in his mouth and searched in the cabinet for a cup. He rolled his eyes as he found the cupboard empty, all the drinking vessels being in the sink along with other soiled dinnerware.

He walked around the corner from his small kitchen area back into the living room just in time to catch a pastel-hued package of squishy feminine products in the forehead. His narrowed-eye gaze was matched by one on Autumn's own face.

"Super thick maxi absorbent? Do you think I'm a hemorrhaging horse?"

"That's all they had!" He bent over and picked up the package.

"Bullshit! Just where did you go?"

"Pickley's, of course. It's on the bag, genius."

"And that's all they had? What kind of bullshit is that? Did you ask if they had any in the back, or—"

"No, I didn't ask. I had a long day at work, got stuck in traffic for an hour, and I was tired."

Autumn put her arms akimbo and stared at him, mouth twisted as if she'd just eaten something sour. "If you didn't want to go, you could have just said no instead of getting the wrong thing on purpose."

His face grew angry, hands held out to his sides. "I didn't do it on purpose. It's not like I'm a tampon expert."

"These aren't even tampons, you dumbass! They're pads."

"Don't they do about the same thing?"

"God, why do I even...?" Autumn picked up the rags and jammed them back into the white plastic bag, then headed for the door. She retrieved her long black coat along the way, swaddling herself in its embrace.

"What are you doing?" Steve asked.

"Isn't it obvious? I'm taking these back so I can get what I actually need."

"I'll go." Steve dug in his pocket for his car keys.

"Oh, no, sir! I wouldn't want you to sully yourself with such a trivial thing."

"It was my mistake. I'll go."

Her face startled him when she turned to face him, brows low over her narrowed brown eyes. "Stop being so damn nice about it! I can tell you're pissed. You're pissed about a lot of things lately. Why don't you let it out?"

Steve stared at the carpet, shoulders slumping. "I'm not pissed at you, okay? I got yelled at by Stoneface, there was a traffic jam and —"

"You're *so* pissed at me." Autumn opened the door.

"Aren't you a little...a little...early?"

"There was blood in my pee and I feel like shit, so I assume I'm having it early, all right? Can I go please?"

He took his hand off the door, not realizing he had shut it just as she was attempting to swing it open. She disappeared out the opening, her stomps fading in the distance. He turned his back to the door and slid down to his buttocks, hiding his face in his hands.

He remained that way for a long time, finally rising to his feet when his rear fell asleep. He munched on a bag of potato chips as he stared at the TV, the images not truly registering with him. When the clock on the wall indicated it was nearly nine thirty, he called Autumn's phone. He left a message when there was no answer.

"Hey, sorry about the spat. I was worried about you. If you're all right and don't want to talk, just send me a blank text or something. I love you."

He set the phone down and stared at the ceiling, eyes hard. With a grunt he rose to his feet and got his keys off the table. Worry drove his limbs as he dashed down the stairs and into the cold, dark night. Suckling the warmth from his body like a hungry infant, it seemed that the night itself was against him.

The leather seat of the car was icy on his back as he roamed the night streets, eyes scanning to either side of the road for Autumn. He followed her path to the store, then back to the apartment, and then checked her other neighborhood haunts. Growing frustrated, he decided to drive to Queens, figuring that even if Autumn was not there he could give Sal a piece of his mind.

He parked on the street before the shop. He spotted Sal's vehicle, a bright green family-sized caravan, parked a few feet down the street from him. The sight made him grow angrier.

The bell at the top of the door tinkled merrily as he entered the parlor, contrasting his black mood. The waiting area was largely empty at that hour, Sal seated behind the receiving desk.

"Hello. Steve, isn't it? We haven't met yet, but I've seen you picking up Autumn. I'm Sal."

Steve strode over to loom over the much smaller man, even more dwarfish in his low seat. His waist was hidden below the desk, but his upper body seemed to be in good shape. Muscular arms covered with tattoos both new and faded gripped his armrests. Everything about him, from his bald and waxed pate to his youthful green eyes and pierced lip seemed to make him a more obvious mate for Autumn. Steve found his bile backing up in his throat, and he wanted to throttle the man on the spot.

"Yeah. So I've heard. Is Autumn here?"

Sal seemed very uncomfortable, scratching behind his bald head. "She's in the back, but she doesn't want to see you right now."

Steve pivoted on his heel, stalked toward the door which lead to the work area. "Where are you going?" Sal asked in alarm as Steve's hand gripped the knob. "Wait —"

Steve ignored him, swinging the door open.

"Autumn?" As soon as Steve looked inside, he froze with his mouth wide open. She stood, filter mask and latex gloves on, next to a young woman in a chair. The stranger had no clothing on from the waist down, her feet up in stirrups. She lifted her face to stare in shock at Steve, then at Autumn.

"Get. Out," said Autumn through gritted teeth.

Steve shut the door behind him, growing red.

"I tried to tell you," said Sal with a nervous laugh, "that she was doing a below the belt piercing."

Glad to have someone on whom he could vent his anger and frustration, Steve stalked over to him and glared. "Why is she working? I thought she just went for a walk."

"She called me, wanted to hang out awhile. I asked if she could help out with this chick who didn't want a dude to see her with her pants off. That's it."

"Hang out awhile?" said Steve, leaning on the counter to loom down at the man. "That's a euphemism for 'wanted to stick my dick in her,' right?"

"Steve," said Sal, spreading his hands out wide, "it's not like that, swear to god."

"Oh, you think you're pretty clever, don't you?" Steve smiled, though his eyes seemed cold. "First you offer her a job, then you comfort her after we have a fight, and then you're in there, aren't you buddy?"

Sal's jovial features turned dark. "I don't like being talked to like this in my own shop. Autumn and I are just friends. That's it."

"Oh, you don't want to hear me say it in your shop? Then how about this: You get up and walk out from behind that counter and we step outside for a minute. Just for a minute, because that's all the time I need to shove my foot up your ass."

"Steve, calm down," said Sal, holding his hands up in supplication. Both of their heads turned as the door opened and Autumn entered the waiting room.

"Nice job!" Her fierce glare took in both of them. "Now she's too freaked out to...What's going on here?"

"Sal's about to get his ass kicked," said Steve with a snarl.

"Steve, leave him the fuck alone," she said, eyes narrowing dangerously. "You don't know shit about shit, so quit acting like an ass."

"It's all right, Autumn," said Sal from behind the desk.

"No, it's not all right! I'm supposed to be cool with him eye humping you all damn day, every day? I don't think so!"

"Why don't you turn off the testosterone faucet?" said Autumn. "You can be such an alpha male douchebag sometimes! I'm not going back to—"

"Let's go," said Sal, putting his hands on his desk and shoving away from the table. Steve's mouth twisted into a mirthless grin.

"Finally! Now you're gonna…"

Steve's words died in his throat as Sal rolled out from behind the counter in a wheel chair. His lower half was skinny to a ghastly degree, his useless legs twisted unnaturally.

"Try not to mess up my face too much," Sal said with a grin.

"Asshole," said Autumn, shoving past Steve and out into the cold.

"Autumn!" said Steve. He turned and gave Sal an apologetic head shake, then ran out after her.

He caught up with her up the street, her arms crossed over her chest and legs moving stiffly. She did not look at him when he called her name.

"I didn't know he was in a…"

"I don't give a shit about that." She spoke through gritted teeth.

"Then what? Tell me what I did!"

"I shouldn't have to tell you, but I will anyway. You don't listen to me, you don't trust me, and you don't respect me."

"What? Just how in the hell do you figure that?"

Her eyes flashed angrily to his. "If you trusted me, respected me, you wouldn't feel the need to go hunt me down just because I'm gone a couple of hours."

"Just because?" He sputtered for a few moments before finding articulate speech. "I was worried sick! I didn't know if you were hurt, or—or raped and bleeding in an alley, or—"

"Don't make yourself out to be noble. You've been just itching to get up in Sal's face about us."

Steve's cheeks flushed red. "That just kind of happened. I was just gonna ask if he'd seen you, and he told me you didn't want to see me, and—"

"He said, and I quote, 'she doesn't want to see you right now.' Because I was up to my knuckles in another woman's cootchie."

He laughed in spite of himself, a ghost of a grin playing at her own lips. "I'm sorry…I guess I do tune you out when the subject of, uh, monthlies comes up."

"Go on."

"And," he said with a sheepish grin, "I guess I have been kind of a jealous douchebag about Sal."

"Kind of?"

"But I do respect you."

"Do you?" Autumn had a slight smile on her lips, but her eyes glistened as if she were on the verge of tears.

"Absolutely! If I didn't, I wouldn't have asked you to marry me."

She looked down at the sidewalk below their feet, chewing on her bottom lip. "I still don't know why you want to do that."

Steve laughed, shoulders relaxing. "Oh, why would I want to do that? Well, let's see, you're the most beautiful woman in the world…"

"Oh, stop."

"…and you're smart, and funny…" He moved his head in near hers, and whispered in her ear for a moment, "…and the fact that it's the best sex I've ever had doesn't hurt."

She laughed, turned her head to gaze into his eyes. Her own seemed to be haunted, or maybe just tired. "I'm sorry, too. I heard your message. I should have responded somehow. I know how you worry."

"Look, why don't we go back to the car? I'm freezing, and this isn't the best neighborhood."

"Okay."

Steve felt his body deflate in relief. Autumn was coming back home.

They spend the ride home making humorous comments about the various people they saw on the street. Autumn's decidedly mean-spirited sense of humor had his ribs aching with inappropriate laughter. By the time they got home, both were wiping tears from their eyes.

"See that Asian over there?"

Steve glanced in the direction she was pointing and saw an angry young man of Pacific descent, leaning against a lamppost, trying to look tough.

"He's just mad because we don't have vending machines with schoolgirl panties in them."

Steve swerved a bit, his eyes tearing up so badly he was momentarily blinded. "Stop," he said, gasping for breath, "please, you're going to get us in a wreck."

"Okay, okay."

They drove in silence for several minutes, Steve still chuckling from time to time. When he had mostly regained his composure, a wide grin broke out on Autumn's face and she spoke once more.

"He's more upset that he found out American women don't have sideways facing vajayjays."

Steve laughed, feeling absolutely horrid about it but also completely unable to stop. He ran up on the curb a bit turning into the parking lot behind his building. Autumn leaped out of the car a split second ahead of him, he being hampered by being out of breath.

"God," she said as she ran around the building ahead of him. "I'm going to piss myself!"

He followed more slowly, taking time to lock his car and turn on the alarm. He stopped at the mailbox and withdrew a stack of paper, mostly ads. He thumbed through them idly while he walked up the stairs, stopping to pick up a glove someone had dropped.

"Autumn?" he said as he found the door wide open. Her coat was lying on the floor near a chair. He picked it up and carefully draped it over the chair back. "Autumn?"

"I'm here." She was standing in the brief hallway between his bathroom and bedroom. Her voice bore a tone of urgency, which spurred him into the darkened room. He took her in his arms, feeling the heat emanating from her.

"What's the matter? God, your skin is burning!"

"I think uh...I think I need to go to the hospital..."

She swooned, and he caught her, carefully putting her on the bed in a sitting position.

"Easy! I'll call an ambulance. Just don't move, okay?"

He dug in his phone and walked into the bathroom. His terrified gaze in the mirror was in contrast to his calm voice as he spoke to the operator.

"Oh my god," he said as he glanced down at the toilet. The water was murky and dark with blood, some of it even on the seat. He dashed back to the bedroom to find her lying unconscious on her back.

"Autumn! *Autumn!*"

chapter 17

Ostensibly, Steve was reading the *People* magazine in his hands. The reality was that he had long ago rendered it unreadable, both by twisting the cover in his massive hands and soaking it with his nervous sweat. He was perched on a hard, plastic chair in the waiting room of the ER. The big man was almost afraid to move, as if the tiniest ripple in the air could hurt Autumn's chances as the staff tended to her.

He had wanted to stay with her, but once the staff found out they weren't married, he was ushered out to the waiting room. Autumn had regained consciousness in short order, but had been groggy and incoherent. Steve had bundled her into his car and quickly driven to the hospital, casting constant frantic glances at Autumn as she drifted in and out.

Steve's mind was drawn back to the present when a nurse came to his side. The elderly woman placed a hand on Steve's shoulder, quietly explaining that Autumn was being admitted. She directed him to the ICU on the eighth floor, adding a pat on his back.

Numbly, he rode the elevator upward, the destroyed magazine forgotten in his hand. He read the numbers above the many doors once he walked into the hall, staring at them with focused intensity until he found the one containing Autumn.

The sight of her in the bed made him cringe on the inside. She was awake, her eyes focusing on him and a weak smile playing at her lips. Her pallor was frightening, and it seemed to take her a great deal of effort just to say hello when he came to her side and took her hand.

"How are you feeling?"

"Been better, sugar. My back's on fire."

Their heads turned toward the door at the sound of someone opening it.

A tired doctor walked swiftly into the room, pushing up his spectacles with one finger. He was not very tall, almost painfully thin, and had a thick mustache with more than a bit of gray showing. He glanced up from the clipboard in his hand, seeming surprised to see Steve seated next to Autumn's bed.

"Good evening," he said in a gravelly voice, coming up to the bed. "How are you feeling, Ms. Winters?"

"Not too good, Doc." Dark circles were heavy under her eyes, the whites of which were an unhealthy yellow hue. Tubes ran from her arm to an IV stand next to the bed. She had the covers pulled up to her shoulders, shivering though the room was not cold.

The doctor peered inquisitively at Steve before looking back to Autumn.

"He's my boyf—" said Autumn, then smiled slightly. "He's my fiancé. You can talk in front of him."

The doctor took off his glasses and rubbed his nose tiredly with thumb and forefinger. His voice was carefully measured when he spoke.

"Ms. Winters, I am afraid that, in your refusal to treat your condition, it has flared up again. Your immune system has nearly destroyed your kidneys, and they are failing."

Steve was stunned, his jaw dropping. Autumn only nodded, closed her eyes and spoke.

"Condition?" said Steve, staring at Autumn. "What condition?"

"How long do I have?" she asked, ignoring Steve's question.

"On dialysis, you could live indefinitely," said the doctor. "The best thing would be for you to go on a transplant list, but…"

"But what?" Steve asked harshly. "Doesn't that take a long time? Shouldn't you be doing that right this second?"

"He can't," said Autumn icily. "I have an incurable, possibly fatal disease, Steve. They won't give me a kidney or anything else."

"Incurable? Fatal? Where the hell is this coming from?"

"I have this thing, Steve," said Autumn, seeming strangely cold as she looked into Steve's devastated eyes. "It's called Lupus. My immune system is overactive, and sometimes it turns against my own body."

"Why didn't you tell me?" Then it suddenly dawned on him. "Wait, that bottle…you said it was for, for female troubles."

"I lied, Steve. Okay? I lied. I didn't want you to know I was sick."

"Why? Did you think it would make the slightest bit of difference in how I felt about you?"

"Look, sugar," said Autumn with a sigh, "I've been living with a time limit, an expiration date, for quite a while now. It can make you do some stupid things, like go bungee jumping, or taking drugs, or…" Her voice became small for a moment. She turned her gaze away from him, as if she could not meet his eyes. "Or make you jump into a relationship before you're ready…"

"So, what? You were afraid that if you only had a little while left, you didn't want to waste it on me?"

"No, you moron," said Autumn, her sickly eyes narrowing. "I didn't want to wonder if you were only with me because I was sick! Okay?"

"Please," said the doctor, "don't upset her too greatly right now."

Steve flinched, having forgotten the doctor was even in the room. New hope flooded his breast as a thought occurred to him.

"Can you give her one of my kidneys?" Steve asked quickly.

"Would that work?" Autumn asked. "I mean, he's a man, would his kidney even —"

"Him being male makes no difference," said Dr. Grossman sadly, "but Mr. Borgia informed us that he has blood type A. The fact that you have different blood types makes it impossible. And there are other factors as well."

Steve's face fell, while Autumn looked calmly at the doctor.

"How long?" she asked.

"Days? Definitely. Weeks? A possibility. Six months…seems unlikely." The doctor turned on his heel and went toward the door. "Please close the door if you need more private time," he said before exiting.

Steve's face grew dark, and he practically spit words from his mouth. "Fucking monster! He tells you, tells you horrible things and just turns around and leaves!"

"Shhh…this is a hospital, Steve. Keep it down. It's not his fault, and I'm sure he has a lot of other patients to see."

He stared at her, flabbergasted. "How can you be so calm?"

She looked out the window. "Because I've been expecting this, Steve. I've been selfish. I'm so selfish…"

"Selfish? You don't sound selfish enough!"

She smiled at him, extricating a limb from under the covers to pat his hand. "I'm not worried about myself."

"Don't worry about me. Hey, it's in sickness and in health, right? I'm going to go on Facebook, Twitter, hell, I'll even dust off my AOL account and ask if there's anybody, anywhere who is a match."

"Don't. Please, just stay here with me. You can do all that once visiting hours are over."

He stopped, feelings of helplessness turning his belly to fire and his tongue to lead. She didn't understand, he had to do something, *anything* to save her, no matter how desperate. However, when he stared into her soft brown, almond-shaped eyes, he knew that his choice had already been made.

"You know," he said, sitting back down, "the first time I looked into your eyes, I fell into them."

She chuckled softly, squeezing his fingers with faded strength. "Such a pu…such a romantic."

"I don't ever want to climb back out. Not ever."

"Then don't," she said, closing her eyes and falling asleep.

Only after her breathing had grown even and shallow with the rhythm of slumber did he leave her side. He felt the hot tears running down his cheeks, his breathing coming in gasps. Not having another refuge, he swiftly went into the bathroom and shut the door, turning on the water to drown out his agonized weeping. Never had he felt such profound despair, such an utter lack of hope.

He slid to his bottom, long legs folded in the small area of the bathroom, tears still streaming down his face.

"This is horrible," said Crawley for the hundredth time as they sat in the hospital lobby.

"I know," said Phil, squeezing her hand.

"I wish we could go and see her. We should have said we were family."

"Steve can get us in."

"How is he?"

"About how you'd expect. Going apeshit crazy. Right now he's trying to find someone on the Internet who can be a donor, but…"

"Autumn has some weird blood type? That's what he said, right?"

"Yeah, a rare type. Might be hard to find a match."

They sat in silence for a time, watching as worried people filtered past them. Crawley sent a message to her parents explaining her absence, and then spent a few minutes chatting back and forth with them. Phil busied himself with posting on his own social media page, trying to find a suitable donor.

He brightened a bit at one of the posts he read, nudging Crawley with his elbow.

"Check it out. This guy says her blood type is recessive. That means—"

"That both of her parents must have had it. Maybe one of them can donate a kidney!"

Phil tried to keep his optimism in check. "I think her mom is dead, though. I'll have to ask Steve."

"There he is now." Crawley looked past him at the tired giant striding out into the lobby. She rose to her feet quickly and left a confused Phil following a moment behind.

"Oh my god, Steve," she said, wrapping her arms around his waist in what seemed to Phil like an overly friendly hug. "Are you all right?"

"No, but I'm not the one you should be worried about, thanks."

"How is she?" Phil asked, giving Steve a side-hug.

"Hanging in there." They moved to the comfortable seating. "They took her for another test a while ago."

Steve's eyes were bloodshot, the skin on his face swollen noticeably. Occasionally he would sniffle a bit and wipe a bit of mucous from his nose. He slouched in his seat, shoulders slack, trying to smile through his pain.

"Thanks for coming, guys."

"Not a problem," said Crawley, patting his hand.

"Bros forever," said Phil with a slight smile. "Steve, are Autumn's parents still alive?"

"Her dad is, but they don't get along. He ran out on her and her mom a long time ago."

"Well," said Phil, "there's pretty much a one hundred percent chance that Autumn's dad has the same blood type as her. If we could find him—"

"We could say, what?" said Steve darkly. "I'm the guy who's banging the daughter you haven't seen for sixteen years. Can we please have a kidney?"

"We have to try," said Crawley.

"Yeah," said Phil, "it might be your only shot!"

"All right," said Steve, cautious optimism dawning on his face. "I'll see if he's online anywhere. Be real convenient if he was on Facebook."

He pulled out his phone, finger swiping rapidly across the surface with his fingers. A joyful smile dawned on his face.

"There's a shit ton of Jonathon Winters! Fortunately, only a couple of them are the right age. So if we narrow those down to people who've lived in New York, we get…just one. Huh. No pictures of himself… not much posted at all, but he does list a daughter named Autumn."

"That's an old person's Facebook page," said Crawley with a bit of disdain. "They don't put any effort at all into them."

"Is his phone number or address viewable?" Phil asked.

"Yes…He lives in a place called…Pow-keep-sey?"

"Poughkeepsie," said Crawley. "My father and I go there all the time to drop off samples."

"Give him a call," said Phil.

"Couldn't hurt," said Steve, hastily dialing the number. The anticipation on his visage soon changed to bitter disappointment. "Damn, this number's no longer in service. Fuck!"

The expletive drew the ire of the other denizens of the lobby, but Steve didn't seem to notice.

"I think," said Phil, "that we need to take a little road trip."

"I'll go and get my coat," said Steve.

"No," said Crawley, putting a hand on his forearm and squeezing it. "Your place is here, with Autumn. We'll go and find him."

"Go and find who?" said a gravelly voice behind them. They turned to stare up into the weathered, whiskered face of the Deathslayer.

"Pop!" Steve surprised the old man by giving him a warm hug. "I thought you were still in Mexico."

Deathslayer stared intently at his son's haggard face, brow furrowed. "Jumped on the first flight available. Didn't even change out of my ring gear. How are you holding up, son?"

"I'm hanging in there. Little tired, but I'll make it."

"Phillip," said his father, turning to shake the young man's hand, "you're looking well."

"You too, Mr. Borgia," said Phil with a smile.

"Pffft," said Deathslayer, "call me Bill, you're making me feel even older."

"Nice to meet you, sir," said Crawley, shyly shaking his hand.

"Always nice to meet a lovely young lady," he said back, giving Phil an elbow in the ribs. "Not bad, kid!"

"Anyway," said Phil, "we should probably get going. We need to rent a car to drive up to Poughkeepsie, and —"

"What's in Poughkeepsie?" Deathslayer asked.

"Autumn's dad," said Steve. "She needs a kidney transplant, and he might be the only match."

"Why do we have to rent a car?" Crawley asked. "We can take my dad's van. It's got plenty of room for you too, Mr. Deathslayer."

"I'll buy the gas," said Deathslayer with a wink.

Steve stared at the faces of his father and friends, shamed. "Thanks... I don't know how to repay any of you."

"Take care of Autumn, son," said Deathslayer, squeezing his shoulder.

"Woohoo!" came an obnoxious voice from across the lobby. They turned to see a teenage boy making the sign of the devil in their direction. "Deathslayer! You rule, man!"

"Sometimes, that gets really annoying," said Deathslayer, before turning to the young man and returning the salutation.

"I need to check on Autumn anyway," said Steve. "Thanks again."

"I should call Susan too," said Deathslayer, extracting his phone, "she might want to go."

"Do you think this is going to work?" Crawley asked as they walked toward the door.

"Hey," said Phil with a smile. "We got the Deathslayer on our team. With all the minions of Hell at our disposal, how can we lose?"

chapter 18

P hil's fingers rattled on his keyboard, typing at a rapid pace. He was in such a hurry he did not even deign to sit on his comfortable chair, instead leaning at an awkward angle with his back twisted to reach the keyboard from outside his cubicle.

"What's up, nerd?" Rich startled him with a poke in the ribs. The confident young man had on a sky blue shirt and burgundy tie. His cup of coffee steamed in his hand, wisps of white drifting past his narrowed eyes. "Why are you dressed casual? Is it casual Wednesday or something? Why didn't I get the memo?"

Rich sat his coffee down on Phil's desk and began to doff the tie.

"Keep your tie on, dumbass," said Phil, hitting send on the report he had been finishing. "I'm taking some personal days. Just tying up some loose ends."

"Yeah, I heard about Autumn," said Rich, shaking his head with what seemed genuine sympathy. "Sucks ass, dude. Hey, you should bring that piece of Asian delight with you; there's nothing like the morbidity of death to bring out a girl's freaky side!"

"How can you think about crap like that now?"

"Oh, I touched a nerve. That's right, Steve was saying you keep fumbling in the bedroom."

"What?" said Phil, his face getting red. How could Steve tell Rich of all people?

"Fumble…fumblerooski, fumbleriah!"

"Shut up asshole!" Phil attempted to duck around Rich and leave.

"Look, dweeb." Rich put his arm out both to comfort Phil and prevent him from leaving. "Believe it or not, I can help you. I know just what your problem with Crawley is."

"Oh, yeah? What do you know about it?"

Rich turned his torso to the side, spreading out his arms. He pointed at the end of his outstretched arm.

"Right here, this is tier one. This is where you're at when you finally dip your dick in pussy."

"Wouldn't that be further along?" Phil ruefully figured that playing along with Rich's stupidity would shut him up faster.

Rich snorted derisively. "Yeah, a newbie like you *would* think that. No, sex is just the beginning my friend. Just the beginning. To move along the tier, to the last step—" Rich indicated his shoulder with a jab of a well-manicured index finger "—you have to be prepared. You have to be a man."

"What's the last step? And what do you mean, be a man? I'm well over eighteen, Rich."

"Tier Fifteen is when your woman is totally, completely satisfied," said Rich with a wistful smile. "Even I, in my supreme natural talent, have only been to Tier Fifteen a handful of times. And turning eighteen don't make you a man. For tens of thousands of years, manhood was something that had to be *earned*. You won't be able to please Creepy Crawley until you feel you've earned your manhood."

Phil cocked his head to the side. Behind the bluster and vulgarity, there seemed to be a kernel of wisdom in Rich's words. It was true that he in many ways did not feel worthy of a feisty, sexually adventurous girl like Crawley. But he had no idea about how to prove that he was, either to himself or her.

"Oh, come on, Rich. How would a Jewish kid from Brooklyn even go about doing that?"

"Well," said Rich, scratching his chin, "there's this South American tribe that lives in the rain forest that makes their young men wear gloves filled with stinging, poisonous ants…"

"Yeah, sure. Great. That sounds like a great plan."

"Or you could go on a vision quest, or great and dangerous journey."

"I think you're making this shit up as you go along. I have to go. We're driving upstate to try and find Autumn's dad, so —"

"That's it!" Rich clapped him on the shoulder. "The universe is giving you the chance to prove your manhood! If you can overcome the challenges on the road trip, you will have earned your manhood, padawan!"

Phil was at last able to swerve past Rich. "If you say so, Rich. Have a nice weekend."

"Walk with the ancients, my fierce squaw!" Rich held his hand over his heart and stared stoically after Phil. "For when you return, you shall be a brave!"

"Mr. Borgia," said the nurse, lightly patting Steve on his shoulder.

"What's up?" Steve sat up in the chair he had been dozing in. He glanced out the window, blinking at the afternoon sun. "It's not after visiting hours, is it?"

"No, sweetie, the chief of medicine wishes to speak with you."

Steve glanced at Autumn's bed, finding her sleeping deeply if not peacefully. The pathos of her pallid, sickly form nearly brought tears to his eyes, but he squared his jaw and followed the nurse out into the hall.

"Her office is on the first floor. Charlene at the front desk can show you the way."

He thanked the woman and walked toward the elevators, lost in thought. He wondered what the chief wanted to see him about, but he also could not help but wonder about the group that had left early that morning, headed for Poughkeepsie. It all seemed so ludicrous, that he should be here uselessly sitting around while others tried to save what he knew in his heart was the love of his life.

Upon reaching the ground floor, he was directed to a cluster of offices in the administrative wing. In short order he was being ushered into a nicely appointed office. The woman sitting behind the desk was middle-aged but in good shape. Her waist was narrow and her skin taut, and her hand strongly gripped his own for a shake.

"Mr. Borgia," she said once greetings had been made, "please sit down."

She indicated a pair of comfortable upholstered chairs. He carefully sat down in one, arranging his long legs under it.

"I understand that you believe you have a donor."

"Nothing is for sure yet, but we're hoping."

"I see." She had introduced herself, but Steve had forgotten her name. Fortunately, she wore a gold name tag on her lapel proclaiming her Dr. Layla Sark. "You are aware, of course, that your fiancée has no health insurance."

"I can take care of her expenses. I have a good job."

Dr. Sark sighed, the sound of someone who was about to act in a manner they were not comfortable with. "Mr. Borgia, we're not concerned about the day to day costs concerning her care. But the transplant operation is very expensive."

"I said I'd take care of it!" Steve's eyes narrowed to slits and his hands rasped into fists.

"The costs are going to be roughly seventy-five thousand. I'm sorry, I don't see how you're going to swing that on a teacher's salary."

"I'll pay it off if it takes thirty years." Steve tried to ignore the growing knot in his belly.

"I'm sorry, but hospital policy is that we have to collect half the money up front. Until we receive it, even if a donor does come through, we won't be able to proceed."

"Are you serious? Look, I'll get you the money. I'll work two or even three jobs, you can cut me open and take whatever you want—"

"Mr. Borgia," she said, holding up a hand. "Please calm down. I'm on your side."

"Calm down? When you just told me I have to watch her die so you can save *money?* And you want me to be calm?"

"I realize this is a difficult time for you."

"Oh yeah? Well, let me ask you something. Have you ever had to watch while someone you love more than anything just wasted away in front of you? Have you ever had your life, your love, your whole future just ripped right from your hands? Because if you haven't, I don't think you realize shit."

Steve rose to his feet, snarling at the inquisitive receptionist as he stalked past. He went to the elevator, still seething, and reached for the number nine button. His finger stalled, hovering near the switch. He turned toward a passing nun and asked her where the chapel was.

Steve rode the elevator to the top floor. He crossed over the fenced-in bridge that spanned the gap between the elevator and the parking garage. Passing by a gaggle of staff who were using the eagle-eye vantage to smoke, he trudged out to the edge of the garage. Though his car was parked several floors below, he kept walking until he was standing with hands braced on the concrete, staring out over the city.

It didn't seem fair to him. So many people deserved to die. Dictators, serial killers, molesters…why did the universe decide that it was Autumn's time? What kind of twisted logic did the celestial bureaucracy running the cosmos use to determine such things?

In his despair, he briefly considered leaping over the side. It was a full ten stories down, and he had no doubt that the impact would be lethal. He felt guilty, thinking of Autumn lying in her bed, struggling to stay alive. He also thought of his father and mother, and what they might feel if he were to kill himself, and thinking about that made him even more upset.

Deciding that Autumn didn't need to know about either the problems with her transplant or his momentary weakness, he spun on his heel and strode back toward the hospital with purpose. He would put on a brave front for her. He would do anything for her.

"That's Steven's sister?" Crawley asked from the front seat as they watched the lithesome woman make her way to the van.

"Yeah," said Phil from his spot next to her, "you met her before, at Rex's house."

"Oh, yeah…I don't remember her being so built."

Susan was wearing tight black yoga pants and sneakers, and had on a snug spandex top. Her hair was pulled back in a ponytail, and she was donning a jacket as she walked. She cut an impressive figure, both from her beauty and her fitness.

"Damn," Deathslayer said from one of the bench style seats, taking up most of it. "She looks just as pretty as her mother did. I mean, does."

Crawley and Phil shot him appreciative smiles at the jest. Perhaps because of the gravity of the situation, they were all behaving a bit silly, cracking jokes and acting boisterous. When Susan entered the vehicle, their levity seemed to annoy her.

"I'm glad you're all having fun. Meanwhile poor Steve and Autumn are going through hell."

"Uh," said Phil, "it's pretty obvious that you don't even like Autumn. Why are you here exactly?"

Susan glared at Phil until he cringed.

"I may think Steve can do better, but I still don't want her to die! Plus, I'm doing this mostly for Steve. Why are you here? You're just his friend because Steve feels bad about your big brother getting killed."

"SUSAN!" said Deathslayer, his bellow filling up the cabin.

"Sorry," said Susan. "I guess I'm more upset than I thought."

"It's all right," said Phil, though he had a hard set to his jaw.

"All right," said Crawley. "Let's get this show on the road!"

She put the van in drive and pulled carefully into the street. Susan turned around on her seat and spoke to her father in hushed tones for several minutes. At length she turned about to face them in the front seat.

"What do you know about Autumn's dad? Is he going to help her, or is he a big fucking jerk?"

"Apparently," said Phil, "he's a big jerk. Ran out on Autumn and her mother when she was just a teenager."

"Great, so now we have to go up to him out of the blue and be like 'hey, can we have one of your major organs? Thanks!'"

"It'll be fine," Deathslayer said from the rear. "Let me tell you something, NO father could tell his daughter no, not even if she asked for his head on a platter."

"*You* wouldn't, Daddy," said Susan with a sigh. "I'm not so sure about Autumn's dad."

The conversation abated, at least temporarily. Crawley put on the radio and they rode in relative silence for a time. Phil consulted their route on the GPS device on the dashboard. It would take two hours of non-stop driving to get to their goal. He leaned back in his seat and sighed.

"Gonna be a long trip," he muttered under his breath.

"Hey, beautiful," said Steve as he entered Autumn's room.

She glanced up from her dinner tray and smiled. "You're just in time for some primo cuisine." She indicated the meal with a shaky finger. A few slices of turkey, covered in a greasy sauce, were flanked by a mound of peas and a gelatinous scoop of mashed potatoes.

"Looks delicious," he said, sitting down next to her. His worn, miserable appearance made her cringe.

"Oh my god, sugar, go home and get some sleep."

"I'm fine." He sat up and slapped his cheeks.

"No," she said, putting down her fork. "No, you're not. Steve, *this* is why I didn't want us to be together. Maybe I always dated jerks because it didn't bother me that someday they'd have to…have to…"

She sobbed, tears leaking from her tightly shut brown eyes. He moved to comfort her, carefully holding her in an embrace.

"I don't want you to watch me die. Please, just leave and go home."

"No," he said, tears streaming from his own eyes. "I won't leave, not ever."

They clung to each other for a long while, tears mingling on their cheeks. She felt so frail in his arms, her life seemed such a fleeting thing that he felt it could slip from him in a moment.

At length, she gently pushed his face away so she could look him in the eyes. "You're too good to me. Most guys would have been out the door a long time ago."

"See?" said Steve, running a hand through her dark hair. "Dating a pussy has its benefits."

"I'm sorry that I didn't tell you sooner," she said, bottom lip quivering.

"Don't be sorry." He wanted to be strong for her, but on the inside he felt his heart was breaking. He tried to keep the hopelessness out of his voice and off of his face. "We're going to get through this, you'll see."

Autumn smiled, then reached for his hand and squeezed it, but the hollow glint in her eyes said that she did not hold out much hope either.

chapter 19

The bare branches of trees seemed to jab at the dark road like accusing fingers. The day had grown overcast, casting a pall over both the van and their spirits. Phil tried changing the radio station to find a more up-tempo background noise, but it hadn't seemed to help.

"This isn't going to work," said Susan out of the blue, echoing their own thoughts and shocking them out of their reverie.

"How can you know that?" her father asked. Deathslayer's brows were arched, his arms crossed over his chest.

"Because it's stupid. This guy ran out on Autumn and her mother. What makes you think he's going to give up a vital organ?"

Deathslayer chuckled. "Guilt?"

"What if that doesn't work?"

"We could always threaten him," said Crawley from the driver's seat. "He probably owes back child support in the five-figure range."

Deathslayer gave her an appreciative nod, then leaned forward to whisper in Phil's ear. "She's devious. I like her." He patted Phil's shoulder firmly and sat back down.

Phil turned his gaze on Crawley. Deathslayer didn't understand Crawley, not at all. It wasn't deviousness that drove her, but a sense of justice. After all, she always played the noble knight classes on MMO role playing games, was always willing to part with rare items if someone else needed them more. Crawley was very *giving* in her own way, very supportive. It was a shame that she came across to so many people as conceited or bossy, but then his own social skills weren't the best. Briefly, he wondered what his life would have been like if he hadn't inherited friends from his late brother. Steve had been a true friend to him, and he felt even more determined to save Autumn.

"Why don't we appeal to his humanity?" said Phil. "If you could save someone's life, wouldn't you do it?"

Crawley glanced at him and smiled sweetly. "You're such a good person, Phillip. But you really shouldn't judge people by your own example."

"Yeah," said Susan. "You're being egocentric."

"Hey," said Deathslayer, "I'm sure he's never even *looked* at another man!"

They enjoyed a good guffaw at the jibe, the van's metal walls echoing with their laughter. Deathslayer and Susan engaged in a spirited debate about the nuances of a headlock. Phil took note of their momentary distraction and leaned toward Crawley.

"I'm not a good person. Or maybe I am, but I'm not a good boyfriend."

"Oh, Phil, you're a great boyfriend!"

She patted his hand and smiled but her comment had the same kind of superficial joviality as always, as if she were holding something back. Phil sighed, wondered just what he might do to move along to Tier Fifteen. He grinned helplessly. Rich had brainwashed him after all.

"You look bored, hon," said Crawley, gesturing toward her tablet in the divider between their seats. "You can use my iPad if you want, you know, to play games or whatever."

Phil picked up the device, grateful for a distraction. He turned it on and squinted his eyes when something popped up immediately.

"Uh, it's on a book or something."

"Oh, uhm…" Crawley had just a hint of red coming to her cheeks. "Just close that app down if you want to find the games. Or, you could read it, I guess, but most of the stories I have are, um…erotic."

"Oh, really?" Phil's his heart jumped in his chest. Finally, fate had handed him the chance to see what Crawley found stimulating. He was aware that such stories were not necessarily a manual for pleasing a woman, but it would give him a place to start. "Maybe I'll check out some of these after all."

Crawley giggled, briefly turning her dark, shining gaze on him before returning her attention to the road.

Steve bent low over the brightly painted table in his classroom, stout arms supporting his weight. Seated next to him was an older black woman, dressed like she was headed for church, complete with hair scarf. The classroom was otherwise empty, it being late afternoon.

"So you see, we're learning the letter V next week and—"

"I think you made a mistake, Mr. Borgia. You're learning the letter X the week after next. Isn't that out of order?"

"Yeah, some letters are a lot easier to teach than others, so I do them early in the year. We don't do the harder ones till the end."

"Well, it's not how I learned, but it's your classroom."

Steve ignored the mild insult and continued to impart his schedule to her. She was attentive enough, but she seemed possessed of an attitude that Steve could not possibly tell her something she did not already know.

"I'll give you my cell number, so if there's anything you need, just let me know."

"Your kids are in good hands with me," she said. "I do have to ask, what is your policy on discipline?"

"Pretty much go by the district standards. Except that I don't really punish the kids. The most I might do is move them out of an area for a while, let them calm down."

"You don't punish?" she said, mouth agape. "Then how do you make them listen?"

Steve grinned, which was a ghastly sight as he had barely slept in the last week. His baggy eyes and gaunt cheeks made him appear like a graveyard ghoul.

"You just have to be creative. If you can't hold their attention, then you don't belong here. You have to differentiate between kids being kids and actual willful misbehavior. If a child isn't listening to you, it may be your fault."

The scoffing snort she gave him seemed to indicate that his children were in for a lot of time outs. He thanked the woman and gathered his belongings.

Steve walked out into the parking lot, almost stumbling on the stairs. He dropped the key four times trying to open the car door, cursing as his fingers shook. Once he seated himself, he popped open a cool aluminum can and drained the energy swill within, grimacing at the bad taste. Slapping his own cheeks, he attempted to psych himself up for another long night at the hospital.

"You can do this." His voice echoed hollowly in the cabin. Carefully, he pulled the car out into traffic. He wondered how his father and the others were doing. He had received a message from them saying that Autumn's father no longer lived in Poughkeepsie but they had been able to discern clues about his possible new locale in Albany. The wait for news was intolerable, preventing him from being able to truly rest.

He arrived at the hospital, and the bright lights illuminating the smooth sidewalk stung his over-worked eyes. The interior of the lobby was only slightly less lit, and his squinting was misinterpreted by some of the other visitors, who gave him a wide berth.

Leaning heavily on the elevator wall during his trip upstairs, he hid his face in his massive palm. Part of him wished that it would all go away, that he would arrive at Autumn's room to find her fit and ready to go home.

As he entered her room, he noted that she was not alone. Sal was there, as well as several of her friends from the parlor. A nurse was checking on Autumn's vitals, and was giving the unusual crowd cautious glances.

"Hey, sugar," said Autumn as he came in, sitting up a bit in her bed.

"Hey, beautiful," he said, kissing her on the cheek. He turned to address Sal and the others. "Thanks for coming by."

"No problem, sir," said Sal, shaking his hand with a surprisingly powerful grip. "We were just leaving anyway, weren't we guys?"

The strange procession filtered out of the room, and Steve moved a bouquet of flowers and balloons out of his path to sit next to Autumn.

"You seem tired."

"I'm fine, beautiful. I arranged for time off, so I'll be able to sleep in tomorrow."

"You're not fine." Her mouth straightened, and her eyes narrowed. "Sal says you went by the shop yesterday."

Steve grinned and arched his brows twice in rapid succession. "I might have done that."

"He says you got a tattoo."

"That's also a distinct possibility."

"Damn it, Steve," she said with more vigor than he had seen in days. "I *told* you not to get my fucking name—"

"It's not your name." He doffed his coat and unbuttoned his shirt. He slowly slipped the sleeve off his left arm, revealing a white gauze bandage. Carefully peeling up the corner, he revealed the design to Autumn.

It was a large image, taking up most of his deltoid region. An oak leaf, its edges crisp and tinged with a brilliantly illustrated profusion of color. Had it not been on Steve's arm, she felt as if it could have been falling gently from a tree. A slow smile spread on Autumn's face, her eyes shining.

"It's beautiful."

"How are you feeling?" he asked, taking her hand in his.

"Not so bad today. Last night after you left, my legs were itching like you wouldn't believe, and I threw up a couple of times this morning, but I'm all right now."

Steve's face was crossed by dark clouds, as he was torn between telling her about the crew trying to find her father or keeping her in the dark so she wouldn't have to worry. He finally decided that she needed to know.

"Autumn, uh…I should probably tell you something."

She squeezed his hand. "You can tell me anything."

"This might not be easy to hear…"

"Oh my god." Her mouth formed an O. "You slept with Eleanor."

"What? No!"

"I was kidding, sugar. It's been a week since I made fun of you; I didn't want you to start getting soft."

"Perish the thought," he said, a bit irritated.

"Sorry. Go ahead and tell me what you wanted to."

He took a deep breath, looked into her beautiful eyes, and blurted it out. "My dad and sister are trying to find your father."

Autumn's eyes went wide. Her mouth opened, muscles playing along her jaw, but no sound came out. Then her brows descended low over her eyes and she crossed her arms over her chest.

"Steve, he didn't want anything to do with me before. What makes you think he's going to care that I'm dying?"

The casual mention of the worst case scenario made him flinch.

"He can donate a kidney, Autumn!"

"Why would he do that? He never cared about me before! You're wasting your time. I can't believe that you would do something like this without even talking to me first."

"I'm sorry. I should have told you."

"Yes, you should have! This is my life you're fucking around with!"

"Oh, imagine that, someone you care about keeping a big secret. I wonder what that feels like."

"So that's it, then. You've got your revenge now, don't you?"

Steve flinched a bit, feeling guilty but unable to let go of his anger. "Well, maybe I didn't tell you for me, and not for you."

"What's that supposed to mean?" Autumn crossed her arms, indignant.

"To avoid *this*, for one thing. Besides, you're stubborn."

"*I'm* stubborn? Me? You're the one who refuses to see reality."

"And what reality is that?" Steve tilted his head to the side.

Autumn sighed, spread her hands out wide as if in exasperation. "I'm dying, Steve. You have to accept that, and all your stupid schemes can't stop it."

He reacted as if struck, causing her fierce glower to melt away. Her mouth went slack, and her eyes lost their fiery glint. Steve shook his head, feeling as if she were not only giving up on her own life, but on him as well.

"You know I can't do that. Why is it a bad thing that I want to save you?"

"I never said it was—" Autumn's voice abruptly cut off. Her head hit the pillow and her arms went slack, one limp hand brushing Steve's arm.

"Autumn?" he said, slapping her hand rapidly. "Autumn!"

He slammed the nurse call button and shouted for help.

"I don't think this is it," said Phil, leaning forward to look past Crawley. The ramshackle structure was a single-story, rough wooden roadhouse. A row of shiny motorcycles stood leaning next to each other, streetlights reflecting off the chrome. Loud music blared from inside the establishment, which bore the correct numbers on its side in fading neon paint.

"It has the right address," said Susan, her hair tickling Phil's nose as she thrust her head right in his way. "Keep an open mind."

"I'll go see what's up," said Phil, opening up the door. Gratefully, he stretched his legs, blood flowing back into his starved limbs. He stiffly made his way to the entrance, pushing open the flimsy door and coughing in the thick smoke that rolled out into the night.

At first no one seemed to notice him. Large, burly men with hair bristling from every conceivable inch laughed boisterously as they drank, played darts, and howled at the football game on the old style television. Phil shuffled between the haphazardly arranged tables and chairs to the bar, getting the attention of a middle-aged bartender. She was dressed provocatively, her large bosom straining against a tight shirt with strategic cut-outs. Her shorts were not any more modest, and when she bent low to wipe up a spill he was treated to a flash of her lace undergarments.

"Excuse me, ma'am, but do you know a Jonathon Winters?"

"What?" The woman eyed him up and down with suspicion.

"Jonathon Winters." Phil patiently tried not to stare at her cleavage. "He was listed as living at this address."

The barmaid put her hands on her hips and cocked at eye at him. "Are you a cop?"

"What? No, I'm not a cop! I'm just looking for Jonathon Winters, have you seen —"

A big, meaty palm dropped onto Phil's shoulder. He turned, staring up the hairy limb it was attached to, into the equally hirsute face of a man who seemed not the least bit amused.

"Is this guy hassling you, Shelly?"

"Just some creep. Get rid of him, will ya?"

"Time to go!" The big man seized Phil's arm in a painful grip.

"Now wait just a minute," said Phil, stumbling along as the man dragged him through the bar.

"Take a hike, queer!" The burly man swung his torso forward and propelled Phil with great speed out the door. Phil hit the sidewalk and skidded a few feet. He stared down at his stinging hands, shocked to find them torn and bleeding.

"Hey!" he heard Crawley's voice say sharply. She dove out of the van, leaving her door standing wide open and rushed to Phil's side. Glaring up at the burly biker, she seemed as if she wanted to throttle the man. "You should be ashamed of yourself!"

"You're with this clown, sweetie?" said the biker. He laughed, then glanced down at Phil. "Either you've got a foot long pecker, or she's waaaaay slumming!"

"You son of a bitch," said Phil, getting his feet under him. He was determined to knock the man's head from his shoulders in his rage. He never got the chance as Deathslayer strode between them. The big biker blanched, staring up into the face of a man much larger than even himself.

"Is there a problem?" said Deathslayer, flexing his considerable muscle and bearing down on the biker.

"Not with you." The man licked his lips nervously. "You're our kind, buddy. Little buffer boy can't come in. That's the way it is."

"No reason to throw him out on his ass," said Deathslayer, putting a hand on the man's shoulder as if he were an old friend. His gaze remained icy, however, as he continued to speak. "I'll take it as a personal favor if you apologize to him."

"Sure, man," said the biker, smiling up at Deathslayer's whiskered visage, "no problem!"

The biker turned his own whiskered visage on Phil, bleary eyes full of fear. "I'm sorry, man," he said.

Phil nodded, too stunned to reply vocally. Steve's father patted the man on the shoulder firmly and then the two of them went into the bar, Deathslayer winking at Phil.

About twenty minutes later, Phil was wincing as Crawley applied Band-Aids to the cuts on his palms. She was cajoling him about being a baby when the door to the bar swung open and Deathslayer came striding out. He pulled the van's side door open, a defeated slump to his shoulders.

"No go?" said Susan.

"Afraid not," said Deathslayer sadly. "The place used to belong to a guy named Jonathon Winters, but he sold it about five years ago. The new owners, well, they never got around to filing their paperwork with the state, it seems."

"Great," said Phil, "I got tossed out like garbage for nothing."

"What are we going to do?" asked Susan. "This was the only lead we had!"

"Calm down," said Deathslayer, "it's not all bad news. One of the boys in there says he thinks Jonathon may have found work with a construction company in Buffalo."

"Buffalo?" said Phil. "We're running all over the damn state!"

"This is just one of those gnats on the asshole of life," said Deathslayer.

Phil and Crawley were overcome with laughter at the colorful analogy.

"What?" said Deathslayer as Susan grinned ruefully.

Steve stood outside Autumn's room, nervously chewing on his knuckle. The frantic sounds from within had died down, making him hopeful that Autumn was well, or at least as well as could be expected. He jumped when the door opened and a doctor exited, flanked by two nurses. Steve's expectant, hollow-eyed gaze asked the question his mouth could not form.

"She's stable. I don't see any immediate cause for alarm."

"What happened? She said she was feeling better, and then…"

The doctor sighed, rubbing his own tired eyes. "Mr. Borgia, when someone is as sick as your fiancée, sometimes the body just kind of gives up."

"Gives up? Where did you get your medical degree? Guam? What kind of fucking stupid ass thing to say is that?"

"Mr. Borgia, please keep your voice down."

"I bet if I had a platinum credit card, you wouldn't be blowing me off like this."

He entered the room, cautiously approaching her bed. Autumn turned her head weakly toward him and tried to smile. She struggled to speak, but the words kept catching in her parched throat.

"Shh," he said, sitting down next to her in his customary spot and taking her clammy hand in his own. "Don't try to talk. I'm here."

Autumn's eyes fluttered closed, though she had a serene smile on her face. Her hand weakly squeezed his own, and soon she had drifted off to sleep once more.

Steve did not budge an inch, even when his bladder urged and the skyscrapers were dotted with light. It was not until a nurse came and politely but firmly told him visiting hours were over that he finally rose from his vigil. Casting one last glance over his shoulder at her slumbering form, he wondered if it would be the last time he saw her alive.

chapter 20

The sun bore down on them cheerfully, as if in mockery of their grim purpose, as the van sped along the highway. They had hastily left the motel rooms they'd rented the previous evening as soon as the sun creased the horizon, and their bleary faces reflected their lack of sleep. Crawley's good mood did not diminish, however, and she seemed to enjoy the change of pace from her day-to-day schedule.

Phil did not. He was a creature of habit, and life on the road was fraught with inconveniences that he found unsettling. Using gas station bathrooms had lost its charm almost immediately, and using cold bottled water to rinse the greasy sweat from his hair was something he was not eager to repeat.

He glanced over at Crawley as she sang along with a song on the radio while he looked at the books on her iPad. Her taste in literature was surprising. There was a definite "damsel in distress" theme in the erotic novels she had, lots of fair maidens whisked away by devious pirates. She seemed more sexually aggressive to him, but clearly she wanted to be in a submissive role. That put his neophyte self in an awkward position. Did she really want him to act like that? *Could* he really be that way? He wondered if this was the test of his manhood that Rich had spoken of, then rolled his eyes at himself when he realized how incredibly ignorant the notion was.

Crawley pulled the van off the highway at the exit they had been waiting for. In short order they were driving through a sleepy village, arriving at the small headquarters for the construction company Jonathon Winters allegedly worked for.

"Jenoine Contracting," said Phil, reading the sign on rickety posts outside the brick structure. "This is the place, but I don't see anyone around."

"Mostly, they just store their equipment here," said Deathslayer. "There should be someone in the office, though."

Deathslayer went around the side of the building to relieve himself in some tall weeds, though his head still poked above the verdant patch. Susan, Phil, and Crawley made their way inside the building, pushing through a glass door equipped with a buzzer. A stout man with a thick neck lumbered up to a long wooden counter and leaned on it. He plastered a cheery smile on his ruddy, sun-wizened face when he spoke.

"Hello there. How can I help you young folks?"

"Hello, sir," said Phil, walking forward and offering his hand for a shake. The man seemed put off a bit by the gesture, but did briefly seize the offered limb in his own meaty paw. "We were wondering if you have a man named Jonathon Winters working for you?"

"Johnny?" The man's eyes flickered in recognition. A second later they narrowed. "Now why do you want to talk to Johnny? What are you about?"

"Please, sir," said Susan, "it's a matter of life and death. We really need to speak to him."

"Oh, give me a break," said the man, his eyes narrowing even more until they were fierce flint like slits. "I know what this is about. You just want to hassle Johnny, like that crew from the SBC last week! You can go to hell, and take your opinions with you!"

"Uh," said Phil, "crew from the SBC? Look, we don't want to cause trouble—"

"Fine. If you don't want to cause trouble, then leave."

"What?" said Susan, striding forward. "Come on, dude! We're not here to—"

"Get. Out. Do I have to call the police? Because the chief is just like Johnny, you know, and he won't take kindly to you hassling him!"

"We'll go," said Phil, swallowing hard at the thought of dealing with police. "Sorry to trouble you, sir."

"We're not leaving," said Susan with conviction.

Phil grabbed her by the bicep and yanked her toward the exit. "Yes, we are. Come on, Susie, there's a better way."

"What do you think he meant?" Crawley asked as soon as their feet were crunching on gravel. "I mean, about the chief of police being the same as Jonathon?"

"Maybe he's a deadbeat dad too," said Susan grimly. "Maybe these SBC goons are from the state or something…"

"I don't know," said Phil as they approached the van, "but I think I figured out a way to find Jonathon."

"How so?" Susan asked, standing with one hand on the door handle.

"I handle the Jenoine Contractors payroll account. I have access to all the employee data, including their addresses."

"Um, sweetie," said Crawley with a touch of concern, "can't you get in trouble for that?"

"Probably," said Phil with a shrug, "but it's not like I'm using their information to open up fake credit card accounts, or apply for a loan. It's for a worthy cause."

"I say do it," said Susan. "We're not getting anywhere with the Skipper."

"Huh?" said Crawley and Phil in unison.

"Skipper," said Susan, reddening in the cheeks. "You know, from *Gilligan's Island?*"

She was met with blank stares.

"Oh, what a couple of nerds! If I'd have said he looked like some Han Skywalker bullshit you'd have laughed!"

"This has got to be it," said Phil as they pulled up outside a ranch-style house with clean white siding. There was a small dog on a chain in the front yard, straining at the end of its leash and barking its head off. Streetlights buzzed overhead as a haze of insects swarmed in their warm yellow light.

"Let's go," said Crawley, starting to get out.

"Wait a minute," said Deathslayer, rubbing the sleep out of his eyes. "We shouldn't all go marching up their sidewalk. Phil, you and Susan look the least threatening, why don't you two go talk to them?"

"I'm threatening?" said Crawley at the same time Phil protested his own label.

"Don't make it a thing, doll. I just think that they're both Anglo, neither have tattoos…"

"I get it," said Crawley, getting back in.

Phil sighed and got out into the early twilight. Susan followed him a moment later. Both of them were haggard, as they had not brought supplies for a two-day trip, but Deathslayer had rented a hotel room the previous evening, so they at least were well-rested. They made their way up the sidewalk, the little dog protesting their presence vehemently.

"I don't think this is the right house," said Susan, stopping to scoop something out of the recycle bin on the modest porch.

"It has to be. There's no other Jonathon Winters who works for Jenoine, and this guy moved in at the right time."

"Yeah, but look at this."

She showed him the *Jet* magazine she held in her hands.

"So? We don't even know if it's his. He could have gotten it by mistake."

"There's thirty more of them in here. I think this Jonathon is bla —"

The front door opened, startling them. An older man stood in the door, his eyes narrowed in suspicion. He had pale brown skin, short curly black hair with a peppering of gray, and was clad only in a pair of boxer shorts and tank top. A dense bush of hair stuck out of his shirt and his legs were hairy as a Sasquatch.

"Can I help you?" he asked in a baritone.

"Uh," said Phil, still holding the magazine.

"Hello," said Susan, smiling prettily, "we're looking for Jonathon Winters."

"Let's say you've found him. Does he owe you money?"

"No," said Phil, quickly interjecting himself. "I'm sorry to be so blunt, but do you have a daughter named Autumn?"

The man flinched, eyes seeming to focus on something far away. "What's this about?"

"Johnny," came a high-pitched voice from behind him, the speaker unseen, "who is it? Are we expecting company?"

The door abruptly swung open wider, and a short, bald heavyset man entered their view. He had a neatly trimmed mustache and twinkling blue eyes. He smiled warmly at the young people on his doorstep.

"Hello, kids. I'm sorry, but we're happy with our non-religious life, so—"

"They're not Jehovah's Witnesses this time," said Jonathon grimly.

"Then who are they?" he asked, addressing the query to Jonathon. He then turned his gaze on them. "Who are you?"

"That might take a while to explain," said Susan, biting her lower lip.

"They seem to know my daughter," said Jonathon, still eying them suspiciously.

"Really?" said the other man, smacking Jon on the arm. "Then what the hell are they still doing on the porch?"

He opened the door wide, despite the angry glare Jonathon gave him.

"Come on in," he said, opening the screen door. "Johnny, go put some pants on for goodness' sake, we have *company*."

They entered the dwelling, noting how cozy it seemed. A modestly sized living room boasted a comfortable sofa with tasteful plaid upholstery that matched the drapes over the large bay window. Two recliners done in black leather were arranged next to each other in front of the flat-screen TV, a small table between them. A bowl of popcorn sat on the table, a few kernels on the floor, and the image on screen was of a movie on pause. Susan giggled at the sight of Nicolas Cage with his nose at an unfortunate angle, his forest of black nostril hairs unsettling.

"You two have a seat right there."

Phil found himself disarmed by the man's charming manner.

"Johnny? Why do you not have clothes on yet?"

"Brad," said Jonathon, "can I talk to you, please?"

"We'll just be a minute," said Brad with a wink, going with the other down a hallway and out of sight. They heard a door slam and their voices raised in a heated discussion.

"Wow," said Susan, "who would have bet that Autumn's father was black?"

"And gay," said Phil. "Guess that explains why he left Autumn and her mom."

"It's still no excuse not to be in the life of your child."

After an uncomfortable five minutes or so, the door opened and both men came into the living room. Jonathon had put on a pair of slacks and a collared shirt, though he kept it unbuttoned. Brad stopped off in their large kitchen and re-appeared with a tray of deviled eggs and crab cakes.

"Would you like some refreshment?" asked the little man, setting the tray on a glass top coffee table near their feet.

"No thanks," said Susan.

"Well," said Phil, his stomach suddenly gurgling, "I think I might partake."

He picked up one of the crab cakes and bit into it, his eyes widening at the delicious flavor. The tidbit disappeared into his mouth quickly, and he found himself reaching for another.

"How is…" said Jonathon, sitting in one of the recliners and scooting it a bit to face them. "How is Autumn?"

"Sick," said Susan, "very sick. It's why we're here."

Brad and Jon exchanged alarmed glances.

"Is it the Lupus?" asked Jonathon, licking his lips. "I heard about her mother. I…wanted to be at her funeral, but…"

Phil cleared his throat.

"We're not here to berate you for your past, Mr. Winters. I'm going to cut to the chase. Your daughter is dying, and you might be the only one who can save her."

"I don't have any money. I wish I could help, but I just don't. Even with Brad picking up hours at the Walmart, I just don't see how—"

"Money is not the issue," said Susan, holding up her hand. "Her kidneys are failing, and with her condition and rare blood type—"

"No one will give her one," said Jon, hiding his face in his hand.

"Honey," said Brad, putting a hand on Jon's knee, "you have to help her."

"I know!" he said harshly, turning to glare at Brad.

"I know…" he said again more softly, staring at the floor. "I just hope she can forgive me."

Early the next morning, the unusual caravan got off on its journey. Crawley piloted the white van, while Jonathon followed with Brad in their yellow SUV. Jonathon had wanted to leave the previous evening, but Brad had talked him into waiting until morning. The decision had not sat well with Phillip, who was tired of sleeping in a strange bed, but no one else had seemed to mind.

"We have a new problem," said Susan, glaring at her phone.

"Now what?" Phil asked impatiently.

"Even if we get Jonathon to the hospital in time, they won't do the operation unless Steve pays them half up front."

"What?" Deathslayer asked. "I thought he had good insurance."

"She's not covered," said Susan, "and even if they got married this second, it would still be a couple of months before she would be on his insurance."

"Motherfucker!" said Crawley, startling all of them. "Sorry."

"I know how you feel," said Deathslayer, jaw set hard.

"Can't you cover it, Mr. B—I mean, Bill?" Phil asked.

Deathslayer seemed abashed, staring down at the van floor. "I don't have much money left, kid."

"What?" said Crawley. "But you're world famous! You sold out the Garden over twenty times!"

"And I blew a lot of cash when I was young and stupid," said Deathslayer. "Between the kid's trust funds, our mortgage and the recession, I can barely break even."

"Daddy," said Susan, "why didn't you tell anyone?"

"Why do you think? I never wanted you to worry. Besides, once the revenue from this new tour is accounted for, I should have a little nest egg built up again."

"But that doesn't help us now," said Susan, biting her lip. "Maybe we can go on Kickstarter, try and fund it ourselves."

"That would take too long," said Phil, sighing. "It's like God himself doesn't want us to help Autumn and Steve!"

Crawley pursed her lips, glanced over at Phil.

"No, God wants to help us. That's why we found her father, why he wants to help, and it's why we're going to succeed."

"That's great, sweetie, but it doesn't solve our problem. Where are we going to get thirty thousand dollars?"

"I could pay for it," said Crawley.

"Come on," said Susan from the back seat.

"No," said Phil, "even if you had the money—"

"But I do have the money," said Crawley.

"Eleanor," said Deathslayer. "There's no way your father has thirty grand just sitting around."

"It's not my dad's money. It's mine."

"But where did you come up with it?" Phil asked.

She grinned at him. "You're an accountant, you figure it out. Let me say this: How many arachnid labs do you think are operating in North America?"

"I don't know," said Phil, "a hundred or so?"

"Try twenty. We have a big market share, and our costs are very low since we work out of the home."

"And you don't pay rent or buy food," said Susan helpfully.

"What's that supposed to mean?" Crawley asked. Her eyes narrowed and her nostrils flared.

"Susie, don't piss her off! Eleanor, that's, that's just the most generous thing anyone has ever done."

"Except for that whole dying for your sins thing. It's not like I need the money, or like I'd be spending all that I have."

Phil shot her a worried glance. "Are you sure this is all right? I mean, we can find another way."

"I said it's fine, Phil! I want to do this. A lot of people who we go to church with pay lip service to helping out those in need, but when the time comes for them to open their wallets they get pretty darn stingy. I'm *not* going to be one of those people."

"Damn, Ellie," said Susan, "and here I thought you were just a know-it-all stuck-up chick!"

"Susan!" said Deathslayer and Phil in unison.

"But I was wrong," said Susan with a sheepish shrug. "You're actually a pretty decent human being. I'm not sure that *I* would come up with that kind of money for someone I'd known less than a year."

"As I said—" Crawley giggled "—it's not like I'll be spending all the money I have saved up."

Phil swallowed, realizing that Crawley now held yet another advantage over him. The journey was nearly over, and he truly did not feel any different. He should have known that Rich was full of crap, that this "vision quest" of his wouldn't bear any fruit.

Deathslayer noted the serious gleam in Phil's eyes, as well as the tension in the air between Susan and Crawley. He cleared his throat and got all of their attention. "Hey, anyone know any good fart jokes?"

Phil burst out laughing, while Susan turned to face her father.

"Daddy!" she said in admonishment.

"Slow down," said Phil, "there's a cop up ahead."

He pointed out the patrol car sitting behind a billboard not far up the road. The front end was just barely visible, but it had the right shape and color. Crawley checked her speed and nodded.

"I always use cruise control."

They passed by the police car, Steve staring hard into the cabin. A middle-aged state trooper was shooting radar across the road. He flashed by too quickly for Phil to notice anything remarkable about him.

They traveled for another minute when Crawley cringed.

"That cop has his lights on!" She pulled over on the gravel shoulder.

"He's not after us," said Phil, peering behind him. "Uh oh, he pulled over Autumn's dad."

"Why?" Susan asked. "There's no way they were speeding if we weren't."

They sat on the shoulder, watching the proceedings behind them with great interest. After what seemed an interminably long time the officer instructed Jonathon to get out of the car. He handcuffed the older man and took him firmly to his squad car.

"Oh, fucking great," said Phil.

Several hours later, the van and SUV were parked in the lot of a tiny sheriff's office. The crew in the van munched on fast food while Brad was inside trying to free his husband.

"Who'd have thunk not paying parking tickets for twenty years would have a negative consequence?" Susan asked snappily.

"Calm down," said Deathslayer. "I'm sure it'll work out fine."

"I think I'll go check and see what's taking so long," said Phil, wiping a bit of ketchup off his mouth.

"I'll go too," said Crawley, getting out of the van as well.

They walked up the stained concrete steps to the one-story building. Phil had seen larger roadside cafés, and wondered where they might be keeping their prisoner. The glass doors swung open and the couple scanned the station. A chest-high counter was directly before them, currently unmanned. The rest of the building looked like an office, with several desks bearing computers arranged around the room. Sitting at one of the desks was the old timer who had arrested Jonathon. He was scribbling on a note pad while Brad talked in low tones with Jonathon. The prisoner was sitting on a long wooden bench, one wrist attached to the armrest with a pair of handcuffs.

"Can I help you folks?" asked the trooper, glancing up from his desk.

"We were just checking on our friends," said Phil, nervously glancing at the two men on the bench.

The trooper's eye twitched, and he shot a stony glare at Jonathon. "Your friend is going to the county jail."

"Over parking tickets?" said Crawley.

"It's clear he won't be able to settle his account today, and I don't have a holding cell here."

"But, officer," said Crawley, "it's a matter of life and death!"

"It always is, sweetheart. I don't need to hear whatever story you have cooked up, no matter how much of a tearjerker it is."

Phil glanced down at the trooper's desk, and his eyes went wide.

"That's not fair!" said Crawley.

"Eleanor," said Phil, taking her by the arm, "let's go."

"But—"

"Shh...We'll be right back, officer."

"We're not going anywhere," said Jonathon with disdain.

Once they were back outside, Crawley pulled her arm out of his grasp and glared at him.

"What do you think you're doing?"

"There's nothing that you or I can say to change his mind."

"Then what are we going to do?"

"Did you notice the action figure on his desk?"

"No, what does that have to do with anything?"

"Everyone has a hero." He smiled at her enigmatically as they headed to the van.

Phil grinned when the seated officer didn't glance up at their entrance right away. He politely cleared his throat, as they approached the desk.

"Welcome back," said the trooper, staring up at last. "I'm not sure what you think you can accomplish, but…"

His voice trailed off, eyes going wide. No words issued out of his slack jaw as the Deathslayer came striding into his office. He did not have his trademark black leather outfit, but he had the distinctive slow, measured walk and thousand-yard stare of the legendary character. The trooper rose to his feet and approached, a stunned smile on his face.

"Unbelievable. Sir, it is a true pleasure to meet you. My son and I are your biggest fans!"

Crawley gave Phil a soft kiss on his cheek.

"What was that for?" he asked, holding his face.

"For saving the day."

"I think it's Steve's dad who's saving the day," he said with a snicker as the trooper posed for a picture with his idol.

"It was your idea. You're such a good friend, Phillip."

"Bah, anyone would have done the same."

"But anyone didn't do it," she said, giving him another kiss. "You did."

Phil was inclined to shrug, but then he noted the light gleaming in Crawley's dark eyes. They were full of adoration, of her confidence not only in him but in both of them, as a couple. It made him feel ten feet tall.

"It's getting late," he said with a smile, hooking his hand in hers. "We probably couldn't make it back to the city before midnight."

Crawley's dark eyes gleamed, and she bit her bottom lip. "We should rent another hotel room."

"Yeah," Phil said, lowering his tone. His hand brushed over her smooth cheek, an electric tingle running through his fingers, "but I think that we should get our own room, you know, so our…snoring…doesn't disturb Bill or Susan."

"Oh? Yeah, I've been known to 'snore' pretty loud…"

She sidled up to him and kissed him on the mouth. Normally, the prospect of intimacy filled him with nameless dread, so afraid was he of disappointing her. This time, armed with the knowledge gleaned from her fiction, as well as the confidence gained from dealing with the state trooper, he felt excited. Nervous, but definitely excited. He silently wondered if Rich had been right after all, that he just needed this journey and its trials to feel better about himself.

Crawley's nimble tongue drew his attention back to the present. The late afternoon sun gave a red nimbus to the outer edges of her black hair, making her appear almost divine. For the first time he did not fear that she would dissipate like so much dew in the sun, and he kissed her back eagerly.

chapter 21

Phil grimaced fiercely, eyes narrowed and teeth bared in a snarl. He jabbed his finger toward the king-sized mattress.

"Get in the bed!"

"Don't say it like *that*," said Crawley with a giggle.

They were in the simple but clean hotel room he had rented, its neon sign just visible through the thick, slightly parted curtains. Both were stripped to the waist, Crawley wearing only a miniscule pink G-string and Phil clad in red boxers. She had her hair put up, her slender neck tapering down to smooth shoulders.

Phil was more than a bit uncomfortable, but gave it another try. "Get in the fucking bed!" he said more harshly.

"Noooo!" Crawley rolled her eyes. "You're not saying it right."

"Then how am I supposed to say it?"

"I don't know! Not so angry. Try being stern, like...like you're a teacher about to discipline a child!"

The comment made him feel a bit guilty, as his teacher friend had called three times already that day and sent several texts but Phil had never checked any of them. He banished the thoughts from his mind, trying to do as Crawley had asked.

"Get in the bed," he said, his voice a low growl, "*now*."

He must have hit the right tone, because Crawley simpered and meekly moved to obey. "Okay. Please don't hurt me."

She got slowly on the bed, sitting on her knees and crossing her arms over her chest. Her eyes were shining, though her face still seemed frightened. He stood there for a moment, unsure of what to do next.

"Oh," she said, closing her eyes, "what are you going to do to me?"

Finding his character, he slipped back into it. "Anything I want," he said, getting on the bed after awkwardly doffing his boxers. His body was about half-prepared for a bout of passion, his cock dangling between his thighs. He put his hands gently on Crawley's shoulders and pushed on them softly.

"Oh!" she cried, flopping on her back as if she had been thrown full force. "Oh my god, please, I'll do whatever you say!"

He grabbed her tiny panties and yanked them down to her knees, then her ankles, finally holding them in his right hand. She gasped as if in terror as her nether lips were exposed, already slightly open and growing wet.

"Oh, you're so big," she said as he crawled atop of her. "Please, don't stick it in my ass."

"I'll stick it wherever I want." He nibbled on her dark brown nipples, teeth pinching hard.

"If you don't stop, I'm going to scream!"

Phil remembered the line from one of her stories, and was ready to play his part. He took the satin underwear in his hand and balled it up. She opened her mouth wide so he could jam them into her orifice, though her eyes seemed to protest the act.

"Scream all you want," he said, grabbing her hands in his own and pinning her to the bed. The sounds escaping from behind her satin panties sounded fearful, and the dewy light in her eyes matched. However, her body seemed to want to press itself against him, and her legs spread eagerly as he slithered over her body. He released one of her hands and ran his own over one small breast, kneading the flesh vigorously. Crawley's muted protests grew more insistent, and she fought against the hand still holding her down. She moved her free hand as if to pull the gag out of her mouth.

"Don't touch that!" he growled, momentarily stopping his exploration of her body to squeeze her hand in his own. "Put your hand under your head."

Meekly, Crawley moved to comply. His hand went back to work, sliding down her toned stomach until he reached her mound. Normally he teased the outside a bit, unsure of how much pressure she would find pleasurable, but now he roughly spread her labia and thrust himself inside her. Crawley gasped behind her panties, eyes squinting tightly shut as her body writhed beneath his own.

He slid himself in and out of her, amazed as always at how soft and tight she was. Crawley tried to stay in character, making pleading noises behind the panties in her mouth, but soon his thrusting had her making sounds of ecstasy. During one particularly passionate cry the panties came out to lay in a sodden pile on the bed next to her head.

Soon all pretense of their foreplay was gone, and he was no longer holding her down to the bed. She became his willing partner, allowing him to flip her over onto her stomach so he could re-enter her from that position. He did seize a handful of her thick hair in his fist, yanking back firmly while still being careful not to pull too hard or too far. Crawley's hips ground into his own, indicating that she was pleased with the forceful gesture even if they had abandoned their kinky dialogue.

Phil was exultant. Finally, he was able to hold his own with Crawley, able to please her just as well as she pleased him. She lurched upward, her body arching against his until their faces were pressed together. Though it was a bit awkward, their mouths found each other amid Phil's energetic thrusting. The taste of her tongue inside his mouth, while their bodies were still interlocked on another level, was amazingly intimate, and for a moment he was not sure where he ended and she began.

Crawley flung herself forward, grinding her buttocks against his hips. Taking it as permission to release, he allowed himself to come, gasping through a shuddering wave of ecstasy. Crawley buried her face in the pillows, but still her scream had the windows rattling in their sills. Lazily, she rolled over onto her back, staring up at Phil with a tired but satisfied smile.

"That was fantastic," she whispered in his ear, punctuating it with a peck on the cheek.

"Yeah." He was surprised at the ring of truth in her voice as well as his own.

"Next time," she said, scooting back on her butt until she was in a sitting position, "when I beg you not to do something, that means I want you to."

"Okay. I wasn't sure about the panties thing, if you could breathe or whatever."

"You did fine." She tousled his hair vigorously. "Remember, if things get too scary I can just use the safe word."

"Doughnut."

"Doughnut," she said happily. "But you'll probably never hear me use it."

Phil nodded warmly, reaching his hand up to stroke her smooth cheek.

She put her hand over his and stared at him, eyes worried. "You're okay with all this, aren't you? I mean, I'm not freaking you out or anything, am I?"

"Of course, not. I love you."

Crawley sucked in a deep breath of air, and Phil's eyes went wide when he realized what he'd said.

"I'm sorry, that just kind of slipped—"

"I love you too!" said Crawley, wrapping her arms around his neck and crushing her lips to his. When she pulled away, a slight grin was on her lips. "I was scared you wouldn't, y'know, be into this kind of stuff."

"What? No! I've had the Internet since I was ten. I'm no Puritan."

"Oh?" She kissed his fingers. "What kinds of nasty, dirty things have you been looking at, you naughty boy?"

"Oh, you know," he said as she sucked on his digits, moaning softly. "Gangbangs, three ways, BDSM…"

She stopped her ministrations, giving him a teasing smile. "Did you know that male spiders have to trap females in a web so they can mate?"

"Uh, no." Phil was uncomfortable with the mention of his hated foes.

"Oh, yes," she said, kissing his salty palm. "You see, it's very, very dangerous for the male. They have to protect themselves, so they tie up the lady spider…"

She trailed kisses down his arm, transferring her attention to his chest when she was close enough. Her tongue teased his smooth skin, shaved and waxed at her request. Her teeth teased his flesh, nibbling at it as she headed for his neck.

"That's a little hard," he said as she bit down with vigor.

"Be a man." She giggled.

Phil did his best to comply, and his best was good enough.

Steve rolled out of bed, rubbing his tired eyes. He glanced out his bedroom window, saw that the first pink vestiges of dawn were breaking on the horizon. His bed clothes were stripped off and cast into the overfilled hamper. One of Autumn's shirts fell off the stack and hit the floor. Steve paused long enough to pick it up before going into the bathroom.

He stopped in front of the mirror, rubbed a hand over his unkempt facial hair. He lathered up his face with cream, and then he carefully gave himself an impeccably close shave. The face staring back at him was still tired and worn, but at least his smoothly shaven skin made him appear neat. The image pleased him. He was tired of seeing a bedraggled bum looking back at him.

Stepping in the shower, he turned on the water, dodging out of the way of the stream until it heated up a bit. He washed his hair and thoroughly scrubbed his body with a loofah. After toweling off, he deliberately brushed out his shoulder-length hair. Feeling like he wanted to dress better as well as look better, he donned a pair of black dress pants and a white collared shirt, adding a black sports jacket he almost never wore. Selecting a gray and red striped tie from his small collection, he fumbled with the knot for several minutes before giving up. He tossed the tie back in his closet and selected one that had a knot already in it.

Back in the bathroom, he used a black elastic band to bind his hair in a tight ponytail. A few spritzes of a fruity smelling cologne that he did not care for but Autumn seemed to enjoy, and he was prepared.

"I look like I'm going to a funeral," he said somberly. He stripped off the tie and jacket, but left the dress pants and shirt on.

The drive to the hospital was blessedly uneventful. He drove without the new radio on, the silence suiting his mood. While stopped at a red light, he watched as a couple passed by laughing and running and holding hands. A sudden spring of grief washed over him, and he felt his eyes grow watery.

Steve had to fight off tears several more times before he hit the hospital lobby. People turned their heads at his dapper appearance, but he didn't even notice. His stomach felt like a ton of lead as he rode the elevator up to her floor.

When he entered her room, putting on his best smile, he was surprised to see Autumn sitting up in bed, applying makeup. She had put on ruby red lipstick and smoky blue eye shadow. Her hair was brushed out and braided in an elaborate pattern down her neck. The cosmetics clashed badly with her blue hospital gown, the tubes sticking from her arms creating further pathos. But when he looked into her soft brown eyes, saw the warmth reflected back at him...

"You look beautiful. Shouldn't you save your strength, though?"

She blew out a razzberry at his assessment, running her eyes up and down his form.

"You are a very handsome man, you know that?"

"For a giant who's a bit of a pussy."

"You don't get to call yourself that," she said, clutching his hand as tightly as she could. "That's *my* job."

They talked idly for a few minutes. For better or for worse, both of them seemed resolved to the strangeness of the situation. The subject of the future never came up, though it weighed heavily on both their minds. At length, Autumn leaned backward and laid her cheek on her pillow, smudging a bit of black across it from her mascara.

"You look tired," he said.

"I *am* tired. I'm also fucking bored. I'm sick of being sick."

"Do you want me to turn on the TV?"

"Naw. There's just soap operas and game shows on this time of day."

"I could go to the gift shop, get you something to read."

"No, just stay with me. Don't go. The light hurts my eyes anyway, so I can't stand to read. Tell me a story."

Steve chuckled. "What?"

"You're a teacher. You must know some good stories."

"Yeah, but I don't think you'll like any of them."

"Then make one up," she said, smiling though her eyes remained closed.

"Uh..."

"Make one up," said Autumn insistently, trying to punch him in the arm. The feeble gesture barely registered with him.

"Okay." Steve cast his eyes skyward as he struggled to come up with something on the spot. "Okay, once there was this big, hairy bear, and everyone was afraid of it because it always seemed angry."

"I like stories about bears," she said happily, brushing her clammy hands over his arm.

"Well, this bear was angry all the time because he was lonely. He was terribly, terribly lonely. One day, a beautiful princess —"

"Stop." She opened her eyes to glare at him. "I know where this story is going and you are soooo not making me a princess!"

Steve grinned, then cleared his throat. "Okay. One day, a winged, tattooed succubus from Hell showed up."

Autumn laughed, which seemed to cause her a bit of pain. "That's more like it!"

"So this succubus, she showed the bear a world he never knew existed. And when the devil showed up, saying she had to come home, well, that bear stood up in the devil's horned face and said, *no way! She's mine, and she's staying with me forever.*"

Autumn smiled as his story wound down, managing to give his hand a weak squeeze. "I like that story. But how does it end?"

Both of their heads turned toward the hospital door as Susan strode jubilantly through it. Steve's voice caught in his throat, but his eyes and arched brows asked the question that weighed desperately on his mind. A moment later his eyes went wide in confusion as an older black man strode up behind his sister.

"We found him!" said Susan, gesturing grandly at Jonathon.

The man walked up to the couple, his wizened face furrowing as he nervously approached.

"Hello, Autumn. It's so good to see you."

"Daddy…" Autumn's eyes welled up with tears. "This isn't right. I was supposed to kick your ass the next time I saw you."

"Let's get you better first," said Jonathon. "I definitely deserve an ass kicking or two."

"But," said Steve, "but we can't afford the operation…"

"That's taken care of too," said Susan.

"Dad?" said Steve.

"Uhm," said Susan, "I don't think it's that relevant right now."

"Is this the right room?" Brad asked, coming inside in his usual energetic manner.

"No doubt about it," said Deathslayer, a step behind the much smaller man.

"Who's this?" Autumn asked as Brad came up to her and eagerly shook her hand.

"Uh," said Jonathon, "this is…"

He seemed to lose his speech for a moment. Brad gave him a sympathetic smile and squeezed Autumn's hand.

"I'm Bradley. I guess…well, I guess I'm your stepfather."

Autumn turned her head toward her father, eyes wide in shock.

He shrugged bashfully. "I didn't think you'd want me around."

"I don't care that you're gay, Dad. I *do* care that you ran out on us and never called."

"I called. Your mother always hung up on me. Then she changed the number, a few years passed, and…I'm not sure how it got to be so long since we spoke. It's the worst thing I have ever done as a human being."

Steve glanced up, startled by the touch of his father's hand upon his shoulder.

"Let's give them some time," said the towering man.

"But —" said Steve, unwilling to leave Autumn's side.

"They have some catching up to do," said Deathslayer, gently tugging his son toward the door. "Besides, wait until you hear about the trip! We had quite an adventure, let me tell you."

They left the room, Steve giving one last glance at Autumn and her father.

Autumn's transplant surgery took place on a cold and blustery February day. Steve paced worriedly in the waiting room as the hours passed. It seemed as though there were so many things that could go wrong. The idea of losing his love on the operating table, after so much strife and effort, made him nearly insane.

His father sat helplessly nearby, watching his son with tormented eyes. Phil was there as well, with Crawley leaning her head on his shoulder. Susan had school, but she called her father every hour on the dot to check on the progress.

At length, a surgeon entered the waiting room, drawing everyone's pained stares. His immediate smile put them at ease, but Steve was still compelled to ask how she was doing.

"The operation was a success," said the surgeon, a bit smugly. "It's really one of the simpler transplants I've done."

Phil shook his head at the surgeon's bravado, but Steve took his hand and pumped it enthusiastically.

"Thank you," he said with such warmth and sincerity emanating from his eyes that the surgeon seemed to thaw a little.

"It's my job, sir," he said with a smile. "Oof!"

Steve hugged the man in a powerful grip, setting him back down and even pecking him on the lips. "Can I see her?"

"She'll be in recovery for a while," said the surgeon, adjusting his scrubs a bit. "But I'll let you know as soon as she wakes up."

Brad entered the waiting room, bearing a cardboard tray laden with coffee. His eyes lit up when he saw their smiling faces.

"It's done?" he asked.

"It's done," said Deathslayer, grinning at the little man.

"Who'd have thought," said Crawley. "A happy ending."

chapter 22

Steve whistled cheerfully as he bore the heavy black garbage bag on his shoulder. He smiled at the small knot of people in the elevator who had to move aside for him and his burden. More than a few inquisitive stares were aimed in his direction, but due to his size and biker-style coat, no one seemed willing to actually speak.

He got off on the ninth floor and nearly skipped to Autumn's room. He found her standing at the wire-reinforced window, a Hello Kitty bathrobe wrapped around her form.

"You're feeling better." He deposited the bag on her empty bed.

She turned halfway around to face him, a somber light in her eyes.

"Better than I have in months." Her tone seemed subdued. "Guess not having your blood filtered can have some consequences."

He raised an eyebrow at her morose manner, standing with arms akimbo. "I, uh…I brought all the stuff you wanted. Why did you need so many clothes just to check out? Wouldn't one outfit to wear home have been enough?"

She turned away from him, hugging herself as if chilled.

"Autumn," he said, coming over and putting a hand on her shoulder. "What's wrong?"

Her tattooed hand gently but firmly lifted his away as she turned to face him. Her soulful eyes did not seem the warm and inviting things he had come to love, but dark spears that lanced out at him.

"Steve, I'm not going home with you."

All color drained from his face.

"What?" Steve blinked several times, then grinned. "Ha ha, haven't made fun of me in a while, that's a good one. Little cruel though."

Autumn hid her face in her hands, her body scrunching in on itself as if she wished to disappear.

"I'm not kidding." Her voice was muffled by her hands, but he still heard her clearly enough.

The truth dawned on Steve, and his jaw dropped open. "You're not...Why? Why are you leaving me?"

Autumn lowered her hands, and though he strained to find it there was not an ounce of remorse in her soft brown eyes.

"I don't love you, Steve. I wish I did, but I don't."

"But," said Steve, his eyes growing moist, "I don't understand, you said —"

She turned stiffly away from him to stare out the window once more. "I thought I was dying. I told you what you wanted to hear."

Steve's hands clenched into fists. "I don't believe you. I *can't* believe you. From day one we've been connecting like crazy, I know you feel it too!"

"Just because we have a good time, doesn't mean we should be together."

He turned away from her, went to the empty bed and leaned heavily against it. Nausea roiled up in his belly, and his body shook as he tried to reconcile the intolerable.

"We were going to get married."

"I know. I'm sorry."

Steve spun around on his heel, face suddenly angry. "So when you moved in, that was just for a place to stay, right?"

She turned to face him, her eyes narrow and fierce even as they teared up. "That's right! I knew you were soft, and wouldn't turn me down. I thought if I was going to be dying soon you'd take care of me. But now I don't need you. I'm moving in with my dad and Brad."

"Autumn...don't do this, please. I love you! Don't you believe that I love you?"

Her face softened for a moment. "I know you do, Steve, and I'm sorry. This is the way it has to be."

"What's going on? Are you sick again? Is there something that—"

"Nothing's wrong, Steve. We're over. That's that."

"I can't accept that. I won't!"

"You need to leave," she said, turning around to face the window again. "You're upsetting me."

"I'll stay right here," he said stubbornly, "until you make me believe you."

Her face, reflected back at him in the window, was distorted and fierce. She sighed heavily and turned to face him. "If you don't leave, I'll call the nurses' station and have you kicked out."

"You wouldn't." Steve crossed his arms and glared at her, nostrils flaring.

Autumn stomped the few feet to her call button and pressed it. There was a reply almost immediately.

"Yes?" came the patient if condescending voice from the other end.

"There's someone in my room and he won't leave," said Autumn.

"Fine!" Steve's voice wavered and his vision grew blurry. "Okay, fine, I'll go. Have a nice life, I guess."

Steve stormed out of the room. He cast one last glance over his shoulder, but seeing the implacable, cruel glare on her face did nothing to make him want to stop.

Steve drove back home, hands tight on the wheel. He felt as if he should be crying, as if his world had come to an end, but for some reason the tears would not come. The cold winter evening was little comfort to the fire in his heart. It just seemed so unfair, that he and Autumn would struggle so hard only to have it end like it had.

When he returned home, he glanced around at his apartment and knew he could not stay. If he peered down, he saw the oriental area rug Autumn had purchased. When he looked at the wall, he saw her paintings and sketches. Even the kitchen had little magnets in the shape of skulls. Everywhere he looked, he was reminded of how much beauty and passion Autumn had brought into his life.

He went right back out the door, stormed down the stairs, and headed on foot toward the local watering hole. Steve proceeded to do something he never did: try to drink himself into oblivion. The bartender cut him off after only two hours, and he stumbled out the one door dancing before his eyes that turned out to be real.

CHRISTOPHER SCOTT WAGONER

Steve ended up walking around his neighborhood, which was not the safest activity, but his size and black mood seemed to keep the urchins at a distance. He found another bar, and then another, and soon the night had turned into a swirl of neon lights and dirty floors.

It was well past two in the morning when he stumbled around the corner and sighted his building. He was singing loudly to himself, badly slurring the words to "Always Look on the Bright Side of Life."

He staggered across the street, barely noticing the woman in the short tight skirt leaning on the wall. Her face was done up in clownish makeup, and there was something off about the way her voice sounded.

"Hey, sugar," she said, making him wince at the sound of the familiar pet name. "Looks like you're headed home alone. I could keep you company."

"No offense, sweetie—" Steve could barely focus his bleary eyes on the husky woman; she was nearly his height, and seemed unusually broad of shoulder "—but I'm real sick of your gender right now."

"Then good news, sugar," she said, stepping forward to run her hand across his shirt front. "I'm a little bit of both."

Steve focused on the hand touching him, noticed the large veins, the black dots that indicated new hair growth, and burst into laughter.

"Sorry." He slapped her hand away a bit hard due to his inebriated state. "I'm not into chicks with dicks. But you have a nice night!"

She stood in his path when he tried to walk around. "What you think you're doing hitting me, motherfucker?" she asked, giving him a shove.

"Keep your hands off me, whore!"

"Whore? You calling me a whore?" Suddenly her hand lashed out, a fist smashing into Steve's nose. Blood poured out of the orifice, spilling down his shirt.

"What the fuck?" Steve was aghast, watching the crimson fluid pour into his open palm.

The transvestite took another swing, which Steve ducked under. He tackled her and knocked her to the sidewalk. They rolled about, biting and kicking and gouging viciously. Neither took notice of the car load of young hipsters who stopped to film the altercation with their cell phone cameras.

Steve found himself hard pressed, due to his drunkenness and the fact that the transvestite was nearly as large and powerful as himself. He managed to end up on top of her, however, raining down hammer fists as she tried to cover up with her arms.

Abruptly, a pool of radiance fell over him. He glanced up, squinting at the bright light that made seeing anything else impossible.

"NYPD!" he heard over a loudspeaker. "Get off of the woman and put your hands behind your head."

"Oh shit," he said, even as he moved to comply.

chapter 23

Phil grinned sheepishly at Steve as the big man walked out of the police station, holding a plastic bag full of ice against the swollen knot on the side of his head. The big man stared sullenly at him, wordlessly walking past him to climb into the taxi. Phil bit his lower lip, wanting to say something but not sure what.

He climbed into the seat next to Steve, noting with heaviness in his chest how his friend seemed to move like he was mired in molasses. His blue eyes, normally fierce and hawkish, were dull and listless as they stared out the windshield. The fight had messed up his face somewhat, but nothing that seemed permanent.

"Did they give you a shot for TB?" Phil asked at length.

Steve turned to glare at him as if he were a piece of shit and then stared forward once more.

"Well, that hooker might have had TB, so…"

Steve grunted away his concerns, eyes focused only on the road ahead.

"I tried calling the hospital," said Phil, "but Autumn's already checked out."

"She left with her dad."

"Her dad? What, to spend some time with him, I guess?"

"No, to stay with him, for the foreseeable future."

"Are you serious? That's…that's ridiculous! Why would she do that?"

"Because she never loved me, Phil. She was using me, just like Susie said she was."

Phil flinched, not just at the blunt words but the pain in Steve's voice. "Maybe she was just coming down off her meds, or something. Have you talked to her?"

"She was the first person I called when I got arrested. She had already checked out of the hospital. When I tried her cell, the number went to voice mail the first few times. Then it stopped ringing altogether. I think she blocked me. Had to dig out a five from my wallet and pay for all the extra phone calls, to boot. Cops only pay for one."

"Dude," said Phil, feeling both miserable and angry. How could Autumn do that? To his eyes, to *everyone's* eyes, they had seemed disgustingly happy together. Remembering that he was still a novice in the dating world, he chalked up his confusion to inexperience. "Do you want me to talk to her, maybe bring Ellie—"

"No!" Steve turned a sharp eyed glare on Phil. "I don't want you involved."

"Well, you should drive up to her dad's place, then. It's not that hard to find once you have the actual address."

"No," said Steve, pressing his damaged forehead against the cool glass of the window. "No, it's over, Phil."

"You're giving up awful easy! I thought you said that Autumn was the one? That you guys were connecting on a lot of levels?"

"Yeah, well, the thing about women is they're fucking crazy, and the only thing worse than them being crazy is they're fucking good at deception. She played me, Phil. She came out and said that she played me."

"She couldn't possibly have meant it," said Phil, remembering the glow that Autumn seemed to have when she was with Steve.

"Dude…" Steve rubbed his nose and seemed quite close to tears. "You didn't see her face when she said it. Cold, cold as ice. Businesslike. It's not like we were together that long. I should have known what was up."

"You love her, though."

Steve glanced up at him, moisture at his eyes. "Maybe I do. But it doesn't matter now."

They rode in silence the rest of the way to Steve's apartment. Watching the large man shuffle toward his door was heart wrenching, and Phil tried one last time to lift his spirits.

"Hey," he said out the window, "hang in there, all right? Try not to do anything stupid…well, anything else stupid."

Steve glared at him, wiping the banal smile off of his face.

Phil looked with disdain at the concentric circles staining his glass coffee table. It was right in the spot where Crawley liked to sit, and he could tell what she had been drinking by matching the color of the rings. White for a latte, brown for coffee, red for pomegranate juice. What irked him further was the cork disc coaster that sat, as it always did, within inches of the cup rings.

Using the damp rag in his hand, he wiped the stains away. They were dried on and it took considerable elbow grease to clear them. When he was finished he checked the chrome legs of the table, eliminating even the slightest smudges. Satisfied, he turned his attention elsewhere.

Crossing the white carpet of his generous living space, he stopped momentarily to pluck a black thread from his cream colored sofa. He went around his apartment, tidying up stacks of magazines and turning his spider plant so the leaves did not touch (and therefore stain) the wall behind them.

His doorbell went off, prompting him to glance over his shoulder at the sink. His dinner dishes were still sitting in the soapy water, but he had no time to deal with them. Eagerly rubbing his hands, he did one last check of his domain. Everything seemed neat and tidy, as long as he didn't glance in the kitchen.

Phil's hand shook slightly as he undid the latch to his door. Crawley still had a way of making him nervous. Her moods seemed to infect her at random, and he often felt he was playing catch up for some unknown slight. Still, his face was covered in a warm smile when he opened the white painted door and beheld Crawley standing in the hall.

He drank in the sight of her with his eyes. She had dressed in a short, flared skirt with a bit of ruffle along the hem. Its lavender hue complemented the violet blouse she wore, a small pattern of flowers around each of its sleeves. Over the ensemble she wore a light denim jacket dyed nearly black, unbuttoned to show off her small but firm cleavage. Deep purple tights covered her legs, accentuating their fine curves. A pair of black pumps finished the look, straps buckled over her ankles holding them on fast. Her hair had been brushed out and styled so that it parted on the side. A long plume of hair almost, but not quite, hung in her eyes.

"Hey, baby," she said, melting into his arms.

"Hey." He was unable to resist kissing her lavender-painted lips. Her body felt good against his, the curves he had never quite fully explored sliding across him. "You look beautiful."

"Thanks." She blushed a bit, though it was hardly the first time he had told her the same.

A noise from the hallway reminded him that his front door was still open. He pulled away from Crawley long enough to close the door and lock it. When he turned around she was walking toward the bathroom at the rear of his apartment. She glanced over her shoulder, her hips swaying more than was necessary.

"I'll be right back," she said. "Why don't you sit on the sofa and cue up the movie?"

"Yeah, okay." Phil knew that they were only going to watch about five minutes anyway. Nevertheless, he turned on his Blu-ray and the words *National Treasure 2* appeared on the screen.

He went into his kitchen and poured two glasses of red wine, carefully setting them both on coasters when he returned to the living room. Plopping down near the center of the sofa, he took a sip from his glass. His nose wrinkled a bit at the flavor. Crawley was a wine aficionado, but to him it tasted like cleaning agent.

Just as he set the glass down, he heard Crawley come out of the bathroom. Her heels clicked on the hardwood in the hallway before being muffled by the carpet as she entered the living room. Phil was about to turn as she came up behind him, but she put her hands over his eyes. A grin spread over his features as she giggled.

"Who is it?" he asked.

"A three hundred pound ex-convict here to rape you," she said in a gravelly voice.

"Well," said Phil, "your hands are big enough."

"Hey!" said Crawley, smacking him lightly on the cheek. "Don't make fun of my boy hands—don't turn around yet!"

"What are you doing back there?" he asked suspiciously.

"Nothing," she said. Her hands came away from his eyes, and she climbed over the back of the sofa and plopped in his lap. Phil's eyes went wide when he realized that while she still wore her heels and stockings, there was not another stitch of clothing on her body. Their chemistry was perfect, and yet they both paused before their hands had even begun to explore each other.

"I'm sorry," he said. "I just can't stop thinking about how miserable Steve is."

"It's all right," she said, sliding off of his lap. "I know what you mean. It doesn't seem right, us being happy when he's so down in the dumps."

"I can't believe Autumn did that to him."

"It just doesn't seem like it's true! When I talked to Autumn about Steve, there was never so much as a hint that it wasn't for real."

"Well, I don't know." Phil remembered what Steve had said in the cab. "Maybe she's just good at being fake?"

"If I was Steve," said Crawley, folding her legs under her and sitting up straighter on his couch, "I would drive up there and demand an explanation."

"I think he's in enough legal trouble now. He got a call not to report to work on Monday."

"Oh, geez. You don't think he'll lose his job, do you?"

"I don't know. I'd like to grab Autumn and shake her for doing this to Steve, though."

"I'd like to punch her in the nose!" She giggled at his reaction. "Well, at least give her a piece of my mind."

"So let's do it." He sat up himself.

"All right, tiger," purred Crawley, sitting up on her knees. She crawled onto him, eyes shining with desire.

"No! I mean, yes, but I meant let's go see Autumn."

"Now?" Crawley asked, glancing up from where she had put her face in his lap.

"No, definitely not now, but tomorrow…"

"I've got church," said Crawley, staring up from her decidedly un-church-like activity, "but I'm sure the Lord will forgive me this once."

She stopped talking because her mouth was occupied, and he stopped talking because he was unable.

chapter 24

Crawley's Eclipse rolled up outside of Jonathon's house just before noon. The sun was near its zenith, casting warm light over the well-manicured lawn. Bees buzzed lazily as they zigzagged through the air from flower to flower. The scene seemed too placid, too calm for the storm that was brewing in Phil's gut.

Phil was not a man who liked confrontation. A memory of himself squinting his eyes and shoving his finger in his ears while his parents argued in the next room rose to his mind unbidden. Shaking the image out of his head, he forced himself to bend his thoughts to the task at hand.

Crawley seemed to sense his turmoil, giving his hand a quick squeeze before exiting the car. Things had been different since the night they spent in the hotel room. He no longer felt like her tagalong, but like a full partner in the relationship. That she was more experienced, had more money, and was more attractive than he was seemed irrelevant. Seizing hold of his newfound confidence, he steeled himself for what was likely to be an unpleasant conversation.

He slipped his hand into hers, and their fingers intertwined. Crawley had suggested they only tell Autumn they wanted to catch up with her, maybe take her to lunch. Saving the big guns, so to speak, until they were in the restaurant. Phil was honestly worried what Autumn would do, even in public, if they sprang the true reason for their visit on her in an ambush. Crawley had insisted that Autumn would not speak to them otherwise, and he had relented, figuring that she knew more of the female mind than he did.

His hand was shaking a bit as he knocked on the glass storm door. In a few moments it opened a crack, and Jonathon's face appeared. After a few seconds, his gaze widened and a smile split his face. Eagerly, he shook both of their hands.

"Ellie and Phil! I guess you guys came to see Autumn."

"Yeah," said Phil, clearing his throat, "we, uh, we're probably not expected…"

"I'll go rouse her. Come on in!"

They followed Jonathon into the cozy interior. A college basketball game was on the big-screen TV, and the smell of something wonderful roasting wafted out of the kitchen. Jonathon bustled out of sight for a moment, and then returned with Autumn.

The caustic young woman did not seem to be herself. Apparently, her brush with death had taken its toll, as she had not bothered to put on makeup of any kind. Her hair was pulled back into a simple ponytail, and she wore black sweats and an oversized shirt that probably had belonged to Steve at one point. Dark circles lurked beneath her eyes, which were dull and listless. She glared at the two of them, and Phil suddenly felt very much the intruder.

"Did Steve put you up to this?" she asked in a voice thick with sleep.

"No," said Phil, shaking his head nervously.

"No, he didn't," said Crawley. "He doesn't even know we're here. We wanted to check on you, see how you're doing."

Autumn relaxed just a bit, but still eyed them warily.

"Moping around the house," said Jonathon as he puttered about in the kitchen, "that's what she's been up to."

Autumn rolled her eyes. "Dad, I had major surgery barely a month ago."

"I got a hole in my back too, remember? I feel fine, and I was back on the links two Sundays later. Why don't you just admit that—"

"Dad," said Autumn, glaring at the man until he held up his hands, palms outward.

"Uh," said Phil, "we were wondering if you'd want to grab a bite to eat?"

"Well, my dad's cooking," said Autumn, glancing toward the kitchen.

"Won't be done for hours, kiddo," said Jonathon, smiling widely. "You kids have fun."

"But," said Autumn, eyes casting about the living room, "but—"

"Autumn, Eleanor is too nice a girl to bring it up, but I will. You're walking around because of her generosity. Now stop being rude and go with your friends. Do you some good to get out of the house for a change."

"Fine," said Autumn, stalking off into her bedroom. Phil expected to have to wait a long time, but she returned a moment later with her black leather purse.

Sullenly, she stood before them, tapping her foot. "Well? We going or what?"

A short time later, they were sitting in a Denny's, watching Autumn destroy a plate of chili fries. Phil picked at his grilled cheese sandwich, while Crawley had ordered only a salad, which still largely occupied her plate. They kept the conversation light at first, asking about her recovery.

"I actually feel pretty good," she said around a mouthful of greasy fare. "My back stopped hurting a week ago, and I went for a walk with Brad this morning. You should see him in his Spandex and headband. You'd *die*."

"Sounds like you're reconnecting with your father rather well," said Phil.

"Yeah, I guess. I mean, I'm still pissed at him, kind of, and I guess I always will be, but he's been pretty cool. Hasn't even bitched once about me not having a job."

"I guess it's a long commute from here to Manhattan," said Phil.

Autumn nodded, squinting her eyes a bit as if she were in pain.

"What's wrong?" Crawley asked.

"Nothing. I may have eaten too fast is all." She stared down at her plate and pushed the cheesy slop around with her fork. Without looking up, and keeping her tone quite casual, she asked, "So, how's Steve?"

"How do you think?" asked Crawley, who had been largely silent throughout the meal. "You broke his heart. He's *devastated*."

Autumn gritted her teeth, and the fork scraped sharply across the crockery plate. "He's a big boy. He'll be all right."

"So you don't care?" asked Crawley. "You don't care about him at all?"

Autumn dropped her fork on the plate and glared at her. "No. I don't. Steve's a nice guy, but he's just not my type."

"Oh, bullshit!" said Crawley, standing up and putting her hands on the table. She loomed over Autumn, seeming much more imposing than her tiny frame would suggest. "When you were talking about him on New Year's Eve, you were practically glowing! You guys could hardly keep your hands off of each other, and you spent a lot of time staring at each other without saying a word! If you weren't in love then, I don't know what it looks like!"

"Uh, Ellie," said Phil, tugging on her belt loop, "maybe you should sit down."

Several of the other patrons had turned to see the outburst, and were quietly whispering to each other now. Crawley seemed a bit abashed, sitting down quickly. For a moment, Phil thought that her words, though harsh, had been well-timed. Autumn's eyes fluttered rapidly, and her mouth twisted downward. A second later her face was crossed by a vile sneer.

"Are you done? I guess because you helped pay for my operation, I owe you —"

"You don't owe me," said Crawley, closing her eyes and shaking her head.

"But you don't get to tell me how to live my life. What makes you think you can judge me, or my decisions? Playing with spiders in your daddy's basement and slaying orcs on a computer screen make you a damn expert on life? You're such a know it all. I don't know how Phil puts up with you."

Crawley's nostrils flared, and her dark eyes narrowed.

Phil felt his ire rising, and glared at Autumn with his fist clenched atop the table. "Don't talk to her like that. You're not even mad at her. You're just mad at yourself."

"Oh," said Autumn mockingly, catching him with her fierce gaze, "look at little Phillip, getting up on his hind legs and sassing me. Too bad you can't rise to the occasion in the bedroom like that, huh Philsy?"

Not so long ago, such a comment would have devastated Phil, but the recent changes in his relationship with Crawley gave him the confidence to merely grin.

"He does just fine," said Crawley, and he was grateful for her support even though he really didn't need it. "No one has ever worked harder to give me what I want."

"Well, look at that," said Autumn, and she did not seem displeased. "So you guys worked things out in the end. That's actually pretty cool."

She sighed, staring into the hands she folded in her lap. "Look, I know you mean well, that you're looking out for Steve, and maybe me too, but…" Autumn glanced out the window, watching traffic as it idly rolled past. "Even if I did have feelings for Steve, that would mean that I should stay away from him. This thing with my kidney, it could be just the beginning. I might get sick again, and what do you think that will do to him?"

"So, you're a martyr now?" Crawley asked, though much of the bluster seemed to have flown from her as well.

"It's not like that. The fact of the matter is, Steve needs a girl who's going to be nice, and sweet, and…presentable to decent folk."

She laughed, tracing a line up and down her inked forearms.

"Steve needs *you*," said Crawley, shaking her head. She dug in her purse and took out a hundred dollar bill and left it on the table. "C'mon, Phil, we're wasting our time here."

Phil rose to his feet, but did not follow Crawley as she exited the restaurant. Instead, he rummaged around in his back pocket and took out a thin newspaper. It was one of the hyperbolic scandal rags that were a staple of the newsstands, ironically one of the few print mediums that still sold well. It boasted a picture of Steve's mug shot, his face bruised and bloody from the tussle with the transvestite. The headline emblazoned across the top read *Son of Deathslayer Pounds Transvestite Hard*. He tossed it on the table in front of Autumn.

"Steve's *not* going to be just fine," he said, turning on his heel and storming out while Autumn stared flabbergasted at the tabloid in front of her.

Steve walked out of the principal's office, the slight swelling on his face the only remaining evidence of his scuffle. He was wearing a suit and tie, for all the good it had done him. In his hand was a stack of papers, crumpled up in his fist. Ruefully he jammed them in his back pocket and walked down the hallway with shoulders slumped.

"Hey," said one of the sixth graders as he passed through the sparsely populated hallway, "here comes Pimp Strong!"

"Pimp Strong, Pimp Strong," they chanted as he walked past. He hung his head in shame and moved more quickly down the hall. He stopped before his classroom, his home away from home for the past six years. He stood with his hand on the knob for a long time without opening it. A sound from down the hall startled him. The janitor was beginning his rounds. Steve sighed and entered the room for the last time.

Using a large cardboard box, he gathered the supplies he had bought with his own money. Down came the plastic-covered hearts, the irony of which was not lost on him. Shelves were emptied of lesson plan books and coloring sheet masters, all plopped unceremoniously in the box.

He came to his desk last, shaking his head sadly at the object. He cleaned out his office supplies, adding them to the pile in the box. He came across a stack of glossy photos held together by a rubber band. The top photo featured Steve and his first group of children.

Sitting down on the yellow table, he undid the band and thumbed through the photos. Though he was a little sad to be leaving, it could not compare with the massive gulf in his chest. Life without Autumn seemed hollow and meaningless. Not for the first time, he briefly considered suicide, but the thought of what such an act would do to his family forced the idea back into the darker corners of his mind.

The door to his classroom opened. Steve assumed it was the janitor and did not look up.

"I'll be out of here in ten minutes," he said, still perusing the photos.

The sound of heels on the tiled floor made him glance up. The photos slipped from his nerveless fingers and tumbled to the floor as Autumn approached. She looked healthy, and beautiful as ever. She had done her hair in pigtails, held near her scalp with glass skull-shaped bands. She wore light red lipstick and blush, and her eye shadow was as dramatic as if she was prepared for a night out. A leather coat that he had bought for her months prior was worn over a faded Ozzy Osbourne T-shirt, which hung over the belt line of a leather mini skirt. Fishnet stockings with holes ripped in them for aesthetic purposes covered her legs, disappearing into black patent leather boots with a towering heel. She seemed embarrassed, her eyes not able to meet his as she approached.

What's she doing here? he thought. Seeing her ripped open wounds that had only just begun to scab over, and his initial shock was being fast replaced with a cold ire.

Autumn stopped a few feet away, arms crossed over her chest. "Hey."

"Hey." Steve strove to keep his face and tone neutral. "I'll have your stuff gathered up tomorrow. I'm kind of busy right—"

"Don't worry about it," she said, walking over to sit next to him on the table. She fingered the Band-Aid across his nose, tsking.

"Ow."

"That transvestite kicked your ass."

"Yeah, well, you should see the other…guy? Girl? What does one call them?"

She chuckled, then became morose, looking at the box on the table. "Did you get fired?"

"Yeah. I thought they'd let me stay until the end of the year, but… well, the union is making sure I get paid till August, so that's something. They know I've had a tough time of it."

Autumn folded under his accusing gaze, dropping her eyes to the painted table. When she spoke, her mouth twitched in a sneer. "How can they fire you for something you did when you weren't on the clock?"

"I signed a contract that said I wouldn't do anything to bring the image of the school down." He grinned without mirth. "I guess I kind of did just that."

"It's still not fair. You were a great teacher. And you're a good man."

He turned his face away from her, and his shoulders shook with mirthless laughter. "Just not good enough for you."

Autumn sighed, stared at her hands folded in her lap. "You're too good for me. I don't deserve a man like you."

"Oh, is that why you left? Because I seem to recall you saying something about how you didn't need me anymore."

Autumn glanced up at him once more. Her eyes were narrowed with anger, but her trembling lips and lack of response seemed to indicate it was directed more at herself than at him. "I'm sorry. I never should have said that. I just…I just wanted you to think I was the bad guy, so you could, you know, move on."

Steve crossed his arms over his chest, hot bile-ridden words wanting to flood out of his mouth and deluge the woman he loved more than life itself.

"Oh, you wanted to be the bad guy? Well, mission accomplished!"

Autumn looked away from him, staring out the window at the street. Her eyes grew moist, and she sniffled. Steve felt a pang of guilt in his breast, and softened his tone. "What you said to me…"

Steve got up and paced away from her, running his thumbnail over the crinkling paper stapled to the bulletin board.

"When you said — well, you were there, you remember — I've never been so, so devastated! Losing you was bad enough. Did you have to go and make me doubt that we ever had anything in the first place?"

"I'm sorry."

He turned back around at her wet sniffling and snatched a Kleenex box from a bookshelf.

"Here." Steve handed her the box and sat back down next to her. They sat in silence for a time as she dabbed at her nose and eyes.

"I don't…" said Steve after a time. "I don't know if I can forgive you for that."

Autumn met his eyes. Her own were bloodshot and wavering. "You shouldn't. I don't deserve to be forgiven. Oh god, sugar, I've been an idiot, not to mention a world class bitch. Those things I said to you in the hospital…I didn't mean it. I didn't mean any of it."

He glanced up at her, eyes wide. Then they narrowed into azure slits. When he spoke his tone was harsh. "Those words hurt. They hurt me worse than I've ever been hurt before. Do you know what the last couple of months have been like? I feel like I can't breathe!"

"I *do* know, because I feel the same way! I love you, Steve."

"And I love you! So why aren't we together?"

Autumn put her hand on his cheek, and despite his reservations he put his own atop of it.

"I…when I was…when we thought it was the end…you looked so sad, so miserable. I didn't want to have to put you through that again."

"Isn't that my choice?" He put his hands on her shoulders and stared deeply into her eyes. "There's no other woman for me. There never could be, not ever."

They stared at each other for a long time, seemingly unable to speak or move. At length Autumn giggled, and patted his cheek. "I should be offended, you know. You wanted to beat me up in effigy, and you chose a transvestite hooker."

"I didn't choose her!" Steve was laughing as well. "That he/she started shit with *me* because I wouldn't be her trick!"

"And you got your ass kicked."

"It was a big transvestite and knew how to fight! I bet she would have kicked your ass."

"Me? The master of the toe crusher stomp? That could totally be my finisher if I was a wrestler."

"Nah, you need something flashier, preferably one that makes the mat shake."

Autumn stopped laughing, bit her lower lip. Her soft brown eyes, which still enthralled him, were pleading. "Steve, will you take me back? Please? I promise I'll never hurt you like that again."

Steve tried to hang on to his anger, his bitterness. As he gazed into her beautiful face, he decided that was a silly idea. Why not let the warmth that wanted so desperately into his heart spread?

He reached up and tucked a stray hair behind her pierced ear, a soft smile playing at his lips.

"Of course I'm going to take you back."

"Steve—" Autumn put a hand on his chest "—are you going to kiss me or what?"

"Absodamnlutely," he said, grinning. Their lips met, softly at first. Slowly, they melted into each other's arms. He drank in her scent, her softness, felt the cool metal of her piercings on his face. For the first time in weeks, he felt a burden lift from his heart, leaving him feeling light as air.

"You've lost weight," she said as her hands caressed his broad back.

"Haven't had much of an appetite." His voice was still haunted by the pain of losing her. He wrapped his arms around her more tightly, as if he were afraid she were going to vanish like so much dream stuff.

"I love you," she said, smothering his face with kisses. "I don't deserve you, but I love you. Does that make me a bad person?"

"No. You're not a bad person, Autumn. I wouldn't say you don't deserve me, but even if you didn't, hell, we're all only human right?"

"Not me," said Autumn, ruffling his hair. "I'm a succubus, remember?"

He laughed until she smothered his lips with her own.

Epilogue

Crawley's fingers danced over the strings as she furiously plucked out the solo to "Freebird." A few feet away on the small stage, Phil grinned as he tickled the ivory keys before him, taking genuine pleasure in her performance. Rex furiously pounded the drums while Sven held the mike stand in two hands, nodding his blond head and tapping his long feet to the rhythm.

Out in the crowded bar, Steve moved past the densely packed patrons, holding two bottles of beer up over his shoulders so they would not be spilled. He skirted around a woman vomiting on the floor, crouched low to avoid an errant limb that was flung up in his path, and finally dashed up the stairs to the balcony overlooking the dance floor.

Autumn smiled at him, seated at a table near the railing, the same seat they had occupied months before. She leaned past a man who had apparently been hitting on her and waved.

"Hi, sugar!" she said cheerfully as he approached. She turned to face the slender hipster who was still leaning on their table. "Still think he's not enough of a man for me?"

The little man swallowed nervously and licked his lips. Steve stared down at him from narrowed eyes, nearly a foot and a half taller than the man. Knots of muscle played over Steve's forearms as he clenched his fists.

"Boo!"

The little man jumped nearly a foot. He scampered away from the couple, not giving a backward glance.

"Thanks, sugar. He left no cliché untrampled."

"Not a problem."

"Crawley's got them hooked." She gestured to the stage below.

"She's got Phil hooked."

"No doubt. Just like I'm hooked on you."

"Now who sounds like a pussy?" he said, taking a long pull on his beer.

Autumn's brows rose high over her widened brown eyes. She slapped her palm on the bottom of the bottle. Steve spilled it onto his shirt, foam rushing out of his mouth.

"That's *our* word," she said. "*You* can't say it!"

Steve laughed even as he sputtered, setting the half full bottle back on the table.

"You're a pain in the ass!" His smile belied his words.

"And you wouldn't have it any other way."

Their lips met across the table in a passionate display that revolted some, delighted others, but that everyone envied.

Acknowledgments

This book wouldn't have been possible without my awesome editing team. Thanks, Sean and Colleen! I'd also like to thank Omnific for taking a chance on this decidedly nontraditional romance novel, when so many other publishers passed on it. Finally, I'd like to acknowledge the late, great Robert Asprin, whose Myth Adventures series taught me to love novels more than.

Why are you reading this crap? Turn the page already!

About the Author

Christopher Scott Wagoner: Strange visitor from another world! Jettisoned from his planet at an early age, he was adopted by a kindly midwestern couple and taught to fight for truth, justice, and the Native American way!

When he's not busy saving the Galaxy, Chris finds time to pen fiction novels. *Forever Autumn* is his first book without dragons in it. He is rumored to enjoy professional wrestling, cartoons, and jokes that fall on the "offensive" side. Unsubstantiated accusations that he used to teach preschool have never been confirmed by him, but he has a lot of pee stories.

check out these titles from
OMNIFIC PUBLISHING
◄ ··· ►Contemporary Romance◄ ··· ►

Keeping the Peace by Linda Cunningham
Stitches and Scars by Elizabeth A. Vincent
Pieces of Us by Hannah Downing
The Way That You Play It by BJ Thornton
The Poughkeepsie Brotherhood series: *Poughkeepsie, Return to Poughkeepsie* &
Saving Poughkeepsie by Debra Anastasia
Recaptured Dreams and *All-American Girl* and *Until Next Time* by Justine Dell
Once Upon a Second Chance by Marian Vere
The Englishman by Nina Lewis
16 Marsden Place by Rachel Brimble
Sleepers, Awake by Eden Barber
The Runaway series: *The Runaway Year* & *The Runaway Ex* by Shani Struthers
The Hydraulic series: *Hydraulic Level Five* & *Skygods* by Sarah Latchaw
Fix You and *The Jeweler* by Beck Anderson
Just Once by Julianna Keyes
The WORDS series: *The Weight of Words, Better Deeds Than Words* & *The Truest of Words*
by Georgina Guthrie
The Brit Out of Water series: *Theatricks* & *Jazz Hands* by Eleanor Gwyn-Jones
The Sacrificial Lamb & *Let's Get Physical* by Elle Fiore
The Plan by Qwen Salsbury
The Kiss Me series: *Kiss Me Goodnight* & *Kiss Me By Moonlight* by Michele Zurlo
Saint Kate of the Cupcake: The Dangers of Lust and Baking by LC Fenton
Exposure by Morgan & Jennifer Locklear
Playing All the Angles by Nicole Lane
Redemption by Kathryn Barrett
The Playboy's Princess by Joy Fulcher
The Forever series: *Forever Autumn* (book 1) by Christopher Scott Wagoner

◄ ··· ►Young Adult Romance◄ ··· ►
The Ember series: *Ember* & *Iridescent* by Carol Oates
Breaking Point by Jess Bowen
Life, Liberty, and Pursuit by Susan Kaye Quinn
The Embrace series: *Embrace* & *Hold Tight* by Cherie Colyer
Destiny's Fire by Trisha Wolfe
The Reaper series: *Reaping Me Softly* & *UnReap My Heart* by Kate Evangelista
The Legendary Saga: *Legendary* & *Claiming Excalibur* by LH Nicole
The Fatal series: *Fatal* & *Brutal* (novella 1.5) by T.A. Brock
The Prometheus Order series: *Byronic* by Sandi Beth Jones
One Smart Cookie by Kym Brunner
Variables of Love by MK Schiller

New Adult Romance

Three Daves by Nicki Elson
Streamline by Jennifer Lane
The Shades series: *Shades of Atlantis* & *Shades of Avalon* by Carol Oates
The Heart series: *Beside Your Heart, Disclosure of the Heart* & *Forever Your Heart*
by Mary Whitney
Romancing the Bookworm by Kate Evangelista
Flirting with Chaos by Kenya Wright
The Vice, Virtue & Video series: *Revealed, Captured, Desired* & *Devoted*
by Bianca Giovanni
Granton University series: *Loving Lies* by Linda Kage

Paranormal Romance

The Light series: *Seers of Light, Whisper of Light* & *Circle of Light* by Jennifer DeLucy
The Hanaford Park series: *Eve of Samhain* & *Pleasures Untold* by Lisa Sanchez
Immortal Awakening by KC Randall
The Seraphim series: *Crushed Seraphim* & *Bittersweet Seraphim* by Debra Anastasia
The Guardian's Wild Child by Feather Stone
Grave Refrain by Sarah M. Glover
The Divinity series: *Divinity* & *Entity* by Patricia Leever
The Blood Vine series: *Blood Vine, Blood Entangled* & *Blood Reunited*
by Amber Belldene
Divine Temptation by Nicki Elson
The Dead Rapture series: *Love in the Time of the Dead* & *Love at the End of Days* by
Tera Shanley
The Hidden Races series: *Incandescent* (book 1) by M.V. Freeman

Romantic Suspense

Whirlwind by Robin DeJarnett
The CONduct series: *With Good Behavior, Bad Behavior* & *On Best Behavior*
by Jennifer Lane
Indivisible by Jessica McQuinn
Between the Lies by Alison Oburia
Blind Man's Bargain by Tracy Winegar

Erotic Romance

The Keyhole series: *Becoming sage* (book 1) by Kasi Alexander
The Keyhole series: *Saving sunni* (book 2) by Kasi & Reggie Alexander
The Winemaker's Dinner: *Appetizers* & *Entrée* by Dr. Ivan Rusilko & Everly Drummond
The Winemaker's Dinner: *Dessert* by Dr. Ivan Rusilko
Client N° 5 by Joy Fulcher

Historical Romance

Cat O' Nine Tails by Patricia Leever
Burning Embers by Hannah Fielding
Seven for a Secret by Rumer Haven

Anthologies

A Valentine Anthology including short stories by
Alice Clayton ("With a Double Oven"),
Jennifer DeLucy ("Magnus of Pfelt, Conquering Viking Lord"),
Nicki Elson ("I Don't Do Valentine's Day"),
Jessica McQuinn ("Better Than One Dead Rose and a Monkey Card"),
Victoria Michaels ("Home to Jackson"), and
Alison Oburia ("The Bridge")

Taking Liberties including an introduction by Tiffany Reisz and short stories by
Mina Vaughn ("John Hancock-Blocked"),
Linda Cunningham ("A Boston Marriage"),
Joy Fulcher ("Tea for Two"),
KC Holly ("The British Are Coming!"),
Kimberly Jensen & Scott Stark ("E. Pluribus Threesome"), and
Vivian Rider ("M'Lady's Secret Service")

Sets

The Heart Series Box Set (*Beside Your Heart, Disclosure of the Heart &
Forever Your Heart*) by Mary Whitney
The CONduct Series Box Set (*With Good Behavior, Bad Behavior &
On Best Behavior*) by Jennifer Lane
The Light Series Box Set (*Seers of Light, Whisper of Light, Circle of Light &
Glimpse of Light*) by Jennifer DeLucy
The Blood Vine Series Box Set (*Blood Vine, Blood Entangled, Blood Reunited &
Blood Eternal*) by Amber Belldene

Singles, Novellas & Special Editions

It's Only Kinky the First Time (A Keyhole series single) by Kasi Alexander
Learning the Ropes (A Keyhole series single) by Kasi & Reggie Alexander
The Winemaker's Dinner: RSVP by Dr. Ivan Rusilko
The Winemaker's Dinner: No Reservations by Everly Drummond
Big Guns by Jessica McQuinn
Concessions by Robin DeJarnett
Starstruck by Lisa Sanchez
New Flame by BJ Thornton

Shackled by Debra Anastasia
Swim Recruit by Jennifer Lane
Sway by Nicki Elson
Full Speed Ahead by Susan Kaye Quinn
The Second Sunrise by Hannah Downing
The Summer Prince by Carol Oates
Whatever it Takes by Sarah M. Glover
Clarity (A *Divinity* prequel single) by Patricia Leever
A Christmas Wish (A *Cocktails & Dreams* single) by Autumn Markus
Late Night with Andres by Debra Anastasia
Poughkeepsie (enhanced iPad app collector's edition) by Debra Anastasia
Poughkeepsie (audio book edition) by Debra Anastasia
Blood Eternal (A Blood Vine series single, epilogue to series) by Amber Belldene
Carnaval de Amor (*The Winemaker's Dinner*, Spanish edition)
by Dr. Ivan Rusilko & Everly Drummond

coming soon from
OMNIFIC PUBLISHING

Something Wicked by Carol Oates
Going the Distance by Julianna Keyes
The Enclave series: *Closer and Closer* (book 1) by Jenna Barton
The Dead Rapture series: *Love Starts with Z* (book 3) by Tera Shanley
The Hidden Races series: *Illumination* (book 2) by M.V. Freeman
Missing Pieces by Meredith Tate

CPSIA information can be obtained at www.ICGtesting.com
Printed in the USA
LVOW11s1400100215

426459LV00001B/194/P